Autumn Prince

(A Tudor Falsehood)

by Anne Stevens

Tudor Crimes: Book XI

Foreword

The year 1537 promises to be a more propitious one for England, and its newly married king. The danger of a northern rebellion is fast receding, after Robert Aske and his co-conspirators have been disposed of by the Duke of Norfolk s swift justice, whilst Henry hears, in March, that his beloved new wife, Jane Seymour is now with child.

After the dark Boleyn times, the court expects a major reversal in fortunes to take place, and opportunity to come knocking on many doors. Apart from the Seymour brothers, Ned and Tom, the king's happy largesse is set to cascade down over many who have had to live under the shadow of danger for far too long.

Thomas Cromwell, now in his fiftieth year, finds his star in the ascendancy once again. The big house of Austin Friars is now established as a breeding ground for the elite few who can run the legal system, and support the crown in more clandestine ways. It is also a meeting place, where deals are struck, and great men can obtain a hearty breakfast, whilst arranging loans.

The denizens of Austin Friars have never been busier on Thomas Cromwell's behalf. The law courts are kept busy with their redefining of English law, the subjugation of the monasteries and abbeys, and the fairest possible re-distribution of the country's vast new found wealth.

In the course of three short years, Thomas Cromwell has increased the worth of the nation four fold, and there is gold aplenty for investment in the new navy, and the furtherance of English aims abroad. New factions within Europe are forming, and great alliances are quickly made, and swiftly broken.

The venal, and corrupt, Pope Clement has been dead for more than two years, and the Church of Rome, now led by Pope Paul III, has settled down into quiet, but unswerving opposition of the protestant movement.

England is about to become the greatest trading nation of all time, as Thomas Cromwell seeks to move it away from an agrarian culture, living on the edge of starvation, to a bold, sometimes reckless, mercantile society. His land reforms, new tax systems, and common laws, will earn him a whole new set of enemies, but they will also change the face of England forever more.

Will Draper has become an almost indispensable support to the king, ensuring that Henry remains untouched by the evil that still threatens disaster, if left unopposed. Miriam Draper has been delivered of a daughter, Emily, as prophesied by Pru Beckshaw, and is spreading her mercantile empire throughout the Christian world.

Rafe Sadler is now a member of the king's inner circle of close advisors, and has his own grand house in Putney. The king knows the worth of a Cromwell trained man, and seeks to use him as an accomplished diplomat, a clever spy, and a highly valued negotiator. Because of this extended line of trust, the king feels able to entrust Rafe Sadler with a most private mission.

The king's young advisor has been sent north of the border, to meet with Henry's sister, who is pressing him for urgent assistance. Margaret, once married to James IV, and designated Queen of Scots, is the mother of the precocious, and unreliable James Stuart, King of Scotland.

After years of dominance over the boy king, she now finds that he has grown into a wilful, and arrogant man. He has thrown her over for better councillors, and set Scotland onto a dangerous course. He courts the French king, François and seeks to woo him with lavish gifts of estates that once belonged to his own mother.

In desperation, Margaret, Dowager Queen of Scots, turns to England for help, and looks to her brother, King Henry, for financial support. It is a narrow path she walks, and one that could easily turn her actions into treason against her adopted country.

Rafe Sadler knows the pitfalls and, with Thomas Cromwell s advice and guidance, he must seek to satisfy all concerned.

1   Done Like a Scot

"Your Majesty, I bring fraternal greetings from Henry, King of England, Ireland and France." Rae Sadler bows low to the Queen Mother of Scotland.

"At last, what has the fat oaf to say for himself?" Queen Margaret asks. "Does he wish to know who it is that writes treason to my son. Or is he too stupid to understand he way of things?"

"Madam, you speak treason against my king."

"Alas, I am in Scotland, and that is not treason north of the border, but simple fact, Master Sadler," Margaret says with a sly smile. "Now, should a certain well known someone be in England when then write to James…"

"You know of someone who conspires with James, madam?" Rafe Sadler wonders who has been foolish enough to deal with James behind Henry's back. "I am sure your brother would be grateful for the information."

Margaret, sister of Henry VIII, once Queen of Scots, and mother of King James V, touches a finger to her lips, and reaches for the quill and paper. The sharpened goose quill goes into the freshly ground ink, and she writes a name down with practiced ease. A quick dust, and the paper is folded, and handed over to the Englishman. Rafe Sadler understands why Margaret writes the name down, for it will sound the same in French as it does in English, and that would be indiscreet, in front of her ladies-in-waiting. He takes a letter from his doublet, and hands it to the Queen of Scots.

"From Henry?" she asks.

"No," Rafe Sadler replies. "From Thomas Cromwell. It is a draft, drawable here, in Edinburgh, for five hundred pounds. Master Cromwell begs me to inform you that, providing you stay in Scotland, he will make this into an annual pension."

"Tom Cromwell, you say?" Margaret smiles. "He was a twinkle eyed clerk for Cardinal Wolsey when I last saw him. I visited Henry before Wolsey fell from grace, you know. I told Hal not to upset him."

"Master Cromwell remembers the time well, madam," Rafe informs her. "He told me that you were the only person who defended his old master. For that, he thanks you, and thus renders this small service in return."

"Oh, then I am due another gift for the name on that paper?"

"Perhaps," Rafe Sadler mutters, and glances down at the name. "Oh, Sweet Jesus, madam, could you not have written any other name than this one?"

"Does it displease you so much, Master Sadler?" Margaret cannot help but smile. They want something from you, and when you give them it, and more beside, they blanch and curse their ill fortune.

"It neither pleases, nor displeases me, madam," he replies, as he slips the paper back into his doublet. I am merely the messenger, and I must deliver this news, good or bad, to the right ears."

"Hal's?"

"Dear God, no!" Rafe stands, and bows. "I shall write to you, as often as need be, Your Majesty."

"They intercept my letters."

"Of course. The king will write pleasantries for them to read in his letters, and I will discourse with you secretly."

"How so?" Margaret asks.

"On the last Sunday of each month, you will find a letter under the bolster on your bed. Burn it, once you have read it. Should you wish to reply, leave it in the same place, on the following Sunday. Write nothing that cannot be explained away, in case my agent is taken."

"You must advise me, sir." Margaret likes the look of this young man, and wonders if he might wish to tarry with her for a few days. "Will you come to supper tonight?"

"My pleasure, madam."

"Oh, I think so, sir," Margaret says with a wry smile. "Why, we might find yet another language to converse in."

This last remark, meant as a flirtatious gambit, goes right over the Englishman's head. He is not the sort of man who understands either love play, or *double entendres*.

Rafe bows again, and is gone.

*

At supper, he explains how she is to obfuscate in her writing. It is a simple code, enlivened with certain phrases. 'Fine' weather means good news, and to speak of 'thunder' means some evil is afoot. The Scottish king is to be 'my small puppy', and various members of the council are to be allotted similar titles.

It is childishly simple, and easy for even a casual reader to see that it is in coded form, but when decoded, it means nothing other than the queen has enjoyed a sunny day, or suffered some other banality of the weather.

"The real secret is this," Rafe tells her. He holds up a piece of virgin paper, and shows it on each side, then he places it close to the fire, and words appear, as if by magic. "The juice of lemons, or sour wine vinegar can be used to write a message. Keep it simple, and write in the margins. Once dry the words become invisible, and the paper will seem like a sister's letter to a loving brother, or friend."

"You would have me spy for you, sir?" Queen Margaret asks.

"Madam, you are English born, of royal blood." Rafe sees no conflict of interest, and wonders at the question. "Henry is your king, as well as your brother. Write only what you think important, and transpose the invisible letters by a given amount, so that an 'A' becomes an 'E', if transposed by four places."

"How will you know the number I use in each letter, sir?" Margaret asks, intrigued at the wickedness of it all. "Must I always use the same one?"

"You are a quick learner madam," Rafe says. "Choose a number at random, and incorporate it in the body of the normal letter. Mention that you might do such and such a thing on the seventh, or the third, and we will have the current key. Change the cipher every two letters you write."

"That is easy enough," Queen Margaret tells him. "My husband is in France, with James."

"It is his duty, I dare say."

"And what of yours, sir?" Margaret Tudor asks of him. "Do you have a wife?"

"Yes, I have, in a manner of speaking," Rafe replies, without thinking. "I am betrothed to a dear lady called Ellen Barré. We are only awaiting the news that her husband is dead."

"Of natural causes?" Margaret asks. After all, a significant number of people in royal circles do tend to die unnaturally, whether from an 'accident', the axe, or a dose of poison.

"He is thought to be dead, but the law demands some proof of the matter," Rafe Sadler tells her. "It has dragged on for some time now, and poor Ellen, who is with child again… my child… wants a speedy end to things."

"And if you find the fellow alive?" asks Queen Margaret.

"That would be rather awkward," Rafe admits. "For it would mean I and my Ellen are adulterers, and sinners in the eyes of the church."

"You might have one of Cromwell's young men pay a call on the unhappy creature, and thus end his misery. A sudden blow to the head, or a unhappy fall?"

"Madam, what is it that you suggest?" Rafe Sadler begins to see his foolishness, and regrets taking supper alone with this dangerous Queen of Scots. She smiles nicely at him, and suggests foul murder without a hint of shame. "There is no need for base murder to be done. We are married, in all but law."

"Said like a true Scot," Margaret mutters, and places a hand on Rafe Sadler s thigh. "The nights are cold up here, sir, and *nae* wed, means *nae* wed to a lonely Scottish woman. Good men are a rare thing in these parts."

"Madam, you mistake my kindness for something else," Rafe protests.

"Do I?"

"You do, Your Majesty," Rafe replies. "Now, if you might excuse me?"

"No, you are not excused."

"Madam, I really must insists that…" The words die away on his lips as the king's sister tugs at the bow holding her dresses neckline in place, and it parts. An ample amount of snow white bosom appears, and he gulps.

"Enough of all your sour lemons, Master Rafe, and come closer to me. Let me see how you would pluck a riper fruit!"

"Poor fellow," Miriam Draper says, but she has to smother the urge to laugh. "How did he manage to escape?"

"He leapt to his feet, and declared himself not to be part of the proposed pension arrangements," Thomas Cromwell explains, and smiles at the thought. "The lady took it in good stead, I am told, and they shall remain friends."

"Then Ellen Barré is a very lucky woman," Miriam decides, "for what man would ever usually turn down a grand queen for a girl?"

"Just so." Thomas Cromwell has called seeking Will Draper, but he has missed him. Instead, he takes the time to catch up on the doings of his extended family. "The boys are well?"

"They are, Master Tom," Miriam says, and seems to glow with pride. "Gwyllam is like his father, but little Thomas is content to watch, rather than do, just yet. I think he will make a fine lawyer one day, and his brother a soldier."

"Not that, for I could not bear it," Tom Cromwell says without thinking properly. Will Draper is a soldier, and as useful a man as ever he has met. "Forgive me, but I have seen too much of war, and would rather have the boy follow a safer occupation, such as Privy Councillor, or Bishop of Winchester."

"I fear Stephen Gardiner has that position, and for some time to come," Miriam says. "One of my boats shipped him across to France last week."

"He is in Amiens on court business," Thomas Cromwell says, somewhat evasively. Gardiner is on a mission to disrupt the King of Scots royal visit, by bribing well placed ministers to whisper against him to King François. It is a forlorn mission, Cromwell thinks, and one that is doomed to failure. Miriam knows when not to pry too deeply, and changes the conversation to mercantile matters.

"Have you arrived at a new fleece tax rate yet, sir?" It seems an innocuous enough question, but the right answer will determine her shipping schedules over the coming months. "I worry that it might be too high. Tax exported fleeces, and the owners will look to have them processed locally."

"Thus robbing your fleet of valuable cargoes," Thomas Cromwell replies. Do not worry. We think another four pennies on a bale will suffice. That still makes it cheaper to send the wool to Flanders. Your cogs will be well employed, my dear, providing you keep your haulage charges down to last year's levels. What about all of your business dealings with the Venetians… still flourishing, I hope?"

"Oh, I buy their wine, and other delicacies, thanks to the trade agreement the Doge bestowed on Will," Miriam tells him, "and I make a fine profit on it, but it will not last much longer, I fear."

"Ah, you mean the Ottomans?" Thomas Cromwell has read all the despatches, and wonders if Miriam is looking at the latest news in the wrong way. "The Turks write angry letters to the Doge, and threaten to cut their trade routes, but it is only to mask their real intent."

"Which is?" Miriam can see Tom Cromwell is scheming, but does not know where his fertile mind is going.

"Their Grand Sultan is a clever old rogue who calls himself Suleiman the Magnificent. The fellow only wants to steal a few of the smaller islands," Tom Cromwell explains. "Though he will, almost certainly, try to capture the larger island of Corfu. It is a beautiful prize, I hear. The Venetians are militarily stretched, just now, and their navy will have much to do. The jewel that is Corfu might have to become… expendable. I hope, and pray, that does not happen. The locals are all God fearing Christians, and would not live comfortably under the yoke of the heathen infidels."

"What are you thinking of? Miriam senses a huge profit on offer, and wants only to understand the dangers she must face.

"A ship owner with courage might fill her holds with black powder, cannon, and victuals," Cromwell muses. "A swift run down to the island might result in a good profit. The Doge has more money than he needs, yet lacks enough ships to save all of his empire. If we were to save Corfu for him…"

"I have enough merchant ships, as you well know, Master Tom," Miriam says. "Though I could never hope to fill them with enough supplies. Then I would need fighting men to crew them, and access to the ports along the way. I would have to seek out partners, and that takes time. I could always…"

"No partners." Thomas Cromwell's sharp reply stops her short. "Have your cogs sail up to the Tower, where there are cannon, powder, and shot enough. Order your captains to sail down the Bay of Biscay, and meet with your great ships, currently in Lisbon harbour."

"You know my own business better than I do, sir," Miriam says. When did my vessels make safe harbour then?"

"The Wild Rover docked four days ago, and her sister ship, Tudor Rose, just the morning before. The news only arrived this morning, and has not yet been heralded." Thomas Cromwell shrugs. "They have come home laden with great bounty, my dear. My shipping agent tells me you should clear about three thousand pounds on the cargoes."

"It is not enough, and taking the king's cannon…"

"You must think of it as a loan from His Majesty. If you succeed, the king s purse will take a fifth part of any profits."

"And if I fail?"

"Then we owe the king twenty culverins, and a few hundred muskets," Thomas Cromwell says. "He will want that replaced, of course, and it would cost us about five thousand Venetian Ducati."

"What have you done?" Miriam can tell Cromwell is up to something. "You do not think up ideas like this on the spur of the moment. How long have you known?"

"My spies told me some six months ago," Cromwell confesses. "I had to wait, until the Sultan made a move, but that did not stop me from writing to the Doge. Dear old Andreas Gritti has replied, in secret, and urges me to act on his behalf. In the event of failure, he promises to cover our costs, and if we succeed, we get a half share of the income from Corfu for the next three years."

"Which is?" Miriam asks.

"About thirty thousand Ducati… or close to twenty thousand pounds." Cromwell smiles at the look on Miriam's face. She calculates her own share, and thinks it a risk worth taking.

"I think my brother would be interested in such a venture," she tells him. "He itches to travel. He knows how to fight, and can keep an eye on our investment."

"As will Master Wyatt," says Thomas Cromwell. "The fellow is a born cannon master. Besides, I think our wandering poet will be better employed abroad."

"Is he in love again?" Miriam smiles at the shallow nature of the poet, who falls in love as easily as a leaf falls from a tree in Autumn.

"Of course, and the lady's husband is speaking of doing bloody murder on him," Thomas Cromwell explains. "The boy is a very poor picker of women I fear."

"The boy is at least thirty, and has a wife and young child at home," Miriam replies.

"We men never really stop being boys, my dear girl," Cromwell tells her. "We often risk everything for a moment of madness. Still… the fellow will be useful to our scheme."

"There is much to be done, of course, and I must…" Miriam tails off, and studies Cromwell's features. "Ah, there is something else. Your drooping face and clever eyes betray you, sir. What have you not told me?"

"I am sorry, Miriam… I really am… but I need Will for something."

"You promised." Miriam bites at her lower lip. "You said you would leave him be. No more danger. No more… no more of anything."

"I know, but this is not for me; it is for England."

"Oh, bugger England!" Miriam slams her small hand down on the table, making the wine glasses and decanter jump. "Why is it always for England?"

"It is just how these things are," Cromwell says. "I need him to travel to France with Rafe."

"Poor Rafe too?" the girl says. "He escapes the Queen of Scots, only to fall into your wicked clutches."

"You make me out to be a terrible monster, Thomas Cromwell says, with real hurt in his voice. "Am I so bad?"

"One half bad, Master Tom… one half."

*

"Cut his throat, and be bloody well done with it, Tam." the slightly built Welshman sneers, as he turns to leave the barn.

"You cut his throat," Tam replies, his voice cracking with worry. "The man is a King's Examiner!"

"A turd on the king," says the angry Welshman. "What would you have us do… let him go?"

"I shall not hang for murder, Rees ap Evans," Tad insists.

"We will both hang for stealing Henry's deer," Evans responds. He will not care that I am of his own blood."

"You are the bastard son of a bastard son's bastard son, and I should know, for my own father was a Williams." The big, booming voice cuts through the two men's conversation.

"Who the hell are you?" Evans steps back from the barn's open door as a huge, bearded man blocks his escape.

"My name is Cromwell," Richard says with a genial smile. "Now, cut Colonel Draper loose, or suffer the consequences."

"It was none of my doing, sir," Tam moans. "See, I am cutting his bonds, even as we speak, Master Giant."

"A timely arrival, Richard," Will Draper says as he rubs at his chafed wrists. "For your Welsh friend was not for listening to good sense."

"It took us a while to find you," Richard Cromwell replies. As he speaks, he takes Evans by the throat, and shakes him, casually, like a dog would a rat. "John Beckshaw thought you already dead, and was for burning down every village from here back to Ludlow, and hanging a few suspects."

"Then thank God I am found," Will tells the big man. "I must be getting old, to let someone come upon me from behind. The deer are penned in the forest, and waiting for a buyer."

"Who is the buyer?" Richard shakes the dangling Welshman until he is half dead, then releases his grip. "Pissant little bugger!"

"Sir Charles Exeter's steward is our man," Will explains. It is something he has uncovered by diligent investigative work, and the distribution of a few silver coins. "Though I doubt we can actually prove Exeter s involvement."

"Can we not just hang him?" Richard grabs Tam and throws him down alongside his comrade.

"Proof, Richard," Will tells his friend.

"Very well. Which one of you heard Sir Charles Exeter give orders for the king's deer to be rustled?" Richard demands. "First to speak will be spared the hangman's noose."

"Me!" Both men cry out in unison, and then glare at one another.

"There," Richard says to Will. "Proof!"

"Sir Charles is a knight of the realm," Will says with a shake of his head. "Which means he can only be tried by those of equal rank, or his betters. A colonel does not outrank a knight. I am afraid that any charges would be dismissed. Your promise to these fellows cannot be kept."

"Spare us both the rope, and I will tell you something about Thomas Cromwell that the king would wish to hear." The Welshman is on his knees, and pleads for all he is worth.

"What does a lying Welsh deer thief know about such matters?" Richard draws his dagger and grabs at Evans' ear. The man squeals in terror, and tries to pull away.

"Hear me out, Colonel Draper… for it will do no harm if I lie. You can hang us both afterwards, if I prove false!"

"Let him be, Richard."

"I will not let the rogue live if he defames my uncle," the younger Cromwell curses.

"Nor will I, if he lies," Will insists. "Now, in the name of the king, put away your weapon."

For a moment Richard contemplates cutting the Welshman s throat without more ado, but knows that such an act would cause a great breach between Will Draper, and the Thomas Cromwell faction. He allows the point of his dagger to knick the fellows ear lobe, and slips it back into his doublet.

"I would hear what the rogue has to say," Richard says. "You must not speak in secret."

"I am not your uncle," Will replies, rather sharply. "We shall hear this Rees ap Evans out, and then each draw our own conclusions. Speak out fellow, and make it good, for the hangman is always waiting for the likes of you two."

The little Welshman steps back out of Richard Cromwell's immediate range, and glances across at his comrade, willing him to speak. Tam is, at best, a reluctant and inadequate thief. He knows he is a worse liar, so decides to give the unvarnished truth, and hope it saves both of their necks.

"I was in *Aberconwy*, three months past, and the town was all bedecked with bunting and flags, in honour of a surprise visit by Master Cromwell."

"How does this concern our present business?" Colonel Will Draper's interest is peaked, because three months ago, Thomas Cromwell was celebrating a notable Christmas holiday at Austin Friars. So lavish were the arrangements that the king came calling, just to see the entertainments laid on. He does not recall a sudden dash across Wales that month, and wonders why Tom Cromwell has not mentioned the unlikely visit.

"He was on a grand tour, according to his servant, and decided to stop off on his travels," Tam continues. "The town made him most welcome, and gave him a gift of silver plate, so that he might decide about the abbey."

"You mean *Aberconwy Abbey*? Richard is now interested.

"Yes. The townsfolk pleaded for the place to be left alone, and after a goodly feast, and more lavish gifts, he relented, and swore to spare the abbey from its fate."

"Most noble of him," Will says.

"Not really," Richard tells his friend. We closed the abbey down last month, and dispersed the venal old rogues who resided within. This is all a lot of lying nonsense, Will."

"There is more," the Welshman puts in quickly, before the knife comes out again. "Tell them about Newport, Tam. Go on, they will not harm us if we tell them everything."

"What of Newport?" Richard says. "I know, upon my honour, that my uncle has never visited the place. I dare say he would need a map to even find his way there."

"He was there, about a month ago," Tam Jones says, and flinches at the ferocity of the look directed at him. "The elders received a day's warning, and he turned up riding a big white horse, and dressed like a great lord. He only had one servant with him … the same rogue as I saw at *Aberconwy*… and he was much vexed. I was not party to all that went on… being only an honest working man… but folk talk, and I heard the best of it, after Master Cromwell had left."

"Honest working man? Will smiles. Despite them being about to cut his throat a few minutes ago, he likes them… if only for their very roguishness. "What came about at Newport?"

"Master Cromwell spoke of treason, and of how the king was bent on ridding the marches of these… *malcolm's tents.*" Here Tam furrows his brow in concentration. "He said he had the king's writ to seek out, and hang all of these …"

" Malcontents?" Will says.

"That is it… bloody malcontenters," Tam replies. "Well, the town council all swore loyalty, and begged to be spared from the king's righteous anger. They also loaded his servant s saddle bags with a hundred marks of silver."

"Pray, tell me, what did this Thomas Cromwell look like?" Will Draper asks. "For I think something is sadly amiss here."

"Truly, it is," Richard Cromwell says. "For he would send me, or Mush, to collect any such revenues… if he ever did accept such a generous bribe … which he has not … ever."

"Hush, Richard," Will says. "Your tongue is making a noose for your own neck. Let the man describe Cromwell to us."

"I could," Tam says, crossing his heart with his fingers, "but there is no need. I told Rees ap Evans my story, and he almost choked on his beer. Tell them why, Rees."

"I used to live in Stepney," the Welshman says. "I learned the hooking trade as a lad, and thought London might prove to be fair pickings."

"You were a hooker then?" Will suppresses a smile. The man has never done a days honest work in his life. Now a rustler, he once plied his hooking skills in the big city. "Were you a top floor man, or a grounder?"

"Ground, sir," Rees ap Evans explains. "The prizes were smaller, but there was less danger. I would have my barbed pole in and out in a single breath, with a purse, or some such dainty caught on it. Top floor hooking was harder, and you were never sure what you might fish out. A mate of mine once hooked a pair of hose, with the fellow still pulling them on. He came roaring out, half naked, and with a sword in his hand."

"Most amusing, fellow, but what does that tell us? Richard growls. He dislikes petty thieves, and cutpurses and window hookers were the lowest scum to his mind.

"That I knew my way about London, Rees ap Evans tells the big man. I used to saunter past the new Whitehall Palace, and hang around Chelsea, hoping for a profitable hook, or the chance to cut a purse string. That was when I saw the king. Out he comes, surrounded by fine gentlemen, into the street, and sets off for the docks... on foot. I was amazed, and we all followed, hoping he might throw a few coppers to the crowd."

"Get to the point, Master Evans," Will advises.

"His Majesty was married to the Boleyn whore, and trying to get out of it. He was waving his arms, and shouting. They were all scared of him, save one fellow, who calmed him, and led him off like a bull with a ring in its nose. I asked who the man was, and they said he was called Thomas Cromwell, who was the coming man at court. So, I knew what he looked like when I saw him again in Ludlow."

"In Ludlow?" Will cannot recall Cromwell being much interested in the town, except when taxes were due. "You saw him in Ludlow?"

"I was stood not a dozen yards from him," Rees ap Evans confirms. He was being larded up by the warden of the castle. I think some money was exchanged."

"This is a mad story," Richard says. "My uncle does not ride about England soliciting bribes."

"He was in Ludlow, yesterday," Tam says. "We both saw him and his servant, lording it."

"My uncle is in London, attending upon the king," Richard says.

"Just so, Master Cromwell," the Welshman says with a sly wink at Will Draper. "You understand, I think, sir. A gentleman of your standing can see what I am saying… can t you?"

"Yes. I understand," Will Draper says. "The king s deer will be released back into his forest, and you two will join my company. I have officers, but few men. The choice is yours."

"With us, or…" Richard motions with his hand, to signify a noose about the neck.

"Your humble servants, Colonel Draper," Rees says. "How may may me and Tam serve you?"

"Return the stolen deer, warn your old master that I am investigating him, then make your way to Ludlow."

"You trust these men?" Richard is wary, and knows something is badly amiss, but he is slower thinking than most.

"They will obey me well enough, if only to avoid the spectre of the rope," Will says to him. "I am for Ludlow now, my friend. Are you coming, or not?"

"To meet my uncle… why not?" Richard Cromwell now sees what Will grasped at once, and his curiosity is quite boundless. The west country is being fleeced by the shadow of Thomas Cromwell, and cowers under his gaze. "We must ask him how many bribes he has taken, and why a tithe has not been paid over to the Austin Friars treasury. After all, if this fellow wishes to be a Cromwell, we must ask him why he does not pay for the privilege."

"Oh, I can think of a few better questions than that," Colonel Will Draper says. "To horse, my friend, and let us pay a call on your famous uncle at once!"

3 Ludlow

Rowland Lee considers dallying longer with the new maid, but the appointed hour is fast approaching, and he must prepare for his meeting with Thomas Cromwell. He rolls from his bed, and slaps the girl on her naked buttock.

"Good girl. You please me very much," he says. "Come to me again, after dinner, and there will be a shilling waiting for you."

"Thank ee, sur." It is the extent of her conversational skills, he thinks, and smiles. He can talk to his fellow bishops if he wants fine conversation. Little Meggy has other, more earthy, skills.

"Help me get dressed." The girl stands up, and strolls about the chamber, quite naked, picking up the bishop s discarded clothing. As she hands him each garment, she licks her lips, and gives him a dirty smile. At a shilling a go, she will be able to buy her own house within six months, she thinks, and be buggered with the filthy minded old cleric.

"Your servant, *sur*, Meggy mutters with practiced ease. She does not find the task of keeping Bishop Rowland Lee happy too onerous, and the coins he tosses to her augment the monthly amount she receives from the Privy Council fund. For a crown a month, she spies on the devious cleric, and sends a full, written report to one of the town's aldermen, who is employed by Austin Friars to be their eyes and ears in Ludlow.

"We are honoured today," Bishop Lee tells her. "The king's first minister is staying at the castle, and wishes me to take him on a tour of Ludlow. Master Cromwell is a very influential man, and I hope to gain his friendship. Why I tell you is a puzzle, for you would not know a lord from a turnip. Boots, girl!"

He watches her, as she bends to retrieve them from beneath the bed, and resolves to find her closer lodgings, so that he might avail himself of her more speedily. With boots tugged on, and a gold crucifix draped around his shoulders, he is ready for whatever the day brings.

*

"They will never fall for it." The middle aged man says, as he strolls out of the castle gate. "Someone will guess, and we will both be for the rope, Master Tully."

"Shut your moaning, Tom Cromwell," Tully replies.

"I hate it when you call me that," the fellow says. "I curse the day you ever saw the resemblance between us. I am Edmund Ambrose, and I will not…"

"Enough." Roland Tully s voice is hard, and has the effect of cowering all who need it. If the voice does not frighten them, his size most certainly would. He stands at a little over six feet two inches tall, and has fifteen years of working as a blacksmith behind him. His broad frame is muscular, and his strength is that of any two men. "I have bought you the right clothes, and taught you what mannerisms I recall. As long as we do not go near London, our little ruse will work, time and again."

"I am frightened. My wife and children never get to see me," the mock Tom Cromwell complains.

"You send them money, do you not?" Roland Tully has no relatives, family, or friends, and does not see their worth. A nagging wife only hampers a fellow, and children are a drain on his finances. "We made almost twenty pounds profit from Newport, and your share was six."

"Why do you take the greater part of what we make?" Edmund Ambrose asks. "After all, it is I who am impersonating a great lord. They will not think to arrest a servant."

"I paid out to get this game going. Two horses, clothes, and fancy baubles to hang about your neck cost me everything I got from the sale of my smithy." Tully is tired of having to constantly deal with Ambrose's petty complaints, and would ring his neck like a chicken, were he not such a fine investment. "I must have my seed money back, before we look at profits. What you say is true, of course. They will only see the great lord … not me, the poor humble servant… and hang you, if we are caught."

"I am scared."

"Yes, but of the wrong thing, Master Cromwell. You fear being taken by the king's men, who would hang you, no doubt, but you should really be fearing me. If I think you are trying to get out of our little arrangement, I will snap off your fingers, and gouge out your eyes. I will hurt you, beyond measure, old friend. Then, once I have done with you, I will pay a call on your pretty widow, and the children."

"You would not!"

"No?" Tully grins. "I like them plump, my friend. Imagine your Edith, brutally swived in front of your boys, and then choked to death."

"Dear Christ, Tully, do not threaten me so, or I will never be able to play my part," Ambrose says, truthfully. He knows what the retired blacksmith is capable of, and knows he would do exactly as he promises. Edith and his boys are all he has, and he dare not put them in danger. "I just think we are treading a dangerous path, and should consider giving it a rest for a few months. You must have made a tidy sum for yourself& and I have enough to keep hunger at bay for a full year."

"Very well," Roland Tully says. "We skin the good aldermen of Ludlow for all they are worth, and ride back to Cumberland. We will take a rest… a rest only… and return to the Welsh Marches in the Autumn."

"Have you ever thought what might happen if Thomas Cromwell falls from power?" Edmund Ambrose muses. "They might cut off his head, rather than mine. My poor face would be worth nothing to you then!"

*

"Why, Bishop Lee, good day to you." The alderman inclines his head, just enough to show a respect he does not feel for the venal old cleric.

"And to you, Master Brackenbury," the bishop replies. "How is your Bessie these days?"

"Improving, Your Grace," Brackenbury replies. His wife suffers from bouts of sickness, which usually strike when she does not wish to accompany her husband on civic business. Like most honest women in Ludlow, she does not wish to be in the company of Bishop Rowland Lee, who is renowned for his lewdness with servants, and for having broken at least eight of the ten commandments on a regular basis.

"I will include the lady in my prayers," the bishop says, and makes a vague sign of the cross with his bejewelled fingers. "It seems that I have the senior title amongst us, alderman, and should therefore greet our esteemed visitor."

"If it so pleases you, bishop," the alderman says, with relief in his voice. "I never like these sudden visits. They never bode well, and usually end up costing we merchants."

"Master Cromwell must have a good reason to call on us," the bishop tells him. "If it were bad tidings, he would be here with a troop of soldiers, and a fist full of arrest warrants."

"We shall see," Brackenbury mutters. Then he points a trembling finger. "He is here now, with but one servant. My God, the fellow is a veritable giant!"

"Welcome, My Lord." Bishop Lee steps forward, into the road, and bows to the king's favourite councillor. Thomas Cromwell smiles, and beckons for the bishop to come closer. When they are only a couple of paces apart, Master Cromwell bows, and takes the bishop's hand. He kisses it, with due reverence, and straightens up.

"I am not a lord, Your Grace," he explains to the startled bishop. "I am but an *esquire*, and must show you the proper respect due your rank. That is why I travel with but one body servant. He is a dumb bastard, right enough, but he has his uses."

"He is of a veritable gargantuan size, my dear sir," Bishop Rowland Lee replies, and Roland Tully gives him a glacial stare in return. The two men, with their similar given names, share a common disdain for the law, and the basic morality of everyday life, whilst one is a common rogue, and the other a consecrated bishop.

"He suits me well enough, and his bearing offers me the protection due to my station. The common people see him, and offer me more respect," says Cromwell. "Nice ring, by the way."

"Oh, this thing? It is a trifling gift from one of the Welsh barons," Bishop Lee replies. "I helped him in a border dispute, and he was thoughtful enough to send me this worthless trinket... pretty though it is."

"God always smiles down on generous men," Cromwell says.

"Perhaps, if you do not think it impertinent of me..." Bishop Lee slips the ring from his finger and hands it to the counterfeit Cromwell. "A small token of Ludlow s undying affection for you. Do not think it to be a bribe... for it is a worthless piece of coloured glass."

"What a charming little gesture," the counterfeit Thomas Cromwell says, and slips the ring onto a free finger. It is a particularly fine emerald, he thinks, worth two hundred pounds or more. "I have nothing sopretty to offer you in return, sir... except for my favour concerning this latest unfortunate border dispute."

"Border dispute?" Bishop Rowland Lee can feel a cold, empty space in his stomach. The disputing of borders can lead to years of wrangling, and bloody skirmishes. "It is the first I have heard, My Lor... Master Cromwell."

"It is not yet public knowledge," Cromwell replies. "It is still under review, and I am scouting the land, as it were. The proposed re-drawing of the boundaries will move the Welsh border to run to the east of Ludlow."

"Christ in Heaven!" Bishop Rowland Lee sees the terrible danger at once. If Ludlow becomes Welsh, his own diocese will be cut in two, with the better estates on the wrong side of the border. "Who has thought up such a simple minded scheme?"

"The king."

"I meant no offence, sir." The bishop cringes at the report that might now be written. The Bishop of Ludlow has called his benefactor, the king, simple minded. "Where is the advantage?"

"With the border region enlarged, the king will have created enough spare land to create a new dukedom, and a half dozen baronetcies," the fake Cromwell explains. There is just enough truth in the tale to make it sound plausible, and Ambrose tightens the noose by explaining what the people of Ludlow are about to face. "The king seeks to disband the Border Council that runs the marches so effectively, and create a large kingdom within a kingdom. Ludlow would be swallowed up in this new region, which will be a vast hunting reserve for the Prince of Wales."

"There is no Prince of Wales," Bishop Rowland Lee exclaims.

"Not yet, but the king is looking forward to the safe delivery of a little baby prince in October, is he not?" Ambrose almost giggles at how easy it all is. "Your power, and the power of the Border Council will be broken. We must discuss it at dinner. I presume there is to be a banquet?"

"Of course, sir. Will you return to the castle afterwards, or would you prefer I found you lodgings here in the town?"

"Oh, that is kind of you, Bishop Lee," the fake Cromwell says. "Take our baggage to the Bishop's Palace, Tully, and prepare my clothes for this evening. Pray tell, Bishop Lee, where will you sleep tonight?"

"I shall manage, sir," Lee replies. In the space of a few minutes Thomas Cromwell has wheedled a ring worth at least two hundred and fifty pounds out of him, and appropriated his house. The signs are there, he thinks, that this fellow might be susceptible to an open bribe.

"Excellent," Ambrose mutters. He is now all Cromwell, and the sense of power rushes to his head. "Pray you, Your Grace, introduce these other good people to me."

"Of course, sir," Bishop Lee says. "Might I name the secretary of the Border Council, Master Brackenbury? This is Master Toby Rowe, an alderman of Ludlow, and this gentleman is …"

The bishop stops in his tracks, and tries to recall who this well dressed fellow is who has just joined the line. "This is … pray jostle my memory, young man, for I fear that I cannot put a name to the face."

"My name is Colonel Will Draper, Your Grace, and I am the senior King's Examiner," Will says, and bows. "It is a pleasure to meet you once again, Master Cromwell."

"Ah, you two have met?" Brackenbury asks, ingenuously.

"Why, I have met the king's first minister many times," Will says. He gives Ambrose a small nod of the head, and the fake Cromwell can feel his legs begin to give way. It is then that the real mastermind of the scheme shows his true worth. He steps forward, takes Ambrose by the elbow, and steers him towards their horses.

"No time to linger, master," Roland Tully says. "We must press on to Gloucester, at once."

"What's that? Oh, yes, of course we must. Must rush, that is. Pleasure meeting you, Your Grace." Ambrose is at the side of his horse. He mounts, and wonders when someone will shout, or try to grab at him. Instead, he and Tully mount, and spur their horses down the road.

"I do not understand," Bishop Lee says. "What is going on?"

Will Draper raises a hand for calm, and explains how they were about to try and bribe a complete charlatan. He also confirms that the king has no plans to dissolve the Border Council, and that the threatened estates are quite safe.

"Thank God you came, sir," Bishop Lee says. Then his face grows red, and he almost screams out the words. "My ring. The rascal has stolen my emerald ring!"

"No, sir," Will Draper tells him, with awry smile. "You gave it, freely, as a gift. I saw it with my own eyes!"

*

"I warned you this would happen one day, Tully," Edmund Ambrose says, once they are clear of the town. They dismount, and lead the panting horses, so as not to tire them completely. "The King s Royal Examiner stared right at me. The man is obviously no fool. Once he works out what is going on, I will be…"

"Shut it, you snivelling turd!" Roland Tully sneers. "They will be after us before dark, and baying for blood. I am for Cumberland, as fast as I can. I shall ride one horse, and lead the other behind me. That way, I can change mounts, and get on my way much faster.

"A great idea," Edmund Ambrose says. "Am I to walk then?"

"You can do what you wish."

"They will take me, Tully," Ambrose tells his partner. "I am not a strong man. If they seek to torture me, I must tell them everything."

"Yes, that is a weakness in my plan," Tully says, and places a hand on his comrade's quivering shoulder. "Like they do say, my poor, weak friend... dead men tell no tales. I will make it quick."

"Christ on the Cross!" Ambrose tries to break away, but he has no strength, and Tully grins at the fear on his face. Though he has killed men before, he has never strangled one to death, and he wonders what it will feel like.

"Calm yourself," Tully tells him. "It will be a swift end."

"Unhand that fellow, you rascal!" Captain John Beckshaw stands before them, hand resting on his sword hilt. "I am a King s Examiner, and would have words with you both."

"You damned Examiners are all over Ludlow, like turds in a puddle," Roland Tully growls. There is but one in front of him, and one, probably, coming up behind. "I have no business with you. Step aside from the road, and let us pass."

"You mean to murder your comrade," John Beckshaw declares, "and I will not have it, sir. Surrender yourself to the king's justice."

"Or what... you vain dandycock?" Roland Tully pushes Ambrose aside, and comes at John Beckshaw, as if ready to strike him down.

"Or face me." Richard Cromwell looms out of the hedgerow, with a dagger in one hand, and a cudgel in the other. Until this moment, he thought himself to be a man of great height and strength, but he sees that this rogue Tully has a good three inches on him, and has a bigger, more muscled chest.

Then I will face you, Tully sneers. He has no fear, and is confident that he can master this newcomer. "What is it to be, you fat ugly turd, knives, or bare hands?"

"Man to man," Richard Cromwell replies, and throws aside his weapons. "Win, and you shall go free."

"This is madness," John Beckshaw whispers as the younger Cromwell peels off his doublet and shirt. "What if he kills you?"

"Shoot him in the balls, Richard says to his comrade, quietly. "I cannot refuse a challenge, Master John." He squares up to Tully, who also throws aside his upper clothing. It makes things easier, as there is nothing then for an opponent to grip, and it also shows that there are no hidden weapons.

"You have but to yield," Tully says, "and I will spare your life. Otherwise, I will knock you about, and break your back. I am from Cumberland, and was county champion at wrestling, three years in a row."

"You northern fellows do like the sound of your own loud prating, do you not?" Richard Cromwell is happy to let the man boast, for what he says acts as a warning to him. The huge fellow will know certain holds, and know how to throw an opponent to the ground, and finish him off.

Roland Tully circles, and watches for an opening. Cromwell drops his left shoulder, to try and wrong foot the man, and grabs at him. Tully twists away, and throws himself at Cromwell, who is not quick enough to avoid a solid thump into his shoulder.

The force of the blow makes Richard stagger back, and he is astonished at how easily

Tully moves. The giant ex blacksmith dances around him, looking for a chance to throw his enemy, then lashes out a foot. It connects with Richard s left leg, high on the thigh, and he grunts with pain. Tully dance away, and laughs. It is proving to be easier than he thought. Richard Cromwell may be a big, strong fellow, but he lacks speed, and the wit to see what is coming at him next.

Tully side steps a crude rush from Richard, who stumbles, and goes down onto his knees. The huge Cumberland wrestler forms his fists into a hammer, and raises them above his head, to deliver the killer blow. Cromwell heaves himself up, pushes his shoulder into Tully s midriff and, to the amazement of both Edmund Ambrose, and John Beckshaw, lifts the Cumberland man right off his feet.

Tully's arms flail, as he is then dashed to the ground. The impact drives the air from his body in a great rush, and he knows he is at Richard Cromwell's mercy. He throws up a hand, as if to stave off the inevitable end.

"Quarter... I beg of you, sir!" Roland Tully cries, and Richard Cromwell nods, and moves away. The cunning ex blacksmith sees his chance, and pulls out the knife he keeps concealed within his boot.

"Beware, sir!" Edmund Ambrose shouts, and Cromwell twists around, even as the deadly blade cuts up at him. He reaches out to parry the thrust, and the sharp edged blade slices open his palm, and scores a hit in Richard s right shoulder. The knife jars against the shoulder blade, and Tully screams like a beast coming in for the kill.

Richard feels the sharp pain, and the solid thud of metal against shoulder bone. He knows that he has seconds to act, before he passes out. He brings his bloodied hand up, behind Tully's neck, and drives his right hand up, under his treacherous enemy's exposed chin. The head snaps back with a jolt, and just before he passes out, Richard Cromwell hears the sharp snap of the man's spine.

*

"You damned great idiot," Will Draper says. "Could you not have just put a pistol to the fellow's head?"

"It was a matter of pride," Richard Cromwell replies, sheepishly.

"Hubris, Will, pure hubris," Captain John Beckshaw says to his commander, as he binds Richard's cut hand.

"That too, I suppose," Richard says. "What of my shoulder… is it badly hurt?"

"He missed the muscle, and blunted the point of his blade on your dense bones," Will Draper replies. "What would I have told your uncle?"

"That I died most honourably?" Richard suggests, and he receives a dark scowl for his pains. "I could not let it pass, Will. I had to fight him… as if compelled by some inner voice."

"Well, that makes it all right then," Will snaps. "You are such a … such a child."

It is the old Austin Friars way. The air is cleared, with the judicious use of a few well aimed barbs. There will be no lasting rift between the two, even though Richard begins to see why his friend is angry. Roland Tully was the mastermind of the scheme, and now, he cannot be questioned.

"What of my bogus uncle?" Richard asks. "There is a certain likeness of features, but close up … I think not."

"From a distance, I thought it to be Master Thomas, even though I knew differently," Will says. "This Master Edmund Ambrose may prove to be a useful fellow to have around."[

"I saved your life," Ambrose says to the younger Cromwell. "Would you put me in chains for that, kind sir?"

"Chains? What, we are not going to hang him right here? Richard asks, and Edmund quails in fear.

"No, I shall have Rees and Tam escort our prisoner to Austin Friars."

"You actually trust those two rascals?" John Beckshaw asks.

"They will be loyal. I have given them a stay of execution, not a pardon. If they fail me, the gallows awaits. If they are loyal, I shall find them a fine uniform to wear, and pay them a florin a week," says Will.

"What next for us, Will?" the captain asks. "We have solved the puzzle of the missing deer, and foiled a scheme to rob an entire town. What else can we accomplish?"

"Back to London," Will says. "I have not seen my children for almost two weeks, and I do miss my Miriam. I expect Prudence will be happy to see you too?"

"She will be waiting at the door for me," John Beckshaw says. "It is uncanny, but she knows the moment I start for home, and seems able to know my wishes, even before I have voiced them."

"That is just love, John, not magic." Richard Cromwell says. "I long to see my own dear girl. He is still conducting an exciting sexual liaison with Lady Jane Rochford, widow of the late, unlamented, George Boleyn, and likes to think of it as a great love affair. In time, no doubt, the noblewoman will tire of him, and seek a more suitable partner.

"Lady Rochford must tax your purse," Will says. "She likes her luxurious furs and fine jewels, does she not?"

"I make a tidy living these days," Richard replies, defensively. His mercantile endeavours are quite profitable, and he makes a good living selling his favours to other merchants. Everyone wants to be associated with the Cromwell faction, and Richard receives fees for little more than the odd signature, or a glowering look at a competitor. Enough, more than enough, to keep an expensive mistress.

"Does my brother-in-law still moon after Lady Mary?" Will asks, but he already has a shrewd idea of the answer. Mary Boleyn is ten years Mush's senior, and looking for a stable future. Once the king has forgotten her, she will petition Thomas Cromwell, and ask him to keep his word. The Privy Councillor has promised her a good, reliable husband, and some worthy estate in Cheshire, where she can hide herself away from the persistent scandals that attach themselves to her family name.

"Not so much," Richard tells him. "In truth, he itches for an adventure. He longs to see foreign lands, and make his fortune from deeds of bravura. I, myself, am too old for such flights of fancy, and am resolved to settle down to a life of being a merchant."

"May we all get what we wish for," John Beckshaw mutters. He wants nothing more than a steady income, an interesting occupation, and a brood of children to keep his family name alive in years to come. "Things around the court are quiet now, and we must hope for a future full of good living."

"There will always be gangs of thieves to take," Will Draper replies. "Murders to solve, traitors to run down, and crimes to investigate. The office of King s Examiner will grow in the years to come, until we have officers in every town in England."

"The law is for the rich," Richard Cromwell says. "There is no profit in the poor seeking our help. We would starve whilst keeping them safe."

"Then they should have it for nothing," says Will. It is an idea much in his head these days, that the law be free to all, paid for by the crown, and he wonders if such a fanciful thing can ever be implemented. "Let us ride, my friends, and see what awaits us, back in London."

The prospect of scattering those whom he holds most dear to the four winds does not appeal to Thomas Cromwell, but force of circumstance dictates his actions once more. Often he finds that the fates direct him away from his favoured course, and he must bow down to their more urgent needs.

"Never heard of the place," Tom Wyatt says, as he pores over an old, crudely drawn, map of the far away Grecian islands. "I am more familiar with those places mentioned in the Ten Labours of Hercules, Master Tom."

"See, here it lies," Tom Cromwell says, and stabs a finger at the poorly made chart. "If you sail from Venice, and travel down the length of the Italian peninsula, you come to the island. It is where the great Greek hero, Ulysses landed, on his return from Troy."

"Would that he were still there," Thomas Wyatt replies, a little too tartly. "For it would save me an unwelcome sea voyage."

"It is Miriam Draper s ships that will do all the voyaging," Cromwell explains. "All you and Mush need do is journey, overland to Venice, then meet the fleet at Puglia. The Doge will make you welcome, and ensure your travel warrants are all in place. It will be an easy ride through beautiful countryside to meet up with our fleet."

"What then, sir?" Mush asks. "We are two lone Englishmen, with three or four merchant ships at our call."

"Packed with twenty canon, muskets, victuals for six months, and a crew of fighting men, Miriam's fleet will be a formidable force." Cromwell knows Mush is keen, and just wants a little encouragement. "Once on Corfu, you simply take over command of the main fortress, and fortify the island against the Turks… who may never actually turn up."

"How many men will we have?" the poet asks. "Fighting men, I mean… not merchants and fops."

"Perhaps three hundred English sailors, and as many again Venetian soldiers in the garrisons, Tom Cromwell says. "Six hundred heavily armed men, with canon, can hold Corfu Castle against an army, if well led."

"Until the food and water runs out, of course," Mush says.

"By then, the Turkish invaders will be a spent force. They will take a few of the smaller islands, and retire, to lick their wounds." Thomas Cromwell can see the lust for adventure in his young men's eyes, and so, he presses on. "With the Sultan's army repelled, the wealth of Corfu is ours, for an agreed period. The Venetians will retain ownership of the island, and in return, the Doge will pay us handsomely."

"How handsomely?" Mush is in it for the adventure, but he also has certain financial outgoings. Neither Master Wyatt nor myself are wealthy men yet.

"You will make twice as much as you made from the Venetian war," Cromwell says. "Enough to buy yourselves a goodly estate in England, and live like lords for the rest of your lives. What say you?"

"Yes, of course." Tom Wyatt has never been free of debt, and the prospect of action, and a fortune in treasure, is more than enough for him. "And what about you, my friend?"

"I cannot let a fool like you loose against the Turks alone," Mush Draper says. "Besides, I have no choice. It is foretold, by Pru Beckshaw."

"That girl *sees* too much," Tom Cromwell mutters. "What does she say now, Mush?"

"She had a dream," Mush says. "She said a chosen one shall overcome a false idol, and walk, unharmed from the furnace."

"Fair enough," Tom Wyatt says, with a silly smile on his face. "When do we start out?"

"Chosen one… furnace?" Thomas Cromwell shakes his head at the vague prophesising. If a girl's idle prattling gets the task underway, then so be it, he thinks. He has chosen Mush and Wyatt, and Corfu is furnace like at any time of the year anyway!

*

Thomas Cromwell is pleased at how easily the Corfu expedition has been arranged, and leaves the minor details for Rafe Sadler and Richard to work out. They will liaise with the redoubtable Miriam Draper, and a plan of meticulous beauty will come into being.

Convincing Will Draper that he should embroil himself in what has become known as the 'Scottish Matter' is going to be an entirely different business. He has forewarned Miriam that he must avail himself of her husband's special abilities, and prevailed on her to invite him to dine with them that evening, so that he might start the steady drip of persuasion.

Two of his sturdier lads escort him to Draper House at the appointed time, armed with daggers, and lighted firebrands. Their sinister black costumes warn passers by to keep on passing by, and deter any would be felons from chancing their arms. The bodyguard will stand vigil, outside Draper House, until the master is ready to walk the half mile back to Austin Friars.

At some point, hot food, and drink will be taken out to them by Miriam's kitchen girls, and they will be as well attended as is their master within. Cromwell knows this, and is content that his lads will not suffer for their loyalty.

"Yes, sir?" Young Adam, Will Draper's servant, answers to the knock, and he peers out into the gloom. "What is your business?"

"It is I, Adam," Tom Cromwell says, pulling off his cap, and stepping inside the large entrance hall. "I am expected."

"Who shall I say is calling, sir?" Adam asks. Thomas Cromwell has a moment of concern, and he wonders if the boy is going addle pated.

"Why, it is I... Tom Cromwell, lad. What ails your eyes?"

"What ails you, sir?" Adam replies. "Master Cromwell is already here, and dining with my master. Who are you?"

"What is this foolishness?" Tom Cromwell thinks the lad has been drinking, and pushes him, gently aside. He steps forward, throws open the door to the great hall, and sees himself digging into a plate of oysters. For a second he can only think how odd it is, as he has never liked the things. "Great Christ... what is this?"

"Who are you, sir!" The oyster guzzling Cromwell declares, as he jumps to his feet. "And, pray tell me at once... what are you doing with my face? Return it to me at once!" The room erupts into laughter, and Thomas Cromwell moves towards his double.

"This is … astounding," he says.

"Quite astounding," the fake Tom Cromwell replies. "You look like me."

"Who are you, fellow?" Cromwell demands.

"No, sir… I ask… who are you?" Ambrose replies, mimicking Cromwell's brusque voice.

"Enough, Master Ambrose." Will Draper rises from his seat, and takes Cromwell by the arm. Come and meet Master Edmund Ambrose, sir… your likeness in so many ways."

"Your servant," Ambrose says, and bows low. He has been carefully schooled in how to behave with Cromwell, if he wishes to live. My fortune is my… or rather, *your* face, my dear Master Cromwell. I perceive that you are, in fact, every bit as handsome as I was told."

Thomas Cromwell takes the seat of honour, and pushes aside the oysters. It was seeing himself eating such a detested food that gave him the greatest shock.

"If you are me, sir, you must learn to eat like me. No oysters, unless the king demands it of you, and I cannot abide poor wine!"

The two Cromwells exchange words throughout dinner, and by the final pudding course, they come to an understanding. The Privy Councillor is a busy man, yet is often saddled with ridiculous tasks at the king s whim. Run down to examine the dock yards, the king says, and there are three days wasted. Ride off to look at the York fortifications, and another week is lost. Even the task of standing on the steps of some small town hall, and shaking hands with an alderman wastes precious time.

Make these visits for me, Master Ambrose, Thomas Cromwell says, and I will find you and your family a house in the country, and a small pension. Otherwise, there is one Thomas Cromwell too many in this world.

"Put in such a charming way, sir, Edmund Ambrose says, "and I cannot refuse. I shall be your double, as duty demands."

"Good fellow. Will, we must never be seen together, after this night's meal," Cromwell says. "Master Ambrose must avoid looking like me, until his peculiar attribute is needed. Now, with the meal finished, I must crave a moment of your own time, for the king has need of your services."

"At your service, Master Tom." Will has eaten well, and enjoyed the jest played on his old master. Now, he is in a cordial mood, and ready to help where he can. In the morning, he might regret his equanimity, but for now, he is eager to please the man who gave him his start in life.

*

God's teeth, Master Tom… not France again?" Will Draper has an aversion to the country, caused in the main, by the fact that every time he visit's the place, someone tries to kill him. "Can you not send Mush, or even your nephew?"

"It is not something I can ask of them." Thomas Cromwell knows how easily he could offend Will, and tries not to alienate him from the start. "It needs a man of rare ability. A man who can think, rather than act… then act without thinking."

"It sounds like you want me to do murder," Will replies. He sees the look in Cromwell s eyes, and curses. "You want me to kill someone for you? Then you are mistaken… for Richard is your man for such a thing. I do not do cold blooded murder."

"No, but you have often killed, to protect England, or the king. Why, I recall how you cut down those who would have slain Queen Katherine… rather than let them kill her, and make Henry's life easier."

"That was a moral decision," Will argues. I could not let them murder an innocent woman, no matter what the circumstances were."

"You killed Malatesta Baglione in Italy."

"I did not." Will Draper is appalled that this vile rumour still persists. "I arrested him, and would have turned him over to the Doge of Venice for punishment … had not one of his vengeful victims administered poison to him. I do not have his blood on my hands."

"Then hear me out, and decide the morality of what must be done," Thomas Cromwell asks.

"Of course, I owe you that, sir, but do not presume I will kill to order. I live, and will die, by my own code."

"Rafe Sadler visited the old Dowager Queen of Scots the other day," Cromwell starts. "The king was worried, lest she has to live in anything less than pomp and splendour."

"Her holdings would feed England's poor for a decade, Will mutters. "God forbid she must lose a castle or two."

"Nevertheless, Rafe visited, and asked for her help. He offered her a pension, in return for privileged information from the court of King James. Her son is a flighty sort, and often involves himself in strange plots. I sought only some foreknowledge of his more peculiar actions."

"I see. She turns spy, for gold, and betrays her son." Draper shakes his head.

"We all have a price, Will," Tom Cromwell says. "To seal the deal, Queen Mary intimated that James was speaking, treasonably, with one of the inner circle of the English court."

"That is an easy boast to make," Will says.

"Of course." Thomas Cromwell knows the queen could well choose any name, out of mischief. "So, I asked some of my agents to investigate. You were not here, so I put others on the scent."

"Who did the Dowager Queen of Scots name?" Will Draper asks. False accusations are part and parcel of his everyday work, and it is often difficult to separate truth from untruth.

"The Duchess of Salisbury."

"Ah, Lady Pole is an easy target," Will says. "She is the daughter of a Plantagenet, and a member of a great Roman Catholic family. She always hated Anne Boleyn, and the king, perversely, admires her for it. I would tread most carefully, until some solid evidence is found."

"Oh, it is found," Tom Cromwell says. "Found in abundance, I fear. Lady Salisbury uses travelling catholic priests to convey letters across the continent. She writes to Rome, to Paris, and to her exiled son in France."

"Treasonably?" This is the crux of the matter, Will thinks. Be she a traitor, or a silly woman passing on gossip?

"She is careful not to mention the king, but deplores the Protestant faith, and wonders at how the Holy Roman Empire, France, and Rome, can hold back their righteous anger," Cromwell says.

"Lady Salisbury sails close to the wind," Will agrees, "but that does not mean she must be killed. One woman, with hysterical views on religion, hardly poses any real threat."

"It is what she writes to King James that causes me the most concern," Tom Cromwell says. "Once we knew she was in contact with the Scottish king, we sought out how she delivered the letters to his hand. Rather than through a priest, she used Scottish merchants, who travel freely across the country. Soon, we knew what was going on."

"Treason?" Will sees that this cannot be heading anywhere else. To write to a foreign king, and in secret, reeks of betrayal.

"She suggests to King James that he visits Paris… and he does," Tom Cromwell explains. "He is there now. She suggests James speaks to King François, and he does. Lady Salisbury proposes a marriage, between one of the French king's sons, and one of her own daughters."

"That is rather an odd proposition, is it not," Will says.

"Not really. It allies the Valois house with that of Plantagenet, and gives them a claim to the thrones of each nation. She also proposes that her third eldest son, who is the great grand-nephew of the last Plantagenet king of England, is married to our own Princess Mary. She plots to steal Mary away, and force the marriage on her. With Tudor and Plantagenet merged, Henry will be ousted by an alliance of France, Spain, and the Roman Catholic Pole family."

"That is utter madness," Will says. "Mary is guarded, and the Pole fellow is in exile. As for her daughter marrying a French prince... I think not. François does not barter his children away so easily. He always wants full value for money."

"Mary is no longer under armed guard," Thomas Cromwell says. "One of the many wonderful things that Queen Jane has achieved, is her step daughters reconciliation to her father. She lives, openly, in the king's own household. Jane Seymour loves her like a mother, and cherishes little Elizabeth."

"You can stop Lady Salisbury's plans easily enough," Will Draper says. "Forbid the Pole family to travel, and post secret guards on Mary for a few months. Henry will be none the wiser."

"Quite so, but the main problem still exists. Lady Pole supports her son in exile, and urges him to attack Henry at every turn. For his part, Reginald Pole is a dangerous man. He connives with the Bishop of Rome, entreats François to threaten us with war, and sends Papist priests into England to disrupt our new church."

"I see why you want him dead, but not by my hand."

"Go to France, Will," Thomas Cromwell urges. "Travel with Rafe, who is commanded to join up with Stephen Gardiner, the Bishop of Winchester. Together, you are to entreat with François, and try to win him away from the Scottish king's side. Once there, you must assess the situation, and act as you think fit."

"You want Reginald Pole dead," Will Draper reiterates, "and I will not do it."

"I do not ask you to assassinate the man in cold blood, my friend," Cromwell says. "Find a way to get him back to England, or dissuade him from any more acts of treason. That is all I ask."

"You should send a diplomat." Will Draper wishes nothing to do with the proposal, but finds it hard to refuse his old master. "Send Tom Wyatt, for he has ambassadorial skills."

"Stephen Gardiner is an adept diplomat, and Rafe Sadler is able to argue our case from a clever legal standpoint, but you, Will, have that certain… common touch. You absorb your surroundings, and adapt yourself to them. Whatever the outcome, I know you will make the right choices."

"Then I will go to France," Will Draper says. He is sure there will be a catch, but that is how Cromwell is. Even in telling the truth, he looks to deceive… just in case. "When do we leave?"

"Tomorrow. All the principles have left Amiens, and are now congregating at Arras. With luck, your unexpected arrival will discomfit the Scottish king, if nothing else!"

"Discomfit him enough to want us dead, perhaps?" Will muses.

*

"I shall miss having you about the house," Miriam Draper tells her brother, as he packs a bag with spare clothes and a couple of extra daggers. "Though Master Tom says you might be back within six or seven months."

"As Tom Wyatt and I are to defeat the entire Ottoman world, I would allow an extra week or two on that estimation," Mush says, tongue in cheek. In truth, he fears that the odds on success are poor indeed.

"Am I expecting too much?" Miriam is Mush's only living relative, and she is torn between opportunity, and love for her little brother. "After all, we are rich enough, are we not?"

"*You* are rich, sister," Mush replies. "I cannot live off you forever. I must make my own fortune."

"They say that the Sultan Suleiman has a thousand galleys, and two hundred thousand soldiers at his disposal." Miriam begins to frighten herself.

"He must hold Egypt, Turkey, and the Greek lands with them," Mush tells his sister. "He will only be able to spare so many for an invasion of Corfu. I doubt he could manage more than fifty galleys, and an army of ten or fifteen thousand men. Once inside Corfu castle, ringed with English canon, we will stand them off until they start to starve."

"You promise not to attack them?" Miriam asks because she knows Tom Wyatt, who can be quick to go on the offensive. "Never open the gates, or chase them, not even if they seem to run away in fear?"

"I promise," Mush says. "Now, let me make my farewells to Will, and the others."

"What of Lady Mary?" Mary Boleyn is on her estate in the south, and unaware that her lover is about to sail half way across the world. Their affair, conducted in secret, for the most part, has survived the turbulent removal of her sister Anne from the throne, and flourished, despite the decade between them. After the death of his beloved wife, Mary seems to be the only woman who can touch his heart.

"I have written," Mush says. Mary owes him nothing, and seeks a good marriage. She is not getting any younger, and must make her choices soon, if she is to have a future of her own. "She will understand, and either wait for me … or not."

"Then I wish you well, brother," Miriam tells him. "Give my fond regards to Tom Wyatt, and bid him behave like a gentleman."

"He is making his own fond farewells," Mush replies, with a lopsided smile. It seems his poor wife is in London… and is heavy with child."

"May God grant him a second fine son," Miriam says, without thinking. All men want a son, if the truth be known, and a girl child is little more than a bargaining token, useful for making family alliances.

"Oh, that is the last thing our poet wants," Mush says, "as he has not been home for these last ten months!"

"The biter has been bitten then?" Good for her, Miriam thinks. The poet has cheated on her for years, and treated her with casual disdain. "I cannot see how he can deny paternity, without becoming the laughing stock of the young blades at court."

"Truly said, sister. He now wants nothing more than to get as far away from England as possible!

*

"God, but I hate Calais." It is an often voiced sentiment, and Tom Wyatt means it as fervently as all those others who have said the same over the years. The town, a piece of England, perched on the rump of France is a disgusting sinkhole of vice, filth, and iniquity, but that is not why the poet hates the place so much.

He hates Calais because it is the starting point of so many of the worse parts of his life, and reminds him of some times he would much rather forget. Considering he is a diplomat, and a love poet, Tom Wyatt has far too much blood on his hands.

"We must only stay the one night," Will Draper says, "before we part company, and each go our own ways. Rafe and I are for Arras, whilst you and Mush are for Venice. You must remember to deliver my letters to the Doge, Mush. Miriam, you, and I, owe him so much."

"A debt we will repay," Mush says. "When we save his precious island of Corfu, he will be in our debt, and I will be rich enough to do what I want with my life."

"Still longing to see the wonders of the Holy Land?" Tom Wyatt asks. "Why, I might even come with you, old friend. Do they have a need for poets in Jerusalem?"

"Who can tell… do you know of any?" Mush smiles at Wyatt's flighty nature. The man would be as at ease in Jerusalem, Constantinople, or Putney. "I hear it is the most beautiful place in the world. Such splendour might inspire you to start writing decent verses."

"And the women?" the poet asks, not in the least affronted. He knows, in his heart, that his best work will only come when he has experienced life to the full. "Are they exotic, and lovely?"

"That is for us to find out," Mush replies.

*

"Until we meet again, brother-in-law," Mush says. "How I wish you were coming with us."

"Would that I could, Mush," Will Draper says, earnestly. "For I have no taste for all this court intrigue. What care I if this Reginald Pole whispers poison into the ear of François, and the Bishop of Rome?"

"Can you not just slit the bastard's throat, and then come with us?" Mush asks. "I know you and your morals, but if the fellow needs damned well killing … then kill him. Shall I linger a day more, and do the deed for you?"

"Not for me, Mush," Will says. "I want no more blood on my hands than there has to be. If it is kill, or be killed, I know what to do, but I cannot murder a man because he does not believe in Henry's new church."

"I hear this Pole is a man of influence," Tom Wyatt says. "I think I might have played with him, as a child, but I do not recall that well. What if he wants you dead?"

"Then I will do all I can to stop him," Will Draper tells the poet. "Now, to horse, my friends. You have a long ride across France, and down into the Veneto. God, but I would love to see Venice again. Its beauty is blinding to the senses."

"Let us hope the Venice we remember is still safe," Mush muses. "With a hundred thousand men at his command, Suleiman the Magnificent may already be the new Doge of Venice."

"Then you must return home," Will says.

"And leave poor Venice in the hands of barbarians?" Mush shakes his head. "No, my friend. We must stop the progress of the

Ottomans now, or soon, they will be sailing their fleet up the Thames. Their faith, though flawed, is a strong one, and glorifies the making of war on any who do not bow to them."

"Then, God be with you," Will says.

"And with you," Mush replies. "May he have eyes in the back of his head during these next few months!"

5   Arras

Will Draper watches as his two friends trot off, into the fertile Calaisis region, and wonders if they will ever meet again. It takes only a random musket shot, or a wayward crossbow bolt to change a man s fate forever.

"Then we are for Arras, Rafe," Will says to his lone companion. "How far have we to travel?"

"Sixty miles, at a rough guess," Rafe replies. "I have arranged for fresh horses along the way, and a stop at an inn, half way. We will be in Arras for the day after tomorrow."

"And what of Bishop Gardiner?"

"He is lodged close to the French court, and pays daily visits to make friends," Rafe explains, and shakes the purse at his belt. "He mutters to their bishops, and intimates that Henry might return to the church of Rome, provided the French help us."

"They will not believe that," Will scoffs. "Henry would rather cut his own throat than go back on what he has ordained. He, and his England, will remain Protestant to his dying breath. What else does he do?"

"He bribes courtiers to speak well of King Henry to King François."

"I wager they all take his silver quickly enough." Will shakes his head in disbelief. "The Scots king will get his way, because Stephen Gardiner, the Bishop of Winchester, does not know how to fight his enemy. We must make all speed to Arras, and turn the tables on King James."

"You have a plan?"

"Of course. It is what Tom Cromwell wants of me. He wishes me to destroy our enemy, by whatever means we have at our disposal. I will not do murder for him, but I am not above playing a few jests on the king s enemies."

"Jests?" Rafe Sadler does not think high politics to be a laughing matter, and worries at what the King's Examiner has in mind. "The French do not have a good sense of humour, my friend."

"Then we must do their laughing for them," Will says with a wry grin. "Let us teach these fellows how our English wit is as sharp as our English steel!"

*

"How are we today, madam?"

"We are both well, sire," Queen Jane says, and pats her stomach with affection. "The child is thriving, according to dear Doctor Theophrasus. I would have him by my side, always, such is his medical skill."

"The man makes for a deucedly fine royal physician," the king agrees. "Thomas Cromwell found him you know. The rumour about court is that he helped Will Draper out in some way, and so came to Tom Cromwell's attention. Thomas will not speak of it, of course, so I assume it was some dark secret, best left undisturbed."

"Oh, that?" Jane smiles, and drops her voice, so as to lend drama to the tiny morsel of information. "The colonel was forced to open a grave, so that he could establish how a man died. The doctor was able to prove murder had been done, simply by observing the dead man, and the culprit was quickly arrested."

"Who told you that?" Henry is baffled as to why his queen should know that which he does not, and wishes an answer.

"Er... the doctor, I think." In truth, it was Tom Cromwell, during one of their rare meetings alone. It is a dangerous game to play, but they enjoy one another's company far too much to desist from the pastime. One day, her dear Tom Cromwell often says, it will all end very badly. "Just idle chatter, I suppose, aimed at helping me to rest."

"I really must speak with this doctor one day," Henry says, gruffly. If there are to be secrets told, then the king believes he has the right to be included, if not actually told first. "Talk of such evil doings is not likely to sooth a lady in your delicate condition, my sweetness."

"He is here now, sire," Jane tells the king. "I shall have him come in." Queen Jane whispers to one of her ladies, and the girl disappears, with instructions for Adolphus Theophrasus to attend her side. Inside two minutes, the doctor is ushered in to the most private inner chamber of Henry's court.

"I know you, do I not?" Henry growls, because he recognises the oriental looking face, but cannot put a place to it.

"It was I who attended your … the other lady, Your Majesty, the doctor says. "I was there when …"

"Ah, yes. No matter. Cromwell likes you, so I like you. How come you to be here … in my court?" Henry demands. "You are not, I perceive, an Englishman."

"I am from Exeter, Your Majesty," the doctor replies charily.

"Ah, special Tom Cromwell documents, no doubt?" Henry is aware that his favourite minister is adept at forging papers, when it suits the good running of the country. He recalls Colonel Will Draper's wife, who is a beautiful, olive skinned, young girl from Coventry… and not a Spanish born Jewess. "Where did your forefathers come from, sir?"

"Abroad, sire… like your own," Jane puts in, and the king grins at the jest, and her sharpness of wit. "Can not a good Welshman be also a great Englishman?"

"By God, madam, but you have a pert tongue in your head, and it pleases me that your wit matches your charm, and your beauty."

"You flatter me, sire," Jane replies. "My wit is honed on your own, and my beauty is in your eyes alone."

"Tosh!" Henry growls. "All the men in court love you."

"For my clever wit… and nothing else, my love." Jane successfully steers Henry away from awkward ground. His jealousy can be a dangerous thing to tamper with these days. "Now, you must let dear Doctor Theophrasus examine you."

"Examine me, madam?" Henry snaps. Then his fear of illness makes him cautious. "Why?"

"Because it is obvious to my trained eye that Your Majesty is clearly unwell," the old Greco-Jewish doctor tells him.

"You think so, do you?" Henry does not like being told anything, and is offended at this bald statement of fact. "How do you know this to be so, sir?"

"Your eyes tell me, sire."

"My eyes, blast you? Henry leans forward, as if to leap up, but he grimaces, and falls back into his seat. "My eyes do not pain me one whit, you dithering imbecile."

"The eyes are the mirror of the soul, sire," Theophrasus continues, ignoring the king's rude tone. "I look into yours, and they speak to me of how you are. The outer edges are yellow, which speaks of too much red wine."

"Damned be your impertinence!" Henry is enraged. "How dare you speak to me thus … you dog?"

"Your leg aches?" Theophrasus smiles as he sees the look in Henry's eyes. "Not magic, sire, but mere observation. You have a touch of gout, aggravated by some injury perhaps?"

"I fell from my horse," Henry confesses, "and it has never been quite the same since."

"Does your usual physician prescribe daily massage, Your Majesty?" Theophrasus asks, then shakes his head. "Obviously he does not. Nor does he warn you of the dangers of red wine. Perhaps a touch of honesty would best help you, sire."

"Men are always afraid to tell me the full truth," Henry laments. "Though Tom Cromwell never shirks from it. Are you like him, my doctor from Exeter?"

"The truth will improve your health, sire." Theophrasus never ceases to be surprised at the stupidity of the nobility. Too much of everything is as bad as too little of anything, and the very poor and the very rich share a common doom. Moderation in everything leads to a longer, happier life.

"You can cure me?" Henry asks.

"Not I, Your Majesty. Some things are well beyond a cure, but I can make your suffering less. Your wrist, sire… if I may?" The doctor grips Henry's wrist, and makes that customary humming noise that denotes a good, expensive, physician is present. "Strong pulse. You have the heart of a lion, sire."

"A Tudor heart," Henry mumbles. "What else have you to tell me, sir?"

"Red wine, in excess, damages the liver, and that makes you jaundiced," Theophrasus continues. "Drink quality white only, and cut it with boiled water. Also, you must eat a lot less red meat. Stick to chicken, game birds, and the more tender cuts of venison."

"What, no beef?"

"In moderation. Everything *must* be in moderation." The doctor releases the king's wrist.

"I will send one of my best apprentices to you every morning. He will massage your leg, and it will ease the pain a little. How are your stools?"

"I have a man for that," Henry says. "It is Heneage's task."

"You have a man to pass your stools for you?" the doctor asks with a mocking smile.

"No, of course not! He collects them, and disposes of them," Henry says.

"Have him deliver a sample to me, once a week," the doctor commands. "Fresh and warm."

"Why?" Henry has childish beliefs about witchcraft, and believes that black magic can be worked if you have certain things, like finger nails, or bodily functions.

"Show me a man's warm turd, and I shall know the man," the old doctor explains. "The eyes… and a good turd, are invaluable aids to a physician, sire."

"It shall be done, just as you say," Henry agrees. "Can you make me so much better?"

"Might I speak of death, sire?" the doctor asks, warily. "I am told by those who know such things, that it is treason to speak of a king's mortality."

"It is treason to wish it aloud," Queen Jane says. "Speak openly, sir, for I wish to know my husband is in safe hands."

"Very well. Keep on eating what you will, and drinking so much red wine, and you will bloat up, and be unable to walk. I say you will be dead inside five years." Henry reels back, as if slapped in the face. "Do as I advise, and you will live another fifteen, or twenty years. Allow for regular massages, and consultations with me, and you will outlive all your contemporaries."

"A stark message, sir. Henry says. "I am of a mind to follow your advice, to the best of my ability."

"A wise decision, sire." Theophrasus turns to Jane, and bows from the neck. "And your dear madam… is she well?"

"Quite well, Doctor Theophrasus, thank you," Jane replies. "I thrive under your ministrations, as will my dear husband."

"No more red wine?" Henry shakes his head in utter bewilderment. "We must hope Colonel Draper s wife can procure a ready supply of the white!

*

"An extra sixteen barrels of the light Portuguese white for Whitehall Palace," Miriam says, and Pru Beckshaw makes a note in her journal. "The king's taste is changing for the better."

"We should buy in some more fresh venison too," Pru says.

"Why?"

"I have a feeling," Pru says, "but that is all."

"It is good enough for me," Miriam replies. "We cannot lay hands on English venison, for it is all owned by the monarchy. My men dare not go hunting in Royal Parks and forests without a permit from the king."

"We could buy a supply from the French," Pru Beckshaw suggests. "Normandy teems with deer, and they all belong to their local lords. We might buy a herd in France, sail the beasts to England, and slaughter them here, as needed."

"Yes, a fine idea. See to it, Pru, whilst I arrange for the victualling of my expedition. There is much to attend to, and great risk attached to the venture."

"There is a rising star, and a waning moon coming," Pru mutters.

"What is that you say?" Miriam asks. "Pru's eyelids flutter, and she blinks up at the early morning sun.

"What was what?" she asks. "Did I speak out loud?"

"You said about a rising star, and a waning moon?"

"Did I?" Pru shrugs. Did not the stars rise every evening, and did not the moon always wax and wane? "I do not recall."

*

"A formidable town," Will says, as they trot through the main gate into Arras. "The walls remind me of Dover, and every other man seems to be a soldier."

"The French king is in town," Rafe replies. "Everyone wants to see him, or impress him in some way. See, here comes our greeting party now." Rafe Sadler pulls out his travel documents, and dismounts as a group of men approach.

"What business have you here?" The voice is neither French, nor English. The guttural twang of a Highland Scot is unmistakeable, and Will slides from his horse, but keeps it between him and the welcoming party.

"My business is with the French king," Rafe replies, with a friendly smile. "Are you delegated to meet us, sir?"

"We are delegated to kick your arses out of Arras," the Scotsman replies. He swaggers back and forth, and gestures to the four men along with him. "I am Jamie Campbell, and these men are all loyal Campbell men. We serve King James, the rightful heir to the English throne."

"A strange boast, Master Campbell," Rafe says. "How comes your boy king to lay claim to a real man s throne?"

"Henry has no living sons. James is his nephew through Queen Margaret," Jamie Douglas responds. "With your fat old king gone, he shall rule in England."

"Yet he crawls to France for help," Rafe says.

"You insult us, sir?"

"I do," Rafe replies. "For I have every right to be here, and will enter Arras either past you, or over you. What say you to that, Colonel Draper?"

"I would agree, Master Sadler." Campbell hears the twin clicks of pistol hammers being cocked. He looks across, and sees the second Englishman is concealed behind his horse. "The first ball shall go between Lord Campbell's eyes, and the second into the next man to move."

"That will lessen the odds," Rafe observes.

"Very much so," Will replies. "Two against three… and they only bare arsed hill Scots."

Jamie Campbell who is a nephew of the head of the Campbell clan of Inverness is not about to back down, but the threat of immediate death gives him some small pause for thought. It is whilst he dithers over what action to take that a deputation of French diplomats, with a dozen armed guards arrives.

"Have I the honour to meet *Monsieur Roaulf Sardlur*?"

"At your service, sir," Rafe responds, handing over his documents. "Might I name my companion to you as Colonel Will Draper, the King's Royal Examiner?"

"I am Jean Messon, Conte de Vallions," the rotund Frenchman says, and I am to escort you to the chambers assigned for your use. It is most regrettable, but the king is unable to fund your visit, and you must defray your own expenses."

"We do not seek to impose ourselves upon King François' good will," Rafe tells the Frenchman. "Indeed, we thought these Scots fellows had been sent to dismiss us… before we could deliver our gifts to His Majesty."

"Gifts?" The count glances at the full saddle bags, and notes that the soldier is still levelling his pistols at the glowering Jamie Campbell. "His Majesty will be most pleased to receive you at court. Perhaps you might wish to clean yourselves first?"

"These stinking English are not wanted at this court," Jamie Campbell snarls. "They seek only to drive a wedge between our two countries."

"Is it the French custom to have but one ally at any time, sir?" Will Draper asks of the count. Or might the king wish to make up his own mind?"

"You lawyer," Campbell snaps. He slips a hand to the heavy claymore hanging at his side. "What devilry are you up to?"

"I come with letters from King Henry, and a letter from King James' mother, the Dowager Queen of Scots."

"That slut is no queen," Campbell cries. "She lies with men, like a common whore!"

"Enough!" Will Draper steps clear of his horse, and draws his sword. You insult the sister of my king, sir, and I must demand a full apology."

"My words were hasty... sir," Jamie Campbell says, but the words stick in his throat. His plan to repel the English visitors has failed, and he is under strict orders not to provoke a fight on French soil.

"Then you apologise?"

"If I must."

"In writing?" Will advances, and is within a few feet of the cocksure young Scotsman. "You can write, can you not?"

"You push me too far, Englishman." Jamie Campbell has his own crude set of principles, and he will not allow himself to be humiliated in front of his own clansmen.

"Do I?" Will Draper turns his back on the Scot. "Really, cowing these highland mongrels is too easy. Have they no courage?" The blow, if it connects, is powerful enough to slice a man in two, but Draper twists away, and riposts, in the blink of an eye. Jamie Campbell squeals, and his great broadsword clatters to the ground. His sword arm is cut open from shoulder, almost to wrist.

"Put up your weapons!" The count's sharp command causes the Scotsman's fellow Campbell followers to hold back. The French soldiery form a barrier with their quarterstaffs, whilst Jamie Campbell bleeds onto the grey cobblestones.

"Rafe, hand me your bandolier." Will Draper ties the heavy sash around the Scotsman's upper arm, and ties it off. "Loosen it after a few minutes, and get to a surgeon, as fast as your friends can carry you, Master Campbell. Swift action will save the arm."

"The Scots gather around their wounded leader, and half carry him away. Will Draper pulls up a handful of grass, growing through the old cobbles, and wipes his blade clean of blood.

"Most brilliantly done, monsieur," the count says, and bows to the King s Examiner. "I have never seen such expert swordsmanship before. You are a soldier, of course?"

"Once, a long time ago," Will Draper says. He slips the sword back into its scabbard. "I have had better welcomes in worse towns, sir. Perhaps you might show us to our chambers now?"

*

"You deliberately goaded him," Rafe says, once in the comfort of their rooms. "Even after he apologised, you pressed him into a fight."

"The lad was foolish," Will replies. "Had he meant to force us away, he should have brought another six men, armed to the teeth. Instead, he showed me his weakness. Never cause insult, unless you are prepared to fight. He lost his temper, and the use of his arm for a few months. Had I desired it, he would be dead."

"I think the whole of the French court will be talking about it by now," Rafe says.

"As I wished." Will lays down on the truckle bed. "The French king now knows that we are dangerous. We do not come, with mincing words and fine manners, but with a magnificent gift in one hand, and a useful blade in the other. Friend, or foe… my message says."

"It is a heavy handed way to draw attention, but it seems to have worked. The count was most impressed."

"The next part is for you," says Will. "I hope the gift is grand enough to catch François' greedy eye."

"See for yourself." Rafe Sadler takes a parcel from his saddle bag, and unwraps the soft silk covering. "Master Thomas says the king has no use for it anymore." Will Draper sits up, and stares at the magnificent yellow jewel, set in a band of the purest Welsh gold. "It once belonged to Anne Boleyn, and was a gift from Thomas Cromwell... a costly bribe to get into her presence."

It is a very familiar object to the ex soldier of fortune. "I once gave this ring to Anne Boleyn, before she became queen," he recalls. "It was my task to hand it over, and make her into a firm ally of Master Cromwell's. Instead, I was forced to cross swords with George Boleyn, and he came off the worst. That moment of bravado made us enemies to the end. It is a damnably unlucky jewel, Rafe."

"That is what Master Tom said." The lawyer holds it up and examines its clarity. "He hopes it will bring nothing but ill luck to the French king, and sour his feelings for King James."

"We can but hope," Will says. "What about our other arrangements?"

"In place. Our agent in Arras has made a most suitable choice. I doubt we will go unnoticed."

"Excellent. Wake me in an hour, so that we might visit this magnificent court that is the talk of all Europe."

"Will, we might impress the French king this evening," Rafe says, "but I fear we will make many enemies."

"Then let it be so," Will says, and closes his eyes.

*

"My dear Lord Pole, James Stuart, King of Scotland, holds out his ring hand for it to be kissed. "How are you keeping?"

"Well sire," Reginald Pole, third son of Lady Salisbury replies. "How was the hunting?"

"Splendid. These endless French forests dwarf those of Scotland," the king says. "I could spend my days in them, and look forward to hunting across the great parks of England."

"My condolences on the rather unexpected death of your wife." The Englishman knows that the Scottish king's marriage has lasted no more than a few weeks, and that the sickly girl, chosen by King François, has succumbed to the Scottish weather, almost as soon as she landed in the country. "Do you come back to seek yet another bride from King François, My Lord?"

"I have my eye on a replacement, Lord Pole," James says, with a sly wink. "Have you spoken with His Majesty yet?"

"I try, but he is constantly hemmed in with jealous courtiers," Pole replies. "I hope to find a chance today."

"The English have sent more men."

"Do I know them?" Pole is always wary of Englishmen, because he fears assassination. He often writes to the Pope, and stirs up hatred against King Henry, which makes him a clear target for retribution.

"My man tells me that one is a lawyer, called Rafe Sadler," James says. "The other is a mercenary called Draper."

"Will Draper?" Reginald Pole curses under his breath, and tugs at his fashionably pointed beard. "He is the king's man. Where Thomas Cromwell is the thin, probing, blade, Colonel Draper is the twin edged battle axe. He roots out the king's enemies, like a pig after truffles, and then destroys them."

"Oh dear," James says. "That does not sound too good for you, my dear old friend." He smiles, and wonders if the man is sent to kill Pole, or another, more valued, target. "He has already maimed one of my Lord Campbell's young nephews. You might do well to carry a weapon with you, whilst he is at court."

"There are no weapons allowed in the king s presence," Pole says. "To bring a blade into the throne room is to court death. This English assassin will have to strike at me well away from the king s presence."

"I doubt he will get the chance, my friend," King James says. "The Campbell clan want his blood, and I have given them my full blessing in their endeavours. The wounded young gentleman also happens to be married to a Clan Murdoch lassie. This demands that her kin exact full retribution too. By tonight, thirty odd men will be after your Colonel Draper s blood."

The stone walls of the great hall are covered with even greater hangings, which depict the glories of France, and the more salacious stories from the Bible. The huge silk sheet behind the royal throne shows a vast battle between brave Christian troops, and thousands of brutal Muslim invaders. It is a popular choice, as victories over other foes are scant enough.

The greatest battles of the last three hundred years have all ended in abject defeat for the French, at the hands of English longbow men. Few this side of the channel wish to savour the battles of Crecy or Agincourt, and the fall of Calais. Even their ultimate victory in the so called Hundred Years War results in nothing more than the retrieval of some of their own lost lands.

King François sits on a throne of ivory, sandalwood, and beaten gold, atop a plump embroidered cushion designed to make him look taller than his scant five feet. He is a squat, frankly ugly little man, who rules absolutely. He is surrounded by a host of clever advisors, and those few relatives who he has not had exiled, thrown into prison, or murdered. Beyond this inner ring of courtiers mill a throng of men intent on catching his eye.

France runs on favours, and a favour bestowed by the king is valued beyond gold. To be allowed access to François, one must bribe his way past his jealous ministers, and then be prepared to offer a splendid gift for a minute's time. Many Frenchmen have been ruined in the attempt, and end their days in poverty. The trick is, to catch the king's eye. There is a blast of trumpets from the great double doors, and all heads swivel to see an astonishing sight.

A lone man advances, and eats fire from a stick as he progresses. Behind him are six tumblers, who perform clever cartwheels, and draw gasps from the crowd. All six are beautiful young girls, and all six are clad in the thinnest of gauze sheaths. They whirl and tumble towards the throne, and the crowd parts before them.

To the rear of this magnificent spectacle are two elegantly dressed Englishmen who proceed to the very steps of the throne unhindered. Will Draper effects a deep bow to the king, and holds up a small, sandalwood wooden casket, with gold hinges and a tiny gold clasp. The half naked girls fall about his feet, and flutter their eyelashes at the king.

"Sire, a gift from your cousin Henry, King of England and Ireland, who implores you to accept this offering, and treat us, his emissaries, with your usual good grace." His voice is strong, and his French is very good, for an Englishman. A couple of the king's ministers gesture for the guards to come forward, but an imperious wave of François' hand stops them.

This gift… is it in the little box, or do you present me with these girls, Englishman?"

"Your Majesty has no need of an English pimp, for your own are much better at the task," Will replies, and some of the crowd gasp again. King François cackles with laughter, which ends with a lung wracking cough. He dabs a cloth at his lips, and waves for Will to come forward.

"I agree, sir. We prefer to use an honest French pimp every time," he says. "Pray, open this pretty box, and show me what cousin Henri thinks my friendship is worth."

"Your worth, as a friend, cannot be fitted into so small a box, sire, but this is a token of the esteem you are held in," Will says, as he raises the lid.

"Beautiful!" King François gestures to the magnificent Turkish carpet at his feet. "Sit with me, Colonel Draper. I would like to hear more. What does Henri seek from me, other than a friendly welcome for you?"

"My king wishes to renew the long friendship between our two nations," Rafe puts in, and the king merely glances at him.

"Our long friendship?" he mutters. Another French king lost twenty five thousand knights to English arrows at Agincourt, and the awful event still burns deep into every loyal Frenchman's heart. "England and France have never been close, Master Lawyer."

"I am to remind you of promises made at the Field of the Cloth of Gold," Rafe persists. "King Henry swore brotherhood to you, and you to he."

"You are a most consummate diplomat, sir," King François sneers, his face set into a stony mask. "Words, words, words."

"Yes, enough of hollow words," Will Draper says. "My companion can only speak those drilled into him by my king s advisors."

"Ah, you mean Tomas Cromwell." François nods his head and fingers his sparse beard as he thinks. "Is he truly as dangerous a man as I am told, Colonel Draper?"

"He is a soulless Protestant," Will Drapet replies. "He eats dry bread, and drinks cold water for breakfast, and frowns on any man who would come between he and his precious Henry."

"Colonel Draper, I object!" Rafe Sadler steps aside, and glares at his comrade. He reverts to speaking in English. "These are not the words we were advised to speak. You must guard your tongue amongst these people."

"Not in my court, you saucy fellow." François says with a sly smile. "My English is quite good … and your diplomatic presence is no longer required." For a moment Rafe Sadler stares at Will Draper, as if about to protest, then thinks better of it, bows, and withdraws a dozen paces.

"A rather stuffy fellow," Will observes. "He has spent too long at Austin Friars. Sadler is still a Thomas Cromwell man, whereas… I am the king's man."

"You are Henri's Special Examiner, I am told," the king says. "What do you examine?"

"Whatever baffles others, sire." Will settles himself on the expensive carpet, and explains. "I look into murders, thefts, and treason for Henry. It is my task to root out the truth for him. In the past, I have saved his life, and his treasure."

"Then why are you here, sir?" the French king asks. "You assault one of my Scottish guests, then present yourself as some slack wristed courtier… an ambassador for your Henry."

"I come, like the yellow jewel, as a gift for you, sire."

"Brother France!" James, the young King of Scotland ,swaggers into the throne room, flanked by Reginald Pole, and a thin faced, villainous looking priest. "Am I too late to formally greet these English visitors?"

"One has already wearied me, dear cousin James," François says. "Though his companion is most amusing. You say you are a gift, Colonel? In what way can this be?"

"I come with a secret, but it is for your ears alone, sire." Will Draper throws a heavy look at James. "Some things are best left to a more suitable time."

"Intriguing." The king leaves his throne and examines each of the pretty girls in the tumblers band. At length, he shakes his head, and turns away. "We are, like dear Henri, happily married these days, and my … appetite is not what it was. I shall keep the ring, of course, for friendship's sake."

"You honour my king, sire."

"Yes, I do. I must dine with King James tonight," François explains, "so please call on me again, Colonel."

"That might prove difficult," Will Draper whispers, as he kisses the proffered hand. "Take care of that which you eat tonight, sire." The whole appearance of the French king's face changes, from one of princely boredom, to a look of timid fear. The French court has seen its share of sudden deaths over the years, and the concocting of poison is almost an art form amongst some of his subjects.

"Come with me," François says, and makes for the small door concealed behind the drapes which back his throne. "My private chambers."

"Sire!" James Stuart, King of Scotland, takes an ill advised step forward, and the king's bodyguards slope arms, effectively barring his way with their crossed halberds.

"Later, cousin … later!" François snaps.

Rafe Sadler sits in the outer court, and wonders what Will Draper will say to the king in private. They have a loose sort of a plan, but it will change, to fit in with the French king's own reactions. The inner court doors open, and there is a sudden egress of courtiers, who babble at the odd intrusion of the dangerous looking young Englishman.

"You, fellow… name yourself." Reginald Pole attempts an assertive tone, but he is, in truth, a gentle, and rather scholarly sort of man.

"Master Pole… good day," Rafe replies. It is I, Rafe Sadler, advisor to the king. We met at Salisbury once, on some cathedral business. Your mother sends her dearest love, and wonders if you might ever return to England?"

"My mother sends me nothing, sir," Pole replies. He might be a gentle sort, but he is not a complete fool. To admit any contact with his family puts them in the worst kind of danger. "We have no contact. Is she well, sir?"

"She pines away, for want of her son," Rafe Sadler tells him.

"Lady Salisbury is a strong woman," King James says, and Reginald Pole winces at the man's stupid indiscretion.

"Then you two have met one another, Your Majesty?" Rafe has scored a point without even trying. James Stuart is the sort who thinks himself above everything, and that posturing arrogance equates to intelligence.

"No… that is…" James sees what he has said, and fumbles away from further confessions. "The lady is an old friend of my mother. The two converse… and I sometimes hear news of her."

"Of course." Rafe bows to the thin priest, who has remained a pace back, and is studying him like a cat about to eat a mouse. "I see you still favour the Bishop of Rome's corrupt church, Master Pole?"

"Father Grimaldi is merely a pilgrim," Pole says. He is on his way to visit the shrine of St. Denis in Paris. As a loyal supporter of the pope, I make no secret of my faith, Master Sadler."

"Would that you did, sir," Rafe Sadler replies. "Many of the old faith live out their lives in England without rancour. The king is a decent fellow, and allows men to worship as they wish, if it be in private. It is only when one of his subjects openly denounces him that he becomes dangerous."

"Why are you here?" James cannot refrain from asking. He is a king, and used to being obeyed. "Do you seek to disrupt my marriage arrangements?"

"Not I, sire." Rafe smiles at the thought. "Though I hear you are unfortunate in the choice of brides. Why, the last one died the moment she breathed your foul Scottish air."

"*Cozzo*!" the black eyed priest mutters. It is a vile insult to utter, which he expects to remain un-interpreted.

"*Va fangule*," Rafe Sadler replies, with a cold stare. "Your tame priest has a dirty mouth on him, Master Pole. I speak Italian, French, and Latin. My German is also quite good. Perhaps your man might employ Arabic if he wishes to insult me?"

"Father Grimaldi dislikes the English," Pole admits. "He sees how they conspire against Rome at every turn. What is your soldier friend telling the king?"

"Am I my brother's keeper, sir?" Rafe Sadler asks. The Scottish king snorts, and turns away. Reginald Pole does too, but the priest lingers a moment too long. Rafe Sadler has seen such men before. They dress themselves in respectability, but have nothing more than murder in their hearts. Of the three men, it is he who is the most dangerous, and must be watched.

*

"Speak." King François says, once they are in his private chambers. He feels comfortable surrounded by his art works, his precious wall hangings, and his many holy relics. "What does cousin Henri want me to know?"

"There is a plot afoot, sire," Will says.

"There are always plots, Colonel."

"This one concerns the death of kings."

"The death of kings, you say?" François notes the plurality of kings, and is suddenly eager to know more. "My closest advisors tell me never to trust a word spoken by an Englishman."

"Do we not all speak the truth, Your Majesty, when it is in our own self interest?" Will Draper tells the king. "Sometimes, the truth is all that can save us."

"You are Henri's man?" François asks. "You investigate certain matters for him?"

"I do, and one such investigation brings me to your court, sire." Will takes a deep breath, and prepares to tell the truth, but with a few minor fictions thrown in to add salt to the dish. "There is a plot to destroy His Majesty. His enemies seek to remove him from the throne of England, and replace him with another."

"You speak of the Princess Mary?" The French king knows how easily the daughter of the late Queen Katherine would be accepted by the leading English Catholics. "I doubt the girl has enough influence to bring this about. She is still but a young woman."

"Let us not fence with each other, sire." Will takes a letter from his shirt, and offers it to François. "This is a copy of a message sent from Lady Salisbury to her wayward son, Reginald Pole. In it, she implores him to marry Mary. To this end, he is to smuggle himself, and a trusted priest into England. Mary will be snatched away from court, and the wedding arranged."

"Fanciful." The French king knows documents can be faked, and such wild tales made up. He needs more than some clever story to make him listen. "What concern is it of mine anyway?"

"Once Mary is married, the Roman Catholic dissidents will move against Henry. They might succeed, if enough barons support her cause, and Princess Mary will become queen."

"Her rightful place, some might say," François replies. He sees that this plot might well discomfort Henry Tudor, and cause the English king some embarrassment amongst his courtiers.

"With a Plantagenet husband by her side," Will Draper says. "The old regime will be back in power."

"Master Pole is a very dear friend to us," François replies, with a condescending smile. "I wish them luck, and might even dance at their wedding, Colonel Draper."

"He is an overtly ambitious Roman Catholic, and a great, great nephew of the fifth King Henry… the man who slaughtered twenty five thousand French knights at Agincourt." Will sees the king s face change hue. To mention such an overwhelming defeat to the French king is the height of bad manners. "Once on the throne, he will want the return of all Plantagenet lands both in England, and in France. Burgundy, Normandy, Aquitaine, and Navarre, will be his, by historical right. He will command an army of fifty thousand men, a thousand newly cast cannon, and a hundred and twenty great men o' war."

"Reginald Pole would never have the nerve."

"No, but your cousin would."

"King James?" François lives with a deep rooted suspicion of those around him, and it does not take much to set his mind working against someone. "He comes to me as a mere claimant. He is a client king… one who begs my help against his historical old enemy, the English."

"What does he offer to you in return, sire?" Will Draper shrugs his shoulders. "Henry sends you magnificent jewels, worth a thousand English pounds, and offers France some valuable trading concessions, whilst James takes away one of your children to wed, and allows her to perish in Scotland. Now he wants to pluck another from your fertile tree. Marriage to your daughter, or some other grand French noble lady, will give him a claim to the very throne that you sit on."

"My son will inherit, sir." François insists. "The Dauphin is of my blood."

"Sons die, sire."

"God above, but you know how to put fear into a man, Englishman. Do you still speak of poison?"

"I have no definite idea," Will replies, "but the threat is always there, sire."

"Then what is it you do know?" The king demands answers, and is in the frame of mind where he will consider all things.

"That King Henry is content with his own kingdom. He is the wealthiest king alive, and his ships rule the oceans. He has no need to swallow up pieces of France. If he dies, and Princess Mary rules … then the Pole family *will* want France. It would only take your death to throw everything into confusion. James would claim your crown, by right of marriage, and invade. Then Reginald Pole and his brothers would land in Normandy, and the two armies would crush all resistance."

"Fanciful… as I say."

"Really?" Will glances over at the lone guard who stands by the door. "All it needs is for you to die, sire … and that is an easy enough thing to accomplish. A determined man could do it in a moment. By the time your man could move, I might slip a knife into your throat … or drip poison into your wine."

"I doubt you would sacrifice your life so readily," Francois says, but his tone is uneasy now, and he puts a table's distance between them. The Englishman is a trained killer of men, and might know a dozen ways to snuff out a life.

"Not I, sire. I bear you nothing but good will. My own king orders me to ensure your safety, at all costs." Will bows. "Your servant, sire… but there are others who are not. Has King James asked you for another bride yet?"

"Yes… and I mean to have him married before he leaves."

"Into your family?"

"Yes."

"And Reginald Pole?"

"A gentle sort of a fellow. He asks only that I send him to England, with his tame priest. He says nothing about any proposed marriage to Princess Mary."

"Of course not. Mary does not love France, My Lord," Will tells the king. "Her mother was Spanish, and she speaks fluent Spanish in her own household. She loves the Emperor Charles, who always supported her late mother. With her placed on the throne, England will ally itself to the Holy Roman Empire."

"Dear Christ!" The lie is so vast that François cannot believe it to be anything other than the truth. "Between England, Scotland, and the Holy Roman Empire, my country will be squeezed to death."

"What I tell you is all assumption, sire," Will says, telling the truth. "None of this may come to pass if Henry lives, and you are kept safe. Refuse James another daughter. Force him to marry outside your immediate family. Deny Reginald Pole the chance to visit England until Princess Mary is safely out of his cunning grasp, and avoid assassination."

"Who would dare?" The king paces up and down. "Every word you utter might be a lie. James might love me like a son, and Pole want nothing but a chance to convert England back to the true faith. Then again, some of it might be true. King James does want another one of my daughters... Pole does wish to slip back into England, and an alliance between Scot, Spaniard, and Englishman might come about. I must speak with my councillors."

"You could always ally yourself to England, sire." Will Draper knows this is the hardest part to accomplish, so throws it in, almost as an aside. "You need not vow any military help, but agree a few simple trade deals. It will warn the Emperor Charles to be wary."

"Agreed. That can do no long term harm to me." François nods his head, and pulls at his beard. "I will detain Reginald Pole in France for a few months, and thwart his insane wish to marry Princess Mary. As for King James … I have the perfect bride for him. A young widow with money and lands. It is the only way he shall own a portion of my realm."

"All this costs you nothing, sire," Will tells him. "It is the last thing that might cost you dear indeed. The plan to murder you might already be afoot, and difficult to abandon."

"How so?" The king is nervous, now that he has accepted the truth of some of what Will says. James is a cocksure chancer, and Pole loves the Pope dearly. Neither man is reliable. "Who would dare order the death of a king?"

"Yes, who would dare, sire?" Will Draper crosses to a map fastened to the wall, and studies it closely. "James of Scotland is not the man to give such an order. He is a scavenger dog, looking for table scraps… not a lion. King Henry is not our man either."

"Why not?"

"Because he would give the task to me, sire… and you would already be dead," Will replies with a broad smile. "No, not Henry. His sister Margaret hates you, but has no real power outside the bedchamber. Even Master Pole has his scruples, and would never directly order your death. What of the Dukes of Brabant, or the dissident German states?"

"All too small," François tells the Englishman. "They do not have the power to strike at me. Only the Emperor Charles would have the military strength. He might seek to kill me, and invade my realm."

"His troops make no move, and Charles is a religious fellow, who much prefers a quieter life," Will says. "Besides, when Henry no longer rules, Mary will ascend the throne, and she is a friendly Catholic Princess."

"Then who else? François demands. "If not Spain, Scotland, or England… who would dare raise a hand against me?"

"Some secret foe, sire, Will says. There is a darkness shrouding this business, and we must throw light into it, and uncover the culprit, before…"

"Quite, Colonel Draper before I am a dead man!"

7   **The Assassin**

"Did he believe you?" Rafe Sadler joins his comrade as soon as he emerges from the king's inner chambers. Will Draper smiles and nods his answer.

"For the most part," he says. "King James will *not* be wed to a French princess, and Reginald Pole's travel plans are now in some disarray. I opted for him being held in France, rather than be allowed to slip into England. If he gets in, without our knowledge, he can do untold harm to the new church… and the king."

"The Scots king spoke to me earlier." Rafe Sadler recalls the brief conversation. "He is a damned fool, and no match for Thomas Cromwell's scheming. If we can cause distrust between him and François, our task is made all the easier. Reginald Pole is another matter. He is, I regret to say, another Thomas More. A deep thinking idealist, who cannot see the real world, even when it bites the end of his nose."

"You think he will still rail against Henry?" Will asks.

"Yes." Rafe knows Pole's type well, and foresees trouble ahead. He thinks it is enough to speak what you think is the truth, and he has no thought to political expediency. "I fear that he sees himself as a living martyr."

"Then we should ignore him," Will Draper says. "Let him rant about the Holy Trinity, and the Mass spoken only in Latin, all he wants. King François will not trust him, and Emperor Charles has enough trouble with his own Protestant enclaves.

"Lady Salisbury's mad wish for a royal marriage will never be fulfilled. The whole thing is a ridiculous mess. What sane person could ever think of gaining any success from so diverse a set of actions?"

"I agree, though I would rather have Reginald Pole a prisoner, and in heavy chains." Rafe looks at people in a most black and white way. They are either for forward thinking Cromwellian ideas, or against them. "Perhaps he will keep his mouth closed from this day on."

"Perhaps." A thought nags at the forefront of Will Draper's mind, and he finds himself unable to keep silent. "Has Tom Cromwell given you any specific instructions, regarding the extended Pole family, Rafe?"

"Instructions?" Rafe raises an eyebrow, as if to signify ignorance of what he is being asked.

"Yes… instructions," Will Draper asks. "Has he asked you to kill Reginald Pole for him?"

"Me?" Rafe smiles, in a good natured way. "Is that not what he wants you to do, my friend?"

"Me?"

"Yes. I do the diplomacy, and you are here to do the murder. Am I wrong?"

*

King James has chambers in the outer walls of Arras, which he shares with Reginald Pole, and a small army of Scots, all vying for the place of honour at his side. The Kerrs jostle with the Campbells, and the McCreadies try to elbow the rest aside. Fifty armed clansmen, all looking for a fight, makes for a volatile situation. They need but one insult to spark them into ruinous violence.

"It is outrageous!" James cries, as soon as he returns from his latest audience with the king. "He seeks to have me marry below my true station in life."

"Who, sire?" Reginald Pole asks of him . He is nervous of the Scottish king's fierce temper, and wishes to calm him down, before his kinsmen sense trouble where there should be none.

"Mary of Guise," James says to Pole. "The daughter of Claude, Duke of Guise."

"I know the lady, sire," Pole says. "She is the widow of Louis, the Duke of Longueville. I doubt she is yet in her twenty first year, and she is of a most pleasing appearance."

"Pleasing, you say?"

"Beautiful, sire." Reginald Pole has seen the girl once, from a distance, but still retains the overall impression that she was of a rare attractiveness. "Fresh as flowers, new cut in May."

"Very poetic, Master Pole."

"The honest truth, Your Majesty," Reginald Pole insists.

"And a widow?" James Stuart is partial to a buxom young woman, and senses that her recent widowed state might be an even greater benefit to the marriage bed.

"Her husband left her with large estates in the north east, and control of a most considerable treasure." Pole makes it his business to know these things, and understands that being a widow will not stand in the way of a good match. "She is a distant cousin to the king, I believe, and therefore of royal blood. There is no dishonour in such a marriage, sire."

"Then I should accept?" James is almost childlike when it comes to making decisions. He will often pay heed to the last one to speak, and believes great age begets great wisdom when, in fact, it denotes nothing but the passing of many years.

"That is for Your Majesty to decide," Pole tells him, "but were I in your boots, I would be signing the pre-marriage contracts even as we speak."

"Very well, we are not affronted by King François' somewhat piquant suggestion," King

James declares. "Will you handle the formal paperwork for us, Master Pole?"

"Of course." Reginald Pole sees now that attaching himself to so poor a king will do him no good. The man is weak, and will never be goaded into war against Henry. Nor will his own proposed marriage to Princess Mary come to anything. The whole scheme, now he thinks about it, is nothing more than a foolish dream of his mother's. He wonders how such silliness ever came to see the light of day.

Reginald Pole thinks back, and recalls the day it was first mooted, then he remembers his mother's letters, and who it was who prompted her to write to James. Come to think about it, and the strands all seem to weave in and out of one another, as if by a common hand. Some might even suspect the Hand of God.

Ridiculous, Reginald Pole thinks to himself. Why would the Holy Father in Rome go to so much trouble? Why create so complex a web of deceit, only to let some blustering Englishman tear it apart?

"What is it, Master Pole?" James asks. "You look as though you have seen a vision."

"Yes, Reginald Pole replies, in muted horror. "A holy vision!"

*

"You have that look on your face, Rafe Sadler says.

"What look?" Will Draper asks.

"That look you get when you seem about to unravel some mystery." Rafe furrows his brow, stoops forward, and effects a comical squint of one eye. "You look as though you need a privy."

"It is just that I feel… used, says the King's Examiner."

"Master Cromwell uses us all," Rafe Sadler says. "It does not mean he is wrong to, or that he loves us any the less."

"No, not by Thomas Cromwell." Will Draper clenches and unclenches his fists, and paces back and forth in the large, deserted ante chamber. "Think of it, Rafe. Do you recall what our shrewd Master Cromwell always says about coincidences?"

"That they are very rare, and should be treated with great circumspection. It is an old maxim, and one that stands a man in good stead. Mistrust that which seems to be mere happenstance, for there is a reason for everything. What often seems like a happy stroke of fate often turns out to be a contrivance."

"Just so." Will Draper produces the copy letter he showed to King François earlier. "Is it not strange to your mind that Lady Salisbury's name came to us from the mouth of Queen Margaret?"

"She sought to use it so as to gain an advantage." Rafe recalls his close encounter with the buxom Queen Mother, and how near he came to succumbing to her potent libido.

"What if someone knew she was going to speak with you during your visit, and gave her the name?" Will asks.

"No, she seemed to be most sincere," Rafe replies. "She divulged the name, only to further her own cause."

"I do not say she tricked you, my friend."

"Then what?"

"Perhaps King James and his advisors allowed the queen to overhear them speak of the Countess of Salisbury... accidentally," Will continues. "Then they might have let Margaret see documents from the woman, also 'accidentally'."

"So that she perceived it to be an important secret," Rafe says, "and thought it worth passing on to me."

"Just so. Margaret tells you, and you report it to Thomas Cromwell at Austin Friars. What if we were meant to investigate, and find how Lady Salisbury writes to King James?"

"Through priests," Rafe tells his friend. "We have known as much for months. Roman Catholic priests disguise themselves as beggars and pedlars, and then roam about England, preaching the old faith. Salisbury often used them as messengers."

"Another fact we uncovered far too easily," Will Draper says. "Once we know how it is done, we can intercept their letters, and learn of their plotting. Someone knows Tom Cromwell will become interested in this illicit correspondence, and send his best men to investigate."

"What do you mean?" Rafe is becoming alarmed at Will s doggedness.

"I mean that they wanted us to come to Arras... for a particular reason." Will sees it all now, and wonders at the cleverness of the plan. "King James is deftly manoeuvred out of the French line of royal succession, at our behest. Then Master Pole is kept close to court, again at our insistence. The French court must resent how easily we have swayed their king, and wonder at our ulterior motives."

"We seek only to foil James' plans, and silence Reginald Pole," Rafe says. "What else is there?"

"Nothing, though they will not believe us. They will think we have struck at our greatest enemies, and mean France some harm too. They might even think… yes, of course, I see it all now. Pray God we are not too late!"

"For what?"

"I asked King François who might be powerful enough to draw all the strands together, and we both, foolishly, omitted one name. Pope Paul has the ability to cause all this. He has caused young James to be put aside, and ensures the infant Dauphin will rule after his father. The child is young, and easily moulded. If Rome rules the Dauphin, they rule France. The Papal states, France and Scotland would make a formidable enemy. It is all about great power, Rafe, and who, ultimately, will wield it."

"If you are right, their intircate plan comes to absolutely nothing, as long as… oh, dear Christ… as long as François lives!"

"Pole is not the villain, nor is King James. They are pawns in the game. Perhaps this newly elected Bishop of Rome seeks to bring France back under the Papal thumb, and would sacrifice King François to that end."

"But how?"

"The priest you told me about… where is the priest?" Will Draper realises that the priest is not one of Pole s creatures, but a tool of another, more dangerous man.

"Father Grimaldi?" Rafe remembers the dead, cold eyes, and the resolute set of the man's features. "He was here, with King James, and

Reginald Pole. They both left with their escorts, but I cannot say what became of the priest."

"He is not here to slip into England and pray for lost souls," Will says. "He is here to kill the French king. With King François dead, the Bishop of Rome can then blame us… two English assassins… and join half of Europe in a holy war against England. We must find him, and stop him."

"There are no weapons allowed in the court confines," Rafe says. "He must mean to uses his hands."

"My soul for a dagger," Will curses. "Let us split up, and run this foul villain to earth!"

*

"How are you, madam?"

"Well, Master Thomas," Queen Jane replies. She is sitting in the rose garden, whilst her ladies stroll around its perimeter, flirting with those single gentlemen who hang about the court in the hope of a good marriage. "They tell me that you can grow beautiful red roses in the Winter months. Is that so, sir?"

"After a manner, My Lady," Thomas Cromwell confesses. "I had the cooks place potted shrubs close to the kitchen fires. It is not ideal, but it encourages late flowering. That is why we have rose petals almost all the long year around."

"You love roses then?" the queen asks. She knows the answer to her question, but asks anyway, in the hope of prolonging the chance of conversation with her husband's first minister.

"Yes, with all my heart, My Lady. I watch the sweet bud open, and drink in its natural beauty," Cromwell mutters. "It is the flowering of love, Jane."

"Do you know love, Thomas?"

"I do now," he replies. "I watch the shoot bud, and await its flowering."

"My son will be king of this realm," Jane says, casually. "He will rule as wisely as his father."

"I pray so." Cromwell leans forward, and adjusts the woollen blanket wrapped about her legs. "I love you," he mutters, and she nods, almost imperceptibly.

"Until the world ends," she says. "Ah, here comes the king. I swear he acts ten years younger since the doctor spoke with him this morning. Dear Theophrasus is the only man I know who can tell Henry that he is fat, lazy, and drinks too much, and is rewarded for the effort. Poor Henry. Has he found a new lover yet, Thomas?"

"No, madam, he has not." Thomas Cromwell straightens up, and assumes his usual tight lipped expression. "I would never keep that from you. Never!"

"Thomas, there you are, old friend," Henry says. "You fuss over my queen like a mother hen."

"I love her as I love you, sire," Tom Cromwell says. "My heart swells when I think of the coming months. I pray daily for the queen's deliverance… and for a son… a strong, healthy son."

"Amen to that, old fellow." Henry sits on the stone bench beside Jane, and places a big hand over hers. "How were my shipyards yesterday?"

"Shipyards? Oh, yes… of course. I almost forgot about the royal shipyards. The inspection went very well," Thomas Cromwell says. Your minister was seen by all, and that always encourages them to labour even harder."

"And what about Coventry?" Henry asks his indefatigable minister. "The land dispute with My Lord Warwick needed a very firm hand."

"It is arranged, sire." In truth, the shipyards needed only a flying visit, and the Coventry business but a seal applied. Master Edmund Ambrose, posing as Thomas Cromwell, has saved him a week of tedious travel, a week better spent negotiating with foreign ambassadors, and making future plans at Austin Friars. "They have to take but one look at me, and your wishes are fulfilled."

"I do not know how you find the energy, old friend," the king says. "A lesser man would be tired of all this galloping about the realm, but here you are... flattering my dear Jane, and smelling these beautiful roses."

"Such loveliness feeds my very soul, sire." Cromwell says, honestly. "Though the roses are pretty too."

"What's that? Ha!" Henry laughs at the clever two edged remark, and several courtiers join in. "Do you see, Jane... how our Thomas compliments you in the form of a jest? He pretends to mistake your loveliness for that of these flowers, and... well, I thought it was funny."

"Her Majesty understands, sire... but dislikes loud displays of humour... for it is not lady like," Cromwell says. "I am sure she will smile to herself, once in her private chambers."

"Well observed, my friend. Call me Hal, or Henry, when we are alone," the king says. "We are most pleased to call you our friend, Tom."

"You honour me, Hal," Tom Cromwell says. In truth, the king does not understand the meaning of friendship. For him, it is enough that a man does as he bids, and always agrees with his wishes. There is a sudden commotion from the far entrance to the garden walk, and Cromwell looks up. "Here are the church's black crows coming, and I must revert to calling you... Your Highness."

A cluster of clergymen, with the Archbishop of Canterbury at their helm, come bustling up, bowing for all they are worth. The Archbishop is glowing with pride, and eager to share that which pleases him so much.

"Well, Cranmer?" Henry guesses what is coming, and steels himself to accept the inevitable march of fate. "What is the considered verdict of my conclave of churchmen?"

"Sire, we can find no wrong in it." Cranmer announces. "The most wicked Church of Rome has lied to us all."

"Of course," Thomas Cromwell says. "If the bible can be read by all, their sins will become clear. The common man will see that purgatory is a foul myth, foisted on them by indolent priests, eager to take their precious pennies from them. Did you find many errors in the text, gentlemen?"

"We found none," Master Cromwell. "The Pope... I mean, Paul, the Bishop of Rome, stated that the English translations of Tyndale are full of glaring errors, but there are absolutely none to be found. We have studied the text, sire, and find it to be quite perfect."

"Then you approve of it?" Henry asks.

"I do," Cranmer says. "Some of the passages make me weep at their simple beauty. Bishop Gardiner also agrees with us. We think it only right that the publication of the Holy Bible into English be made legal, as soon as possible."

"That is a matter for the lawyers, sire," Thomas Cromwell whispers into Henry's ear. "The written word is a wonderful weapon, and must remain within our power."

"What do you suggest, Thomas?" Cromwell almost cries out in joy. If the printing of the book is merely made legal, some of the bigger churches will purchase a copy, and the spread of the English bible will take several decades. He wishes the very opposite to happen.

"Let a great Holy Bible be printed, at your explicit order, sire. Command every church in England to have a copy of the book in its pulpit. Order every priest to read from it… and allow readers for those who cannot read it for themselves. Let every church have the word of God in it … by your royal command. Let King Henry's Great Bible become famous, throughout the civilised world."

"Excellent. My Lord Archbishop… you will see to it. The idea of naming it for himself appeals to the king's over weaning vanity, and any opposition he might have for the massive project melts away. In truth, the 'Henry Bible' will never become a popular title, and the common folk will always call it, more accurately, 'Tyndale s Bible', after the man who gave his life to see that the word of God could be read in English.

"Sire, such an undertaking is beyond my experience." Thomas Cranmer is a church man, not a printer, and this new form of mass communication is beyond his powers of comprehension. "I know nothing of printing, or how to illuminate texts. It seems that the Flemings and the Germans have a monopoly."

"Not so. I know a very good man," Thomas Cromwell says to the small gathering. "Master Coverdale can have the printing blocks made up, and begin printing bibles, within six months. A year after that, and every church shall have its own English scriptures, gospels and psalms."

"Then make it so, Thomas," Henry says, "for I weary of this constant strife with Rome. When will they ever learn to leave us, and our faith, in peace?

*

Will Draper has warned François against the possibility of assassination out of mere mischief, but now hopes the king listens to him. In the meantime, he patrols the half deserted halls, in the hope of spotting the perfidious priest, Grimaldi.

He pauses for a moment, and looks out of a beautifully stained glass window. It is growing dark, and soon the court will have to make ready for dinner. The outer halls will fill with people, and the murderous priest will be able to move about with far more freedom.

"Where is the fellow?" Rafe Sadler asks. "We have scoured the outer halls, and he is nowhere to be found. He cannot be in the king's inner chambers, for there are guards all about. Perhaps he thinks to strike at dinner, when the king is at his most vulnerable?"

"I doubt it. This priest is no holy martyr, and he will wish to survive the attack," Will Draper reasons. "He will want to strike at François, and have enough time to slip away. For that to happen, he must have the king all alone, and completely at his mercy."

"The king is never left alone." Rafe realises he is still clutching his parchment and sharpened quills, and stuffs them into his broad leather belt. The power of the written word cannot help in such a dangerous situation. "Even when he attends his private chapel, there is a single priest in attendance."

"Christ!" Will Draper sees it all at once, and takes to his heels. Rafe Sadler understands, a moment later, and gives chase. If he wishes to escape, Father Grimaldi must be alone with François for a while, and where else, but as father confessor, in the king s own private chapel?

*

The King of France is a living dichotomy. On the one hand, he believes he is the divine choice of God, put in place to rule the greatest kingdom since the time of Charlemagne, and on the other he is a frightened little child, who fears for his immortal soul, and fears to meet his maker.

He does not bow the knee to pray, but prostrates himself on the cold Milanese marble floor of the chapel, and begs God above for salvation, like any other miserable sinner. It is a most undignified position for a great king, and he allows no other witnesses, save for a single priest, changed each day, to hear his usually mundane confession.

Father Grimaldi approves of the king's devotion to God, and almost regrets what he must do, but the stakes are high, and it is not his place to contradict the wishes of his master. King

François, who sits at the centre of Europe, and holds power beyond his meagre abilities, must die. The priest is unarmed, of course, but it does not matter. He has been an assassin for ten long years, and knows how to improvise.

He unfastens the sash at his waist, and holds it in one hand, loosely. At the given moment, he will throw the corded sash about the king's neck, and give it a sharp twist. François will die, and the brash Englishman, who has already drawn so much attention to himself, will be blamed. Not only the French, but King James and his men, will wish to run the man to earth.

Father Grimaldi, a trained assassin, and a member of the feared Sardinian Brotherhood will melt away into the night, and slip out of the country. His fee, ten thousand Venetian Ducati, awaits him in a Veronese banking house, and will keep his Brotherhood in funds for the next couple of years.

Powerful men attract powerful enemies, and Grimaldi and his Brotherhood of Sardinian assassins will always be on hand to work for the highest bidder. To date, he and his comrades have slain an untold number of men, from merchants and bishops, to famous lords, but today will be their first royal commission. The priest wraps the cord tightly about his left fist, and prepares to strike.

Footsteps sound in the outer corridor. Father Grimaldi curses, and steps back into the shadows as the sound of running feet approaches. He snatches up a silver candlestick, with his free hand, just as Will Draper bursts into the chapel. The priest thinks fast, and is quick to act. He steps from his place of concealment, and swings the heavy thing like a mace.

Will Draper senses the hurried movement to his left, and tries to twist away from the blow. The heavy silver candlestick catches him a sharp crack on the temple, and then crashes on into his unprotected shoulder. He gasps, and falls down to his knees. For a moment, he thinks he can recover, and make it back to his feet, but a second solid swipe connects with the side of his head, and he tumbles down onto the cold marble floor. I have failed, Will thinks, even as the blackness closes over him.

King François leaps to his feet at the sound of the sudden commotion. He stares, myopically, into the gloom, and sees the big Englishman, Draper, laid out on the hard ground. A gaunt young priest has felled him from behind, and is advancing on the king.

"Sire, are you safe?" the priest says, his voice cracking with concern. "This vile rogue was creeping up on you. Thank God I was here. May God praise the sure swiftness of my hand."

"Father…I owe you my life." King François holds his arms out wide, and steps forward to meet his death. Father Grimaldi smiles, and sweeps the cord up, and around the king's neck. François has no time to scream for help as the moment of his violent death approaches. Then the cord is miraculously loosened, and the priest is rolling on the floor in a flying mass of arms and legs.

King François staggers backwards, clawing at his neck, where the cord has started to bite, and he screams out for help. The men on the floor roll over once more, and the king discerns that it is but two men, locked in a death struggle. There is a soft, almost apologetic cry, and one of the struggling shapes staggers to its feet.

"Bugger me, but the dog almost won!" Rafe Sadler is an unlikely looking saviour, but François does not mind. He throws his arms around the English diplomat, and calls for his guards again. A half dozen armed men rush in, and surround their king.

"Colonel Draper is wounded," FranÁois says, and points to the fallen Englishman. "See to him at once. You, sir… how came you to be here so fortuitously?"

"The colonel guessed your life was at risk, sire," Rafe explains. "He came to save you, but … all is now well. The wicked priest is dead."

"Yes… but how?" Rafe Sadler smiles, and crosses to the body. He puts a toe to the dead man's flank and turns the dead body over. There is a quill sticking out of the man s heart.

"A gooses quill?" François is astounded.

"Forgive me this trick, sire, but arms are forbidden inside the court," Rafe says. He pulls a fresh quill from his belt and tries to flex it. There is no movement. "A steel pin, Your Majesty. I dared not let us go unarmed, so inserted one into several of my hollow quills. They make a most deadly stiletto. One has but to place the palm of the hand so & and thrust. I sought to wound the rogue anywhere. That I struck his heart was the purest luck."

"No, sir, not luck. God was watching over me. François has regained his courage now, and wants to see how Will Draper is faring.

"These bastard Englishmen have thick heads, sire," the captain of his guard says. It will take more than saving his king's life to give this Frenchman a change of perspective. The English are the enemy, and to be reviled at every opportunity. "See, the bone headed swine is sitting up already, Your Majesty." Will staggers to his feet, and throws a dirty look at the big captain of the guard.

"Better never than late," he says, pointedly, and the soldier glowers, and looks down at the ground. "Thank God two bastard Englishmen were here, sire!"

"Who would dare such a thing?" François understands that his death was well planned, and he is furious as to who might make so bold an attempt.

"Not my king, sire," Will says, rubbing his temple. "He means you nothing but friendship. Otherwise, as I have already said, it would be I with the rope, and you would not have lived.

"Your courage will be well rewarded, gentlemen," François says. "Now, who must I strike back at? Who hired this fraudulent priest to kill me?"

"The Pope, sire," Rafe explains. "We believe he seeks to set himself up as the de facto ruler of France, with the young Dauphin as his prisoner."

"Had it been Clement, I would believe you," François replies, "but Pope Paul is a most humane man. He demands fair taxes for the poor, and succour for the starving. He even funds the priest, Ignatius Loyola, so that he might raise an army of priests to do holy work in the Americas. It is yet to be made public, but we have just signed a treaty with Rome. Why would he now want me dead?"

"Who else would dare?" Rafe asks. "The Emperor Charles owns more land than France, and has the wealth of the New World at his fingertips. Besides, he is a God fearing man, and would not endanger his immortal soul."

"Yet the Pope would?"

"Perhaps he thinks himself above we mere mortals?" Rafe says. He has no love for Rome, and does not wish to retract his accusation.

"I have recently ordered my fighting ships to visit this New World," Francois muses. "Charles thinks it is his own private estate, but my captains have orders to take possession of any land not under Spain s control."

"Then there is your motive," Will says. "I was wrong. The Pope is innocent, but someone else wants you dead for the same reasons. With you gone, sire… your son rules. He is not yet able to stand up to the Holy Roman Empire."

"Then it is Charles?" the French king asks.

"No, I think not," Will says. "Charles has no idea of the day to day business of his vast empire. You seek to threaten the Americas, and that would cause the flow of gold to dry up. Only one man would really suffer in that case."

"Who?" François is baffled. "Name him, sir, and his days are done."

"Anton Fugger." Will thinks he understands it all now. "The banker has crossed swords with Cromwell in the past, and seeks to cause as much ruin as he can now. He wishes to protect his mines, so plots your death. With you gone, France will draw in its horns, and leave the Americas alone.

"Further, he drives a wedge between England and Scotland. If your murder is seen to be at English hands, France must, for honour's sake, go to war with us. With the whole of Europe at each other's throats, Anton Fugger can only prosper. He lends money to Spain, and hires troops for Rome. He has Charles support either us or France, and war is the order of the day. Fugger owns the mines, and he owns the foundries that make the imperial cannon."

"Merde!"

"Quite so, sire," Will concludes. "Anton Fugger and his family are the richest people in the world, and seek to rule it from the shadows. We must always be on our guard."

"This man must die."

"Easier said than done," Rafe Sadler says. "Besides, kill him, and the next Fugger will continue in his place. We must hurt them in a way that curtails their ambitions."

"How?" François asks. Rafe shrugs his shoulders to show that such planning is beyond his ability.

"We must ask a wiser man."

"Who?" the king asks. "Who can possibly match this Anton Fugger's intellect?"

With the might of the French court at their complete disposal, it is an easy matter for Will Draper and Rafe Sadler to trace the prior movements of the would be assassin, Father Udo Grimaldi.

Reginald Pole professes to be shocked at the entire affair of the murderous priest. The English papist swears his complete innocence in the matter, and says the priest came to him with a letter of glowing recommendation from the Holy Roman Governor of Lower Silesia.

"Where, in Hell s name is that?" Will Draper asks, and the rebellious Roman Catholic shakes his head to signify his lack of this particular geographical knowledge.

"The emperor's lands are vast," he confesses without prompting. "I saw the Holy Roman seal on the letter, and so took the priest at face value. He seemed most intent on helping me spread the word of God, back in England. It was he who suggested we leave Paris for Amiens, and then prompted a visit to Arras, to speak with the French king."

"You have been played for a fool, Master Pole," Will says.

"Go home now, and you might be forgiven," Rafe adds.

"I cannot. England must return to Rome, or I will continue to wage my lonely war." Pole has his views, and will not deviate one whit from them.

"The English church will never return to Rome, Master Pole."

"God will guide me," Pole insists.

"One day, you will die for your stubbornness," Will Draper says. "This priest and his master care nothing for God, or how we worship Him. You have been sorely used, sir. Return to England, and beg mercy of the king."

"The mercy he showed to Katherine of Aragon… Robert Aske, or the Boleyn whore?" Pole replies sharply. "No, thank you sir… but no. I shall travel on to Rome, and entreat with the new Pope. His Holiness will have important things for me to do."

"As you wish. My task was to stop you meddling with English affairs, and I have done that, without recourse to your murder. I am quite content." Reginald Pole bows, and leaves the chamber. Will smiles across at Rafe. "Will you report back that I let him go?"

"Not I," Rafe says. "I shall report the truth. You have no power to compel the man back to London, yet you did your best to turn him from his ill chosen path. Thomas Cromwell knows you, Will. He will see how things are, and be content with your actions."

"The priest had papers supplied by the Holy Roman Empire," Will muses. "Anton Fugger is behind this. We should take ship at once, and speak with Master Cromwell."

"King François wants us to stay. He has already laden us with bags of golden Louis coins."

"How much?"

"About four hundred ducats… or one hundred and sixty pounds apiece."

"My Miriam makes that much, every time one of her cogs makes landfall," Will moans.

"She is right when she says that cleverness is better than brute strength."

"Perhaps, but cleverness seldom stops a sword thrust, or a lead pistol ball." Rafe ponders for a moment. "We could just slip away, and ride for Calais. By the time François realises it, we will be across the water, and eating breakfast back in Austin Friars."

"A good idea, Rafe," Will replies. "We will set off at dawn, as soon as the town gates are opened."

*

"Good day to you, gentlemen. A fine old day for a ride, is nae it?" The big, bearded Scot sits astride his horse, with a hand across the butt of his long pistol. "D'yea ken which road you are on?"

Will Draper glances to right and left. There are a dozen men on each side of them, all armed with pistols, or the broad Scottish claymore sword. The clatter of horses hooves tells him that the road behind is now also closed to a retreat.

"Why, it is the Calais road, sir," Will calls. "Might we not ride together, Sir Iain?"

"You know me, laddie?"

"You are Sir Iain Campbell, of the Clan Campbell," Will says. "You are the great laird of Inverness-shire, and advisor to King James. I make it my business to know about the great men I must deal with."

"Och noo, I am not here to deal, but to deal with you, Englishman." Sir Iain says, and several of his men laugh at the rather lame jest.

"I doubt King François will look kindly on any belligerent act," Will offers. It is unlikely he can avoid a fight, and odds of some twenty to two are poor. "King James might even…"

"A turd on James," Campbell snaps. "He is a mean minded little fellow, who hates many of my own kin. James ordered me not to look for revenge when you sliced open my nephew's arm."

"For which you should thank Colonel Draper," Rafe puts in.

"Thank him? A few growls, and some laughter is accompanied by the solemn clink of swords being drawn.

"Yes. The boy was a fool. My friend disarmed him, and chose to let him live." Rafe sees the look on Sir Iain's face, and makes a shrewd guess. "What did his men say? Did they tell you how they were overcome by us, with the help of the French, and of how they fought bravely to save their wounded friend?"

Sir Iain sits, ramrod straight on his horse, and digests all that Rafe has said. After a moment, he turns in the saddle, and glares at the man sitting to his rear.

"Dougie… is this true?"

"The damned *scally* lies, sir!" Dougie Campbell is an open faced Scot, and his expression betrays him.

"God blast ye, man!" The laird is shaking with anger. "Six of you, and never a one with a scratch, save for my nephew. I should have known."

Will Draper senses a change in the balance of events, and decides that attack is the best form of defence. He dismounts, and swaggers towards the laird, with his hand on his sword.

"Your nephew tried his hand, and I spared him," Will calls out. "The others did not linger to try their own luck, but ran away, like frightened rabbits. Perhaps they might wish to take their chance now. One by one, or all at once … it is no mind to me, sir."

"Dougie, and Big Gregor," Sir Iain says. "You two boasted the most. Now show me how hard you fought this Englishman."

"Och, but we were five … Dougie starts, then realises he will only make things worse. "Will ye have him dead… or just cut up, like he did to Jamie?"

"What say you, Colonel Draper?" Sir Iain asks. "Will you take them on to first blood, or death?"

"Wait!" Rafe Sadler holds up a sheet of new vellum. "Let me make a contract, sir. A contract between two gentlemen."

"What is this lawyer nonsense?" the Scots laird growls.

"The colonel seldom fights, unless there is a fee attached," Rafe says, ingenuously. "He might kill every one of your fellows, and not earn a penny piece. Let him have their purses, their horses, and their boots. I will write it down, and we shall sign it."

"My boots?" Big Gregor asks.

"You will not need them where Will Draper is going to send you, fellow," Rafe replies.

"Sir Iain… we only sought to save face. The Englishman is a trained killer, Dougie says. I have no wish to die."

"You were willing enough to come on this little outing though," the laird replies. "Would you have hung back, and let real men do the job for you?"

"Sir… we are sorry."

"Then the Englishman spoke the truth?"

"Yes."

"That is a novelty in its own self." Sir Iain Campbell shakes his head at what has been said. "Colonel Draper, I find I have no quarrel with you, or your lawyer friend. If you still wish to fight these two fellows you may, but I wash my hands of them. Neither will ever be welcomed back on my estates, and their family will know of their shame. Five to one, and him nothing but an Englishman… t'ch!"

The laird pulls the head of his horse to one side, and clears the way. Will turns to return to his horse, and both men charge him from behind. There is a loud bang, and Dougie screams out. The lairds pistol shot has smashed his spine. Gregor is still moving forward, more in blind panic than anything else, and Will Draper is able to draw a dagger from his doublet, and effect a perfect underhanded throw.

The point takes the second Scotsman in the throat, and he tumbles down in a welter of arms, legs and blood. He tries to stand, convulses once, and dies.

"Och, and cowards too," Sir Iain says. "My apologies, sir. A true Scot always looks his enemy in the face."

"Thank you, sir." Will retrieves his knife. "If England and Scotland ever settle their quarrels, I will be first to greet you as a friend."

"Well spoken, laddie," the Campbell chief replies. "Now be on your way, before the Frenchies find you are gone."

"Then you know we are slipping away?" says Rafe.

"Yes, and that cunning swine François wants you delayed, so he can use you for his own ends," the Scot says. "Ride for Calais, my friends, and God s speed to you both!"

*

Henry draws the bow string back, with practiced ease, and sends his yard long arrow into the centre of the butt. There is a polite ripple of applause, and the Duke of Suffolk curses under his breath.

"Another five pounds you owe me, Charles," the king beams. "I have my eye in today, and no mistake."

"You have the luck of kings, Hal," Charles Brandon, Duke of Suffolk responds. "God looks down on you, and heaps blessings on this kingdom. You are king, your wife is with child, and England is safe from harm. The sun shines, and the crops grow in the fields."

"Then we are content," Henry says. "Six months ago, a rebel army sought to ruin us all, and starvation threatened. It is truly miraculous how things have changed about."

"We must thank Thomas Cromwell for some of it," Suffolk says. "He leads the way in closing down the greedier abbeys, and the worst of the monastic houses. I am sure it was he who brought Norfolk into line too. Old Uncle Norfolk was a little too friendly with Aske and his followers for my liking."

"Perhaps, but they are all dead now, and by Norfolk's hand," the king says. "The common people see his cruel hand in those deaths, not mine. My conscience is perfectly clear, Charles."

"Of course. It was the Duke of Norfolk who caused most of our ills," Charles replies. "You would do well to keep him on a short tether, my dear friend."

"Tom Cromwell thinks the same, and my wife thinks him to be altogether too vain for his own good." Henry knocks another arrow, and sends it into the target. "Damn. A little to the left."

"You did not take account of the breeze, sire," Thomas Cromwell says, as he comes, half running, across the immaculate lawns. "My Lord Suffolk must have distracted you... else you would have put a wetted finger in the air. Thus!" Cromwell licks his fore finger, and holds it up to the breeze. "Ah, what is this? A warm wind blows in from France, sire!"

"Oh, Thomas, is your little jest meant to tell me we have news from Arras?" Henry asks, and Thomas nods like an excited child.

"The best of news, sire." Cromwell wags a rolled document at the king. "Your dear cousin James is married again."

"Damn!"

"To Mary of Guise," Cromwell continues.

"Who?"

"Mary of Guise, sire." Thomas Cromwell can hardly contain his pleasure at the news. "She has some money, but no claim to the French throne. King James must return home with a long face, and no royal princess. France will not go to war with us this year... not because of Scotland."

"Well done, Thomas. How ever did you manage it?"

"Our diplomatic envoys reasoned with the French king, sire," Cromwell explains. "Master

Rafe Sadler showed François how dangerous it might be, having a perfidious Scot for a dependent son-in-law."

"Rafe Sadler... by God, I shall do something for the clever fellow, Thomas. Perhaps a knighthood, or a fertile estate.. a small sized one... somewhere."

"The Scots offered some affront to our party, and came off worse," Cromwell continues. "It seems Colonel Draper was not happy with them. I believe they lost two men, with another sorely wounded."

"Dear Draper. Did I ever tell you how he once fought with me, and almost bested me?"

"Sire, I was there."

"So you were." Henry is in a fine mood now. His men are putting the Scots to the sword, and France distrusts King James. "Was not your son involved?"

"You knocked him down, but spared him any real harm, sire... for which I thank you."

"Where is he now?"

"He is just back from Cambridge, sire," Cromwell says. "I was hoping you might..."

"Of course. What ever you think fit for him, old fellow. Is he trained as a gentleman?"

"He is still the son of the son of a blacksmith, sire, but we have knocked away all the rough edges. My Gregory will make a fine clerk to the Archbishop, or a secretary to Lord Audley."

"We must reward Colonel Draper too," Henry says. "What do you suggest? I cannot think he wants an estate, for his wife is already quite rich, I believe."

Ah, but someone has been talking out of turn, Cromwell thinks. He never mentions Miriam Draper to Henry, but her great wealth has been drawn to the king s attention.

"She owns a few channel cogs, sire. A woman, try as she might, cannot be a man. She is held back by her children, and her husband's needs. What little wealth she has accumulated is more by luck than good management. During this last hard winter, she foolishly dissipated her gold on food for the poor."

"I see." Henry scowls. "Then I have been misinformed. It seems that her fortune has been over exaggerated by jealous tongues."

"Might I ask who it is who claims to know Mistress Miriam's fortune better than I... the godfather of her poor children?"

"Young Surrey."

"The Duke of Norfolk's idiot son? Thomas Cromwell sighs at the king s naïve outlook. "The Earl of Surrey is a dissolute drunkard, and a vile fornicator, sire. He rents the Draper's old house, which is alongside their new one. I believe Your Majesty once visited?"

"By God... I recall a fire. Did I not take to my barge, and run down the arsonists?"

"Yes, sire. You ran his boat into the bridge, and he was killed." Tom Cromwell adjusts the truth to suit the king, and make him out to be the real hero of the piece. "Since then, Lord Surrey has coveted Mistress Miriam's goodly appearance. He often boasts of how he would, forgive the indelicacy of it, sire, *treat* her."

"Then the wretch tries to ruin her?" Henry is as salacious as the next man, but has a prurient interest in the taking of a woman's virtue. He reviles the would be rapist, whilst being excited at the prospect of taking by force.

"She is a commoner, sire. From Coventry, as you will no doubt recall. I guess Surrey thinks she should give in to him. He is a Howard, of course, and they are an arrogant lot. Norfolk often grumbles that he must sit below you at table, and his son is no better."

"The fellow is an ass," Charles Brandon puts in. "He tells lies about a sweet lady, who often supplies your table, sire."

"Custards!" Henry suddenly recollects the aftermath of the fire, and the beautiful girl with the most delightful pastries he has ever had. "She supplies custard tarts to my kitchen."

"She bakes them herself, sire," Cromwell says. "As for her so called fortune… it is Colonel Draper who earns the real money in the family. He has two hundred a year from the treasury, and made a small fortune in his soldiering days. He fought in Ireland, Wales, France and Italy."

"He was an officer in Ireland, and fought for the Venetians in Italy, at your instruction, Hal," Suffolk adds.

"And he is my man," Henry says. "My very own Royal Examiner. I have a mind to enlarge his office, just to spite young Surrey. How does it currently stand, Master Thomas?"

"He has another officer, sire, and a couple of Welsh rogues who do his dirtier work for him. The colonel often wishes he could raise another half dozen men."

"See to it."

"And his budget?" Cromwell is pleased with this turn in events, but reminds himself to write Surrey s name down in his little black book. "It is five hundred a year now, and he would need another seven hundred to cover his costs."

"Can we run to that?" Henry spends as much on his falcons each year, but is wary of fiscal waste.

"Easily, sire… if we let the Spanish pay." Cromwell is ready to unveil his master plan, and prepares to explain.

"The Emperor Charles is not that generous, Thomas," the king says, then smiles. "You have a scheme, do you not? A Cromwell plot is always worth a listen to. Tell us."

"Whilst in Arras, Colonel Draper foiled a murder attempt against François. The king is grateful, and has agreed to join forces with us, for the next sailing season.

"Assassination?" Henry's blood runs cold. He fears this kind of death above all others, and dreads hearing of such attempts on another king. As the absolute monarch, he feels his life should be sacrosanct. "Who would order such a terrible thing?"

"It seems the Fugger banking family are behind it," Thomas Cromwell explains. "They seek to disrupt the French incursion into the New World, and throw the blame on England. It is a clever enough plan, but one that has been foiled. Now, we are going to have our turn, sire."

"We cannot strike at Anton Fugger," Suffolk puts in. "He lives in an impregnable castle, surrounded by Emperor Charles' armies on all sides. To attack him means war with the Holy Roman Empire. That means the Spanish, as well as most of the German states. The Hanseatic League have almost as many fighting ships as we, Henry."

"We must not go to war over France, Henry says."

"Quite so, sire." Tom Cromwell unrolls a map, and points out certain places. "Charles might have more ships than us, but they are mostly traders… not men o war. We have twice as many warships as he, and he does not even know he is at war. Anton Fugger, in his arrogance, has done this without his lord's knowledge. Now, we must make him pay the price."

"How?" Henry studies the map, which seems to be mostly water, with the odd scrap of land penned in.

"We fight a war at sea," Tom Cromwell says. "We place our ships at key points on this chart. The Fugger mines bulge with gold, which he has shipped back to Spain, or the Netherland parts of their domain."

"Then we raid his mines?" Suffolk asks. He is not the sharpest of intellects, and it takes time for anything complex to seep into his mind. "We must have hundreds of soldiers for such an undertaking… and brave officers."

"No, we let Anton Fugger's men mine the gold, refine it, and ship it back home," Cromwell explains. "We intercept his treasure ships on the high seas, confiscate the gold, and take the vessel into our own merchant fleet."

"Can we stop them all?" Henry asks.

"I doubt it," his minister replies. "We might catch one in every ten. That means we will take two treasure ships in a sailing season. Each one will be carrying about a hundred thousand pounds worth of gold, and the ship itself is worth at least another three or four thousand."

"And the cost?" Henry loves a profit, but hates expenditure of any sort, unless it is upon himself. "A ship at sea can cost me a hundred pounds a day."

"We have our ships manned anyway," Tom Cromwell tells the king. "We must have them rigged, and victualled, and pay our men, no matter what. So why not put them to work?"

"Charles will be angry." Henry contemplates this for a moment, then smiles. "Yes… we shall do it. Retribution for past hurts… what? Give the orders, dear friend. I want my men o' war at sea, as soon as possible."

"Certainly, sire." Tom Cromwell bows. "It only remains to appoint another couple of admirals. We have Lord Norfolk as Commander of the Fleet, and Admiral Sir Roderick Travis is a proven man. Might I suggest we put the Duke of Leinster, and the dearly loved Earl of Surrey in command of the northern flotilla? It might keep young Howard from making any more idle talk."

Splendid, Thomas… quite splendid." Henry moves his finger over the map, and stabs it at a long island on the far edge. Where is this, my friend?"

"I believe the Spanish call it Hispaniola, sire."

"It looks bigger than England."

"It is, I think."

"Get it for me," Henry says. "I might give it to my new son, when he arrives."

"I shall see what can be done, sire."

"Good man," Henry says, and returns to his longbow. A tropical island in the far away Caribee lands will make a fine present, and give his son more subjects to rule, even though they might be a mixture of godless natives, and defeated Spaniards. "We shall think of a suitable new name for the place."

9   The Buccaneer

Sir Roderick Travis is his own man. He is in his fifty second year, and has spent forty of them at sea. As a younger man he raided the Spanish islands, and took many prizes, then came home to a hero s welcome. The knighthood, and his share of the booty kept body and soul together for some time, but it was a chance meeting with Thomas Cromwell that has revitalised his flagging career.

Cromwell is a good judge of men, and knows the old sea captain will be a willing ally. After nudging him into the command of the southern fleet, the Privy Councillor has used him to put the fear of God into the French, and to attack the fortress of Tangiers, so that the Portuguese might sign a peace treaty with Henry.

For his part, Travis cares not who the enemy is, just so long as there is one, and the pickings are sweet. That is why he now pounds the poop deck of the *Henry Grace a Dieu* in mounting frustration. His captain, and those who must be on deck, hold their breaths and wait for the customary outburst of anger directed against the rolling waves.

"God curse this empty sea!" he cries. "Almost two months, and nothing to speak of, but a lone Brabant trader."

The pride of the king s fleet, known to all as Great Harry is almost twenty two years old, and is still the most powerful warship in the northern seas. She has a compliment of two hundred and sixty five sailors, forty excellent gunners, and a hundred and fifty trained soldiers. Under full sail, she can outrun almost any other vessel, and she caught the Brabant merchant with ease.

With secrecy being of the uttermost importance, Sir Roderick has no recourse but to confiscate the small craft's mixed cargo, and lock her twelve man crew in the Great Harry s hold. The small boat is worth less than three hundred pounds, and is a small compensation for the weeks of searching.

The Great Harry, along with the Sovereign, the Silver Greyhound, the Kingmaker, and the Regent are stretched in a line from Trafalgar Point to a position thirty miles off the friendly port of Lisbon, in Portugal. In all Thomas Cromwell has thirty great warships, and a dozen smaller, faster galleys strung out across the unforgiving Atlantic.

"Sir!" Captain Hastie cries, and points to a position off the starboard bow. "A sail, or I'll eat my liver!" A moment later, and the watcher in the high crow's nest confirms the sighting.

"What ship is she, damn it?" Sir Roderick Travis demands to know from his crew. Shouts go back and forth, and men strain their eyes to make out the ship which is heading straight at them. "Is she a Spanisher?"

The lookout ignores the cursing from below, and stares at the horizon with practiced calm. After a moment, he is sure of his facts, and leans out to call down his news.

"Cap'n… she be one of ours. The Arrow, by her flags and rigging," the man cries. "She is under full sail, and coming at us."

"What is this?" Travis thinks hard. Why would one of his small galleys behave so? Then a thought comes to him, and he makes an instantaneous decision. "More sail, Captain Hastie. The sprat is fetching us a fresh mackerel."

"Sir?"

"She runs from a larger ship, you fool!" Travis cries. "The Arrow is leading her onto us. Run out the guns, and have them primed. Call the soldiers to arms, and have them fill the topgallant with muskets. Master Crow… what see you now?"

"More sails, sir," the man cries. "Dear God… but she is a full rigged frigate, and has the wind behind her well and true."

"How far, and how fast?" Travis calls.

"Two leagues, sir… and maybe making ten or twelve knots." Sir Roderick smiles. It can only be a Spanish ship, giving chase to what her captain thinks is easy prey. An English warship as a prize will make him popular at the Spanish court of Charles, the Holy Roman Emperor. The Spaniard will cram on all the sail he can, to catch the Arrow, and will be at close quarters before he realises his danger.

"The Spaniard is coming on too fast for her own good," he explains. "The sun is at our backs, gentlemen. By the time she sees us, it will be too late for her to veer away. We will turn across her bow, and rake her with cannon fire. Each gun must fire as it comes to bear. Her own guns will be mounted broadside, and useless to her, until we come alongside."

"Then she will discharge thirty cannon into our belly, sir," Hastie says. "Will even this Great Harry be able to take such punishment?"

"Our rigging must be thick with muskets," Travis replies. "It is up to them to fire down onto the enemy canon. Let them mark out their gunners, and kill them first."

"And if we do not get them all?"

"Then we lash ourselves to her, and go a boarding, sir. Have you never used that cutlass?"

"Not I, sir. Nor have many of the crew."

"God's teeth. All hands on deck, and have them armed with anything that can kill. I shall lead them over myself."

"That is my place, Admiral," Hastie replies, coldly.

"Then the honour is yours," Travis says. "I shall be second on the Spanisher s deck."

"Double load!" Jack Fenn snaps out the order, and a dozen pairs of eyes turn to him in surprise. "Yon frigate is made of the finest weathered oak, lads. We'll only have the one chance to breach her planks. Now, double load, lads, or taste my anger!" The loaders see their gunners nod, and ram home a second sack of coarse black powder. They follow it with wadded cotton, and step aside as the ball monkey heaves the shot up, and into the muzzle. The lad jumps away, and the rammer drives it into place.

"Ready!" Gun number one wins the race, as it should do, and a smattering of calls show the rest of the broadside to be double loaded, and ready to fire a few moments later.

"Hold fast, lads," Travis shouts. "Gunners are to fire as we cross her bow." The Great Harry heaves about, and cuts across the Spaniards bow. Someone shouts out that they can see men at the prow, and another sees the name painted on her side.

"Santa Maria … something or other, the man informs his mates, as he clutches a hanger in his fist. It is a short, cutlass type sword, both sharp, and heavy, which can be deadly at close quarters. Others have grabbed up axes and short pikes. Down the side of the ship, men hold grappling hooks, tied to lengths of rope.

"Fire one!" The heavy fourteen pounder belches smoke, and a tongue of fire licks out at the Spaniard. The solid shot punches through the thick oak planks, and rips into the inside of the Spanish ship. It smashes through everything in its path, sending wood splinters, and men in all directions. The second cannon goes off with a fearsome crash, and another lead ball rips into the treasure ship's bleeding heart.

Fire three. Fire four. The orders ring out, and a dozen rounds are spewed into the Spanish ship, demolishing below decks, and killing or maiming scores of men. Then the Santa Maria's bow hits the stern of the Great Harry, and makes the English ship swing around. As they come alongside one another the Spanish captain raises his sword to cry out the order to fire. There is a volley of musket fire, and six of his gunners fall back from their guns. Others look up, realise they are being picked out, and try to run. More muskets bark, and men begin to die at their positions.

One Spaniard braves the hail of shot, and touches a smouldering brand to his cannon. It roars, and punches a hole in the English ship's side. The shot passes through the breadth of the hold, and emerges from the far side, without further harm.

The Arrow, having led the quarry into the snare, swings about, and discharges its own four smaller cannon into the leeward side of the Spaniard. These smaller shot crack against the timbers, and bounce off into the sea.

"At them, lads!" Hastie sees the grapples are tied in place, and the two ships are locked in a deadly embrace. "Clear their decks" He leaps across the narrow gap, and is confronted by a half dozen armed Spaniards. Even as he lands on their deck, another fellow hurtles past him.

Sir Roderick Travis is a born buccaneer, and knows that feint hearts never won anything. He ploughs into the Spaniards, cutting at them with a sword in each hand. One man screams, and the rest fall back. Hastie rushes forward, to lend a hand, and more men leap the divide. What follows is a bloody slaughter. The Spanish sailors are not fighting men, and the best part of them are press ganged Genoese, enslaved Moors, or Spanish peasants.

They throw down their weapons, and prostrate themselves on the deck. Some are killed where they lie, until Captain Hastie's roaring voice stops the slaughter. The English boarding party find themselves arranged just below the raised poop deck of the Spanish ship. They fan out and await the final command.

The Spanish captain and a half dozen officers hold this last deck, armed with swords and pistols. One rush would see them overpowered, but it would be a hard fight, and cost some English lives. Sir Roderick loves his crew, and values them above gold. He knows now that they will follow him around the world, if he but asks. More death is pointless. He steps forward, and bows to the Spanish captain.

"Señor, I am Admiral Travis, of the English fleet. We have your ship. I claim it in the name of King Henry."

"This is piracy, sir!" The Spanish captain responds. "You will hang for it."

"Not so, sir. You were attacking my galley, the Arrow, and we defended her. Let us not talk naval law. You must surrender, or die for your ship. What is it to be?"

"We cannot surrender," the man replies in faltering English. "We have ladies aboard. Their honour is our prime concern."

"I understand your concern," Admiral Travis says. "You have my word, as an English gentleman, that you, and your good ladies will be safe. Surrender, and you shall be conveyed to Bristol, from where you can arrange a safe passage home to Spain."

"And my ship?"

"A prize of war, sir." Travis smiles then. "Your hand, sir. All the gold in the Americas is not worth another life."

"Very well, I accept your terms, sir." The captain goes to lean over the low rail, and grasp the admiral's hand. As he does, a young Spanish officer, who speaks no English, sees his chance. He steps forward, and fires his pistol into Sir Roderick Travis' face.

There is a moment of silent horror, then the English boarders surge forward and butcher everyone on the upper deck. The Spanish captain dies, even as he tries to lean back, and his wife, his daughter, and the wives of his officers cower back in terror.

"Enough!" Hastie calls, but to no avail. In seconds the deck is slick with innocent blood. The young Spaniard is dragged to the side of the ship, where the men hack at him, until he is a bloodied mess. Then they tie a rope about his neck, and haul his kicking body up into the rigging.

There are thirty survivors of the fight, and they are all either enslaved Moors, or indented Portuguese and Genoese prisoners, save one man. Dick Selkirk is a Scot, taken in a press gang raid in Bilbao, ten years before.

"You are free men now," Hastie tells them. I ask only that you help crew this ship back to Bristol. Do this, and you will receive a half share each in the prize."

"Sir, I have no wish to return to Scotland, might I sail with you? I did not offer you any opposition, and welcome the outcome of this day. Though I deplore the death of your commander."

"You can sign on, once we are safe back at Bristol." Captain Hastie selects a dozen men to bolster the crew of the Spanish treasure ship, and puts his first mate in charge.

The body of Sir Roderick Travis, England's greatest buccaneer, is wrapped in a winding sheet, along with a cannon ball, and dropped into the sea. The crew salute his passing, and wonder what their share will be from this day's work.

Captain Hastie settles down in what was once the admiral's cabin, and starts to write up a full account of the day's events. It is his duty to report to his masters, as well as make an entry into the ship s log. When he comes to describe the final confrontation, he pauses. It will not do to recount how his men, enraged by the death of their leader, despatched the last few Spaniards, and of how they butchered the women and children. He thinks for a long while, then begins to write.

*

Henry takes the despatch from Thomas Cromwell's shaking hand, and examines it for himself. It is terse, and to the point.

On this thirteenth day of July, in the year of Our Lord 1537, we have fought a great sea battle with the Spanish, and by His Good Grace, God granted us a most happy outcome. I can report that the enemy did fall on the galley Arrow, without provocation, and we were compelled to attempt her rescue.

After much warring with cannon and musket shot, we enjoined with them, hand to hand. His Majesty's sailors boarded the Santa Maria de Bilbao, and overcame the enemy after a fierce combat. The Spanish officers and their crew fought very well, and died to the last man.

Upon opening the holds, I found there to be upwards of a thousand ingots of gold, and six hundred of silver. Also was found a great quantity of treasure. Precious coloured stones of all hues fill two sea chests, and there are many personal pieces of silver plates, goblets and ewers that must belong to the ships officers. My purser values this bounty at one hundred and seventeen thousand pounds, eighteen shillings, and four pence. The ship, a fine frigate type, with twenty cannon (Venetian cast), will make a goodly addition to His Majesty s navy.

Our losses were light, and such was the ferocity of our attack, we suffered only one death, and a half dozen wounded. The king's men did acquit themselves with great honour, and by their deeds did further enrich His Majesty's already fearsome reputation.

It is with regret that I must record the sad death of our commander Admiral of the Fleet, Sir Roderick Travis. He fought alongside his men, and died, at the moment of victory, by a cruel trick of fate.

"Sir Roderick was your man, was he not?" Henry asks, and Cromwell can only nod. He recalls how they met, and how the fellow was not happy unless he had a deck beneath his feet. "I see it in your eyes, my friend."

"He was a fine seaman, sire," Cromwell replies. "The French and the Spanish were in awe of him."

"We must see his family do not suffer."

"He had none," Thomas Cromwell says. Travis has lived a not dissimilar life to the Privy Councillor, devoting it to the furtherance of his country. "Perhaps we might put up a plaque for him?"

" A plaque?"

"Nothing grand, sire. A memorial to him in a church near his home would suffice. The cost can come from his share of the prize, which now devolves to the treasury."

"Very well… see to it, Thomas," Henry says. "Now, what can you tell me about the new lady to our court?"

"Lady Gerta Van der Floss, sire? The lady is the daughter of a very rich Flemish merchant, who wishes to ingratiate himself into our English court life. To this end, he is quite willing to sacrifice his daughter's honour. She is a decent, God fearing girl. I believe she prays an excessive amount, and … perhaps I should not say… for it is not my place."

"What is it?" Henry asks. "He is toying with the idea of taking a mistress, until Jane Seymour's pregnancy is over, and finds the girl to be both attractive, and rather unintelligent. Cromwell taps a finger to his temple, and rolls his eyes comically. "Dear God, the girl is simple minded?"

"Not as such, sire," Cromwell affects a doleful look. "It is only that there are rumours of madness. In the family, you understand. I cannot say for the girl or her father."

"But you see signs?" Henry fears madness even more than the prospect of assassination. It is a commonly held belief that the mad can pass on their malady, as if it were a winter cold. "Is she contagious?" Cromwell shrugs, and glances over to where the girl is playing with little Crommie, Queen Jane s pet dog.

"I doubt it, sire," he says. "Though it is a brave man who dallies with that family's past history."

"They say that is how Richard Crookback went mad," the king says. Richard III was neither mad, nor a hunchback, Cromwell thinks, but the story helps his own cause. He does not wish Henry to take mistresses, in case it weakens Jane's position at court. The king is notoriously fickle, and needs a son to keep him faithful.

"Yes, they say he dallied with a Warwick girl, and her affliction turned his mind, thank God."

"Thank God, Thomas?"

"Yes, sire. Had he kept his wits about him, he might have won the day at Bosworth, and slain your father," Tom Cromwell replies.

"Then the hand of God touched my father that day," Henry concludes. "I am… bored, Thomas."

"The queen will soon be delivered, sire, and then your days will be filled with things to do. Remember that your lady loves the man, not the king. If you think abstinence will damage you, might I suggest you avail yourself of a clean working girl?"

"I cannot go about my realm, hiring whores, Thomas."

"No, sire, but I could find a suitable girl." Cromwell wonders if Henry is contemptible enough to accept such an arrangement. "A clean girl, who is discreet… for a fee."

"What if… what if the queen finds out?" Henry fights between his lust and his own dented code of morality. "No, I must not. Though I thank you for the offer, Thomas. You are a true friend."

"Would that all my friends were like you, sire," Cromwell replies. Now, I must arrange for our ships to be met. "This news came by fast galley, and the Great Harry will be in Bristol Sound by tomorrow evening's tide."

"What will be my share, Thomas?"

"After the crew are given their share of the prize, Your Majesty will be the richer by some ninety five thousand pounds." Henry is staggered by such an amount coming to him, and wonders if his other ships will be as successful. He receives only twenty thousand for an earldom, and they do not become available that often.

"I must have something fine for Jane, and I want to give Hampton Court Palace a new look. The French style is attractive, but expensive, I hear."

"As you wish, Your Majesty." Thomas Cromwell suppresses a sigh. Easy come, easy go, he thinks, and all it has cost is the life of a dear friend. "Might we now discuss our response to the emperor?"

"Our response?" Henry is confused. "Has he written to us?"

"He will, sire. He will want to know how we come to take his treasure ship, and why. We must have a lawful answer for him. It will not do to admit to piracy."

"Dear Christ, piracy?" Henry swings from pleasure to dismay in a heartbeat. "Is that what they will say of me?"

"Charles will want answers, sire, Cromwell says. He already knows how he will handle the issue, but it does him good to watch the king squirm a little. "He will ask why we attacked the

Santa Maria on the high seas, and we must answer him.

"How, sir?" Henry asks.

"Why, we shall tell the truth, Cromwell says. "We are Englishmen, and our word is our bond. The Spaniard fell upon one of our galleys, and the Great Harry sailed to save her. The Spanish fired at us, and holed our ship, which forced us to board her. In the ensuing fight, the Spaniards all died."

"That sounds a just enough reply," Henry says, "but will the Emperor Charles not demand the immediate return of his ship, and its precious cargo?"

"Once the crew were gone, the Santa Maria de Bilbao was at the mercy of the waves," Thomas Cromwell explains. "Our men were free to salvage her, and secure her for the crown. If the prize reaches our port, safely, she is ours. Charles has no legal right. The cargo can be seized, and used to defray our immense costs."

Henry's eyes are glazing over. It is enough that Cromwell knows what to do, and the king can contemplate how he shall spend his portion. The pretty Flemish girl strolls past, with a yapping Crommie in her arms, and gives him a sly little wink. The king groans with discontent.

10   The Night Caller

Thomas Cromwell has his own private chambers near the king, but still prefers to spend his evenings in the comforting confines of Austin Friars. The death of Admiral Travis makes him feel downhearted, and he hardly touches his food. He sits by the fire that evening, and sinks into a slough of despond.

"Master Thomas… the ambassador is here to see you." The lad delivers his message, and awaits an answer. It is rare for anyone to be turned away from the house, but Cromwell is not himself these last few weeks.

"Which ambassador?" he asks, and a splendidly attired little fellow pushes in to the old library.

"How many do you know who would come calling?" Eustace Chapuys says. "How many do you call 'friend'?"

"Forgive me Eustace… was I expecting you today?

"You should be expecting a Spanish army knocking at your door," Chapuys replies. "When the emperor hears of this, he will be tempted to go to war."

"Calm yourself, my friend," Cromwell says. It is time for diplomacy, and he must defuse the dangerous situation. "Our two nations have no need to speak of war."

"The Santa Maria de Bilbao was…"

"*Salvaged*," Thomas Cromwell puts in. "The crew were gone, and she was a lawful prize. The ship, and her cargo become English property. Had your crew stayed aboard…"

"What of the crew?" Eustace asks. He sees the expression on his friend's face, and he scowls at him. "All of them dead? This is infamous, Thomas. How can you justify this act of piracy?"

"Your vessel attacked one of our galleys." Cromwell is on safe ground now, and unfurls his story. "It sought to take the Arrow as a prize, and the Great Harry happened to be close by. The two ships fought, and your crew died bravely. Admiral Travis was killed just as victory was ours."

"I see, and you have proof of this?"

"Come with me to Bristol tomorrow. We shall view what damage there is, and you shall be able to question the captain of the Great Harry. Captain Hastie is an honourable man, and will show you his log, and answer your questions."

"The Emperor Charles will not be pleased," Chapuys says.

"You mean Anton Fugger will be angry at the loss of his gold," Tom Cromwell replies. "You know how Fugger tried to murder François, do you not?"

"I have heard certain stories."

"He sought to turn France against us, and set the Scots at our throats," Thomas Cromwell continues. "Were I to behave in that way, my king would say it was treason… and with the greatest justification. It seems that this scurrilous banker rules the Holy Roman Empire, old friend."

"He is very wealthy."

"Charles should not have granted him such sweeping powers," Cromwell argues. "He brings across a dozen treasure ships each sailing season, and the gold and silver amounts to almost three million ducats a year. Three million, Eustace. How much does your emperor see of that?"

"The Fuggers pay a tithe to the emperor," Chapuys admits.

"A mere tenth?" Thomas Cromwell laughs, and lurches to his feet. "Would that I could be so great a rogue! And the ships?"

"They are the emperor's own fleet."

"So, Anton Fugger has leases for the mines in Peru, and uses the emperor s own ships to haul his gold home?" Cromwell is almost shaking with laughter. "Poor Charles is either a fool, or advised by one."

"He assigned the leases when we needed money for the last war against the French," Chapuys explains. "Fugger handed out loans on generous terms, and the emperor thought it a good deal."

"Then your poor Charles is in a bad place," Thomas Cromwell says. "For I intend halting every ship I can, and stripping them of their treasure. What is a tenth of nothing, plus the loss of a fleet, my friend?"

"You goad me, sir?" Eustace Chapuys has never seen Cromwell like this. The charm, and the civil manners seem to have faded away, and in their place is the hard hearted son of a blacksmith, intent on destruction. "My emperor has fifty thousand soldiers at his command."

"The moment they try to take ship for England, the French will sweep across, and steal away your northern provinces,"Tom Cromwell says. "No gold, no ships, no army, and no empire. I think Charles would like to hear of a better future than that."

"You seek to bargain with the emperor, through me, Thomas?" Eustace Chapuys sees now that the hard words are meant to soften him up for that which is to follow.

"No, I wish only that you communicate an offer to the emperor," Cromwell says. "You must assure him of Henry's devoted friendship. Tell him that England is at war with Anton Fugger, who has done us much mischief over the years, and the time has come for a great reckoning."

"What is this?" Chapuys scoffs. "I know the tale, Thomas. I know how Fugger crossed you once, and of how he sought safety in his stronghold. The story tells of how he went to bed, surrounded by his bodyguard, and woke up to find a dagger buried in the table by his bed. Most dramatic. Master Fugger has slept with armed men in his rooms ever since, and seldom leaves his stronghold. You can have him assassinated whenever you wish."

"Another of the wealthy Fugger clan would only take his place," Thomas Cromwell tells his friend. "I have come up with a much better form of retribution. The king s navy numbers over sixty men o' war, and I can spread them, like a net, across the great span of the ocean. It is likely that our fleet shall take half of these treasure ships, or even more. Fugger will be inconvenienced, but it is the emperor who will lose out the most. His tenth share will dwindle to nothing, and he will lose half of his best ships. We will take them, and make them into English warships."

"And you say King Henry loves my master?" Eustace Chapuys stands, and makes as if to leave. He knows Cromwell has a clever scheme, and seeks to hurry him on to it.

"Your emperor must know which ships are carrying gold, and when they are due. Let him give us this information, so that we might capture more of his ships."

"Are you mad?"

"In the best possible way," Tom Cromwell says, and smiles at the confused Savoyard diplomat. "Have him issue orders that no defence is put up, to spare lives, and we will take the ships as salvage. If he agrees to this, we will sail his ships to our nearest port, remove three quarters of the treasure, as a prize, then send the craft on its way."

"How does this help the emperor?"

"We will deliver his ship back to him, unharmed, and with a quarter share of the treasure in the hold. That is better than a tithe, is it not, my dear old friend?" It is a scandalous proposition, and one that the emperor can never put his seal to. Eustace Chapuys adopts his best affronted look, and hopes Cromwell understands his silent message.

"What monarch can say yes to such a thing?"

"I understand," Tom Cromwell replies, as if reading the man's mind. "We shall keep our dealings at an ambassadorial level, Eustace. All Charles need do is nod his head at you, and the deal is done. The emperor will find himself better off by at least a half million Ducati a year. Fugger will not be able to understand why so many of his treasure ships are taken, and the emperor need never elucidate. In fact, he could still demand that the Fuggers pay the tithe to him. A good lawyer, such as yourself might argue that the tithe is due, irrespective of whether the ship arrives, or not. This tithe is, after all, a tax, is it not? A farmer must pay his due, even if a few of his pigs go astray. Yes?"

Eustace Chapuys is the most famous lawyer in Savoy, and has dealt with the crowned heads of Europe for two decades, but he has never yet met the equal of Thomas Cromwell. The plan seems to be flawless. If the ships evade capture, the emperor still receives his portion, and if they are taken, he gets them back, with an even bigger cut of the gold.

"Yes," Chapuys says, and the deal is sealed. "Though I must ask you about your visit to the shipyards at Deptford, Woolwich, and Portsmouth."

"Oh, merely a case of showing my face, old friend." Thomas Cromwell is satisfied that Anton Fugger is about to be punished for his transgressions and, for once, does not see the trap he is walking into. "The king's ships are coming on well."

"Yes, I know," Eustace Chapuys replies, with a sly look. "I thought you were every bit the Privy Councillor… right down to snubbing me, twice."

"Ah… yes. You must forgive my rudeness, Eustace, but I…"

"What were you wearing at Deptford?"

" What is this, old friend?"

"I spoke to you. I stood less than ten yards away, and hailed you. You nodded at me, but I could see you did not know me," Chapuys says. "Later, at Woolwich, I came closer, and hailed you again. You might have ignored me, had not your fellow, Kel Kelton, whispered my name in your ear. You greeted me then, but the voice was quite wrong. It sounded gruffer."

"A cold, I fear."

"A double, more like," Chapuys replies. "Once I admitted the possibility, I started to see other minor faults. That way you have of dropping one shoulder when you orate is not there. Tell me I am right, Thomas. Who is he, and how came you by him?"

"Happenstance," Cromwell admits. "He was using my name to defraud foolish townsfolk, and so was taken by Will Draper. Now Master Ambrose fulfils some of my daily tasks. In this way, I can attend to important matters, without putting lesser affairs aside. Now, I fear, my little secret is out."

"No one shall hear of your trickery from me," Eustace Chapuys says. "Though you must see that your double knows all those he should. You might also wish to note another more serious failing, my friend."

"Really, what is that?"

"Why, the fellow is much better looking than you," Chapuys tells him. "He must scowl more, and try to make himself appear to be much uglier!"

*

Miriam Draper returns from the nursery, her bare feet making gentle slapping noises on the oak floorboards. Emily, Gwyllam, and little Tom, are all fast asleep, and their nurse is about to retire to her own bed.

"Well?" Will Draper asks.

"They sleep," Miriam replies.

"You worry too much about them," her husband says. "They are healthy, and a source of pride to us. Let us repair to our own bed, and join them in sleep." He has already unbuckled his sword, and removed the three daggers concealed about his person. He pulls his shirt up, and over his head. Miriam looks at his muscular body, and frowns when she sees the healed over bullet hole, and many small sword and dagger cuts that are part and parcel of his life.

"Sleep, dearest?" she says, and drops her linen shift to the floor. The candle light dances across her naked body, and gives her beautiful olive skin an enticing glow. Will looks at her, and feels the old familiar desire. Even after three children, she still has the soft curves of a young girl, and he wants nothing more than to enfold her in his powerful arms.

"Well… rest then?" he replies.

Later, he cradles her slender body in his arms, and asks her why she is so quiet. She sighs, and hugs him tightly to her, as if he were about to slip away.

"It is my brother," she confesses. "He is hundreds of miles away, and riding into danger."

"He is perfectly safe, until he leaves the Veneto," Will replies. "In truth, he hates the thought of not being with Mush, and Tom Wyatt on their sojourn to Corfu. He is a trained soldier, and should be at their side. "Then he has only to lock himself up in Corfu castle, and defy a few hundred of the these mad Mussulmen."

"So, they have but to close the gates, and wait for the enemy to tire?"

"Absolutely," Will confirms. "Corfu castle is built like our own Dover fortress. Mush must worry about nothing, save a degree of boredom."

*

"Where is the wall?" Mush Draper is on a low hill which gives a fine view of the fortress of Corfu. The great castle consists of a stone rectangular outer wall, and an inner tower. To the left of the fortified gate, there is a twenty yard stretch of rubble, where the fortification seems to have been bombarded. "What has happened to my fortress?"

"There was a tremor, sir." The Venetian captain explains to the two Englishmen. "The earth shakes sometimes, and such damage can come about. It is not too bad, I think."

"Not too bad?" Tom Wyatt surveys the yawning gap. "How is that supposed to halt a determined attack?"

"Now you are here, with all your men," Captain Lucretto says, with hugely misplaced confidence, "we can rebuild the outer wall."

"*Cozza!*" Mush curses. "Are you blind? Twenty yards of wall, ten yards high, and five yards thick… and you expect us to repair it? Why did you not tell us sooner?"

"Well, signor, you might not have come."

The Doge, who is even wilier than Thomas Cromwell, has duped them into an untenable position. He has known of the extent of the earthquake damage for weeks, but kept it secret from the ever so willing English war party. After all, he must reason, even with the fortress almost indefensible, a strong English force might still deter the Ottomans, or at least, delay them until more troops become available.

"Just so," Tom Wyatt says, and laughs. "We have a dozen cannon, and two hundred men, Mush. Do we turn around, and sail away, or do we stay and fight?" Mush wonders how he always seems to end up in someone else's mess, and evaluates the altered situation. The chance that they might be able to return to the harbour, and slip away before the enemy realise is slight, and the possibility of holding Corfu Castle is even slighter.

"We stay," Mush tells his friend.

"Then we will almost certainly die," Tom Wyatt replies.

"Miriam's ships will not have waited for us, old friend," Mush says. "They will sail around the island, and try to slip away, back to Genoa, or some other safe port. They will not return until the appointed time."

"Then we must secure the fortress," the poet says. "How long do you think we have?" Mush shrugs his shoulders. News of their arrival on the island will spread quickly, and it will only be a matter of days before the Ottomans know what is happening.

"If they have a fleet ready, they might be here inside a week," Mush says, "and if they are already at sea… we might only have a couple of days."

"The seaward side is virtually impregnable," Wyatt muses. "I shall position my ordinance to cover the gate, and the breach in the wall."

"I will put everyone I can on rebuilding the wall." Mush kicks his horses flanks, and urges it down the hill. Behind him, trains of horses drag along the cannon borrowed from the Tower of London, and two hundred Englishmen form ranks, shoulder their pikes and muskets, and trudge after their commander.

"Look at that bloody great hole!" One of the pike men grumbles. "That'll need patching up, and guess who they will want to do it."

"I shall not complain," his comrade says. "When those buggering great infidels start coming at us, I want to be behind a huge stone wall."

"They say they are all a head taller than Christian men, and care not about dying," the grumbler replies.

"I saw one once," his friend tells him. "The poor fellow was no more or less a man than I, save for his skin, which was as black as charcoal. They pray on their knees, and do not love Jesus Christ."

"That is why they are heathens," his friend says. "What make you of this cock-a-dandy of a poet?"

"I fought alongside him in France, a while ago," the pike man says. "He drilled us until we knew how to keep close order, and acted as cannon master against an army of foreign mercenaries. Now then, that was a fine day for killing. We cut their cavalry down in swathes, and charged them head on. Good pickings, Wilfred."

"Let us hope these heathens like to wear their gold about their necks then," Wilfred concludes. "I am not getting any younger, and I need enough to settle me down."

"Then let us hope for a mighty slaughter, one of the younger men calls from the rank behind."

"Of them, God willing, and not us," Wilfred mutters. "At least the moat is wide enough." His observation is true. Once the Venetians take possession of a new territory, they employ their skills as fortress builders to secure each gain. The old fortress, on a promontory next to the town of Corfu has been separated from the mainland by the construction of the *Contrafossa*, a narrow canal, which acts as a moat. Corfu Castle now sits on an artificial island, and would be impervious to attack, were the wall facing the narrow *Contrafossa* still intact.

*

"Where is the French army now?" The Ottoman Sultan Suleiman, who likes to style himself as 'the Great', demands. A thin, effeminate courtier, one of the Janissary class who run the civil service of his empire, scurries forward and jabs a long stick at the ornately painted map hanging on the wall.

"Here, Your Magnificence," the man squeaks. "They have raided deep into Piedmont, and threaten to capture Genoa from the Spanish King-Emperor."

"What of our fleet?" Suleiman asks. "Has it not yet reached our allies at Genoa?" The courtier takes a deep breath, and prepares to speak an unpalatable truth. Telling such things to Suleiman the Great has often, in the past, proven to be fatal to the bearer of bad tidings.

"It suffered a small set back, Your Magnificence."

"How small?"

"Andrea Doria the Genoese pirate…"

"How small a defeat?" The Ottoman Sultan snaps.

"Thirty ships burned, and a dozen more taken as prizes," the man says, and receives a sharp slap across his face. "Doria drove us back, and relieved the city. The French complain that we are not doing enough, Your Magnif…ugh!" The savage blow sends the Janissary servant crashing to the marble floor.

"We do not do enough?" the Sultan cries. "What are we doing at Naples? My men have the city surrounded."

"Oh, Your Most Benign Magnificence, great master of the world…" The advisor cowers, and waits for another blow, which does not come. He dares to raise himself up onto his knees. "Naples starves, and will soon fall. Our forces are raiding in Puglia. The French ask only that we strike against the Venetians, so that they might withdraw their troops from supporting the Holy Roman Emperor."

"If I sail my fleet up to Venice, we will be destroyed," the Sultan argues. "They have faster galleys, and use Greek Fire to destroy my fleets."

"Sire… what about Corfu?"

"Corfu?"

"A beautiful island, Your Magnificence," the Janissary advisor tells his lord. "There are but a hundred men holding the land, for the Doge, and the castle is a ruin."

"A ruin, you say?" Suleiman likes the sound of this. With a ruined fortification, and barely a troop of defenders, the island should be easy pickings. "How soon can we take it?"

"The remainder of the Genoese fleet are already under sail, Your Highness," the advisor explains. "Forty ships, and six thousand men, will reach Corfu in three days time."

"Order the fleet raiding Puglia to join them."

"That will make the force seventy ships, and twelve thousand strong," the Janissary says. "Once the island is taken, the Venetians will have nowhere for their ships to shelter in these waters."

"What if the Doge knows this, and has sent an army to occupy the island?"

"He has about three thousand soldiers to the south of Rome, and he cannot afford to let them withdraw, sire." The advisor has seen the latest reports, and knows that the Venetians have not decamped.

"But he might." Suleiman thinks the Doge is a miracle worker, and seeks to nullify him completely. "How far away is the Anatolian squadron from Corfu?"

"Three or four days sail, at the most, master," the advisor says. "Should you wish, we can move them against Corfu too. That would make sixteen thousand foot, two thousand cavalry, and over one hundred cannon."

"Cannon we can use on land?"

"Some, yes, but the majority are fixed aboard ship, sire," the man answers. We could sail up the east side of the island, and bombard the fortress from the sea."

"That sounds best," Suleiman the Great says. He is not a soldier, and tends to make his battle plans up as he goes along. "We will bombard the castle into rubble, then storm it with my faithful followers. If the Christians wish to surrender, I shall allow it... but only if they convert to Islam."

"Allah Akbar," the Janissary mutters. Yes, God is great, he thinks, but he does not suffer fools easily. The way forward, as any military man could tell the Sultan, is to strike into the heart of the Italian peninsula, drive away the small Venetian army, and lay siege to Rome. The Pope would sue for peace, and abandon all hope of saving the southern lands, or any of the Venetian holdings near Greece. Unfortunately, the Ottoman way is to blindly obey the Sultan Suleiman, and there is no one brave enough to tell him he is mistaken. "Might I suggest we give overall command to Admiral Barbarossa, Your Highness?"

"Yes... the man never fails me." Suleiman smiles and nods his head. Corfu shall fall, and the Christians will convert, or be put to the slaughter. *Insh allah*, he thinks.

It is the will of Allah.

11   The Lull

Mush Draper believes that leading his men from the front encourages them to greater things, so takes his turn at the wall rebuilding. He is stripped to the waist, and heaving slabs of dressed rock into place when Tom Wyatt finds him. The poet knows all about the impact of cannon balls on granite, and wishes to gauge the defensive capability for himself. He sees that only a thin outer layer of stone is yet in place, and shakes his head in utter horror.

"One well placed ball will punch straight through that," he says to Mush. "You need it to be another yard thicker, and much higher, my friend."

"Remember Tom Cromwell's infamous alchemist?" the young Jew says, as he wipes the sheen of sweat from his brow. "He tricked us into believing that which was not really there. If these Ottoman dogs see a wall, they might well think it is at full strength. We can shore up behind with timbers, and present a formidable looking frontage."

"Then build fast, my friend," the poet says. "Some fleeing peasants have arrived, and say that the Sultan's ships are off the northern coast. If they make a landing in Govono Bay, we cannot oppose them. They will be here within two days."

"Then we have two days of calm," Mush says. "We must bring in all the livestock we can find, and make safe our water supply. Do you have your cannon in place yet?"

"Almost done." Tom Wyatt gestures to the western approaches. "We can fire across the moat, at will, but the seaward side will have to take its chances. The Venetians have a few older cannon, and something they call Greek Fire.

Captain Lucretto says he is sworn to secrecy as to the formula, but insists that it is a most formidable weapon."

"Yes, I have seen it used before," Mush says. "Pine resin, quicklime, and sulphur, are mixed with other, completely secret ingredients, and the liquid is sprayed onto enemy ships. It burns like the pits of Hell, and sticks to all it touches."

"Like flaming arrows?" the poet asks.

"A thousand times worse," Mush replies. "God help any who are foolish enough to make an attempt on our seaward walls."

"I have turned the *Castel Vecchio* tower into a powder magazine," Wyatt says. If your men run low, they must send word, and my lads will bring powder and shot, where needed. I have also mounted two cannon on top of the *Castel a Mar*. They are trained on the drawbridge, should the worst happen, and we are breached." The Turks are adept at storming fortresses, and will first make an attempt on the main gate. Once forced, they would be able to destroy the fortress from within. Mush understands all this, and doubts if two cannon will hold them off for long.

"We have less than five hundred men, and only two hundred of them are English," Mush muses. "Our lads will fight to the last, but I worry about these Venetians. They do not seem to have the same martial fervour as those we met before."

"Against the Condottiero Malatesta Baglione, they were fighting for Venice," the poet explains. "This is just an island, which has not been Venetian for many years. Lucretto and his men do not want to die so far away from home."

"Will they fight?" Mush asks.

"We have no choice," the young Venetian officer says. He has come upon them secretly, and heard their debate. Beside him is a beautiful pale faced young girl of about sixteen years. "We cannot sail away, for your ships have left us to our fate. Nor can we hide out on so small an island. If we let the infidels in, they will either kill us, or enslave us. My dear sister here, and the other Christian Venetian ladies will be most horribly abused by the infidels. My men will fight until their last breath, sir. My oath on it."

"I meant no offence, Captain Lucretto." Tom Wyatt wonders how long their fragile alliance will hold, and how long it will take the coming hoard of heretics to overwhelm them all anyway. "We must prepare for the islanders, who will want shelter."

"We must bar the gates to them," the Venetian replies. "They are … what is the word … *inutile*?

"Useless?" Mush is horrified at so callous a remark. "You would turn away even the women and children? What kind of man are you, Lucretto?"

"A pragmatist, Signor Draper, Lucretto says. "We have neither the food, nor the space for them. They must hide in the hills, and hope the infidels do not catch them. Our task is to hold this fortress, and deny the Sultan this island."

"An island without a population?" Mush argues.

"I have my instructions," Lucretto says, but he seems less bombastic now, as he thinks of several thousand innocents at the mercy of the enemy.

"I cannot agree to turning away these people," Mush tells him.

"Please your self," the young Venetian replies. "You may admit as many as reach the drawbridge … but you must feed them with your own victuals."

"In Mush's homeland, his God would send manna down from heaven," Tom Wyatt teases. "Mayhap we should pray?"

"No need in this case," Mush retorts. "All the supplies in this castle are the property of the Draper Mercantile House, my dear Lucretto. You, and all of your men are fed entirely at our cost."

"As you wish." The young Venetian turns on his heel and stalks away. His sister lingers behind, and curtseys to Mush.

"Forgive my brother, sir. Gianni has never fought before, and worries that he might not be up to the task. He has orders, which sit badly with his conscience. I too wish to save as many of the island s people as possible."

"My name is Mush Draper," Mush says.

"Yes, I know. I asked one of your men," the girl replies with a pretty blush. "Will you join us for an English supper, gentlemen?"

"An honour, Mistress Lucretto," Mush says.

"Isabella," the girl replies, and blushes again. "The seventh hour then?"

Mush watches the girl pick her way delicately, over the rubble strewn inner courtyard, and is reminded of his late wife's way of coming to the point. Isabella is slighter, and a little darker than Gwenn, but the similarities make him catch his breath. He finally turns back to his men, who are standing about, and grinning at him knowingly. Even Tom Wyatt has seen how struck Mush is by the young Venetian beauty.

"An August day,
yet lightening falls,
to strike our Mush,

and true love calls," he mutters, and receives a glowering look of menace for his poetic efforts.

"Come on lads, let us get our thin wall bolstered with timbers," the young Jew shouts. "A bag of silver pennies to every man if the Turks cannot get in!"

Almost two hundred voices are raised in a cheer, and the English soldiers of fortune bend to their task once more.

Tom Wyatt, who prefers to supervise, rather than break his fingernails, slips away, to inspect his cannon emplacements one last time. Mush ponders over what Gianni Lucretto has promised, and decides not to completely trust the Venetian captain. He beckons over a trusted sergeant, and has him post four men at the main gate, with orders to make sure that any refugee islanders are let in.

"What if them bloody Venetians object, sir?" one of the big soldiers asks.

"You have my permission to land a few blows," Mush tells the fellow, but nothing more than that, Flinders."

"As you say, sir… a little slap, to encourage them."

*

"Are you well, madam?" Thomas Cromwell asks in a formal manner, but he longs to sit down with Jane, and question her more intimately. It is all he can do to resist taking her little hands in his, and declaring how much he worries for her health, and that of the expected child.

"I am, Master Thomas," Queen Jane replies, and gives him a sweet little smile. "The doctors say I might be ready in the early part of October. For my part, I think the eleventh, or twelfth of the month."

"Ah, an Autumn child," Thomas Cromwell says. "Do you want for anything, My Lady?" Another banal question, he thinks. Jane is queen of England, and adored by an expectant king. She wants for nothing.

"A little solitude," Queen Jane says, softly. "I cannot turn about in a chamber without bumping into some courtier or other, intent on my comfort. It seems the king has given strict orders for me to be watched, night and day, lest I suffer some mishap."

"He wishes your child to be born safely, madam."

"He wishes for it to be a boy," Jane replies. "Let us not beat about the bush, sir. If I bear a female child, I will be relegated to a degree of historical obscurity. Henry will lose all interest in me, and I can look forward to a life in the shadows."

"A comfortable life, madam," Cromwell promises. Even if the king wants it, the Church of England will not stand for another divorce. Nor will anyone listen to sordid lies about your honour."

"Am I then blameless, good sir?" She smiles up at him, and recalls the few intimate moments that have made her life worth living these last months. "Are we not all guilty of something?"

"Only if found out. No investigation can ever be invoked without either my permission, or the involvement of the King's Examiners Office. Your brothers are each lodged in powerful positions, and will protect you."

"Do they love me so much?"

"I cannot answer for that, madam … but they fear me, and that will suffice." Cromwell stands by Queen Jane, and watches as the courtiers parade around the garden walk. The king is strolling, and chatting away to Suffolk, and a recently chastised Norfolk, who is eager to worm his way back into Henry s affections. "I see Uncle Norfolk is still trying to get his son excused from naval duty."

He calls Henry 'dearest cousin' at every opportunity, as if to remind my husband of their supposed kinship."

"That will not save him," Tom Cromwell says. "He should look to Harry Percy, whose ill luck has never recovered. Then he might ponder on how much the king loved Henry Norris, Thomas More, Anne Boleyn, and young Weston. The king, I fear, is a rather fickle master."

"What if he turns on you? I could not bear it."

"Hush, my … madam. Henry needs me, and that will keep me, and all my Austin Friars people safe." Cromwell ponders for a moment. "In seven or eight weeks, you will give birth, and we will all be basking in the king's reflected glory. Give the king a son, and you may name your own price."

"A small house, near Wulfhall… with the man I love?"

"Ah, that is beyond price, Your Majesty," Thomas Cromwell says. "See, here comes the king. Sire, you look very well."

"Never better, dear Thomas… never better." Henry belches, and scratches at his still red beard. "How do things stand?"

"The French are struggling to hold that which they have taken in Italy. The Emperor Charles is moving a great army south, towards Milan and Genoa, and his fleet have defeated the Turkish Sultan off the Italian coast."

"Then is it time for us to join in?" Henry asks. He has a treaty with Venice, and the Holy Roman Empire, to protect Italy from the infidels, and is eager to gain some of the spoils before the war peters out. "Our navy is the equal of Suleiman's… is it not?"

"Greater, sire, but it is busy with *other* matters."

"Oh, yes." Henry finds it hard to keep up with all of Cromwell's schemes, but the capture of treasure ships coming from the Americas is one dear to his heart. He is almost a half million pounds better off, since the sailing weather arrived, and has no wish to spoil things. "Then can we not land troops in Brittany, or Normandy?"

"The emperor s forces do not seem to need us just yet," Tom Cromwell says. "I think we might content ourselves with a small expeditionary force to Corfu. The Doge is grateful for our help, and we might yet make a profit from the adventure."

"Who commands our people?"

"Captain Draper, sire."

"Will Draper?"

"His brother-in-law, sire."

"Ah, the Jew."

"I grant you, he looks the part, Your Majesty, but he is as English as Doctor Theophrasus… who hails from Exeter, I believe."

"As English as you or I," Henry says, and chuckles at his own lame jest. It is true that the Tudor clan are Welsh, but Thomas Cromwell is English born, and only Welsh through marriage.

"Just so, sire." Cromwell raises a fist to his mouth, and clears his throat. It is a rare sign of nervousness, and passes unnoticed by the king. "Might I indulge our friendship with a small request, Your Majesty?"

"Ask, Thomas." Henry wonders if his minister is finally going to request a title for himself, and is interested to see how high he might aim. In the seven or eight years you have served me, I have never known you to beg a personal favour."

"I ask only for your blessing, sire," Cromwell says. "My only son, Gregory was wedded, a week ago."

"I shall send him a gift." Henry knows Cromwell will choose something nice, and see the boy has it. "Might I enquire whom the lad has taken? Some pretty country squire s daughter, no doubt?"

"Sire… he has wed Lady Elizabeth Ughtred."

"He has done what?"

"I have only now found out. It is my fervent wish that both you, and the queen look kindly on my son's rash action. It must be true love that has addled his brains so."

"The Lady Elizabeth is only widowed these last six months past," Henry says, somewhat taken aback. "Her husband's body is still warm. Your son is a fast mover, sir!"

"Oh, Henry … and how long did we tarry, sir?" Jane puts in with a touch to his elbow. She knows that marriage to a member of the royal family, without permission, is a dangerous business, and seeks to help Tom Cromwell out of a tight corner. "Give them our blessing, and some land to go with it… for my sister's late husband was almost penniless."

"You are soft hearted," Henry grumbles. "In truth, he has met Jane's younger sister on several occasions, and was contemplating having her brought to court, where he might develop a closer relationship. Jane understands how these things work, of course, and recalls how Mary served the king before her sister Anne.

"She is better off wed," Jane replies. "Otherwise, some licentious gentleman of the court might think her a worthy catch. I think young Gregory is a perfect match for my sister. It will make a man of him, and bind him ever more closely to you. The father serves you very well, does he not… and the son will have his uses."

"You speak wisely, madam, Henry says. Though I would wish you did it in private some times. It seems we are now related, Thomas… though I am not sure how."

"I am the father-in-law of your sister-in-law, sire," Cromwell says. "That makes me as much of a relation as poor old Uncle Norfolk."

"Ha!" Henry explodes with laughter, and his sides shake at the sly insult aimed against the duke. "You jest well, Tom. Would that all my relatives were as quick with a pithy comment. As his father, you must chastise the lad for not asking your permission, but as his king, I will see to his comfort. If I cannot endow the father, then let me treat the son. What have we spare?"

"Some estates in Rutland, sire," Cromwell replies. He has chosen his moment well, and the small lie about not knowing has made the story more interesting to the king. He will think Gregory Cromwell to be a clever rascal, like Suffolk or Wyatt, and love him for it. Kings always love rascals. "For my part, I have a small farm in Leicestershire which he can have. I am seldom free to look after it these days."

"Excellent, for it is not seemly that a queen of England's sister should live in abject poverty," Henry says. "I should have thought of it sooner." Without another word, he stomps off, and blithely interrupts a private conversation going on further down the rose garden. After a moment, he is back slapping one hapless courtier, and casually resting his hand on the rump of the poor fellows female companion.

Cromwell turns to Jane, and they exchange small smiles with one another. The business of marrying Cromwell's son into the Seymour family has gone well. Jane's impoverished sister has a fine new husband, and the couple will have about a thousand acres of excellent arable land, spread across two counties.

"Your servant, madam," Cromwell says, and he bows from the waist. Queen Jane nods back, and they smile again. On the other side of the quadrangle, Tom Howard, Duke of Norfolk, throws Cromwell a poisonous look. Over the last few months, he has found himself blocked at every turn by the scoundrel, and now finds his son is to be banished to the fleet.

"Thomas Cromwell," he mutters to himself. "Always Cromwell. God's curse on you, and yours… you lowly bastard!" He looks about, to see if there is anyone to whom he can turn, so that he might form an alliance, and sees nothing but Cromwell men. Since the execution of his niece, Anne Boleyn, Norfolk has become increasingly marginalised. Even his old comrade, Charles Brandon, seems now to be firmly in the Cromwell camp. Suffolk goes out of his way to support the Privy Councillor these days, and seldom lingers to speak with his old friend.

Dangerous days call for desperate measures, Norfolk thinks, and it might be time to return to his family roots, and seek out those survivors of the old regime. The Plantagenet name might be a part of history to most, but the bloodline still carries on. Lady Salisbury is still a power in the land, and her son, Reginald Pole has the ear of the new Pope. Perhaps, he wonders, the time has come to make his move.

*

"Is it always so hot?" Mush asks the pretty girl sitting to his left at table. I wonder anything ever gets done."

"I have only been here for a few months, but my maid tells me it is like this for ten months of the year. Then they have heavy rain, and many mosquitoes," Isabella says. Since first seeing the handsome young Englishman, she has wanted nothing more than to be in his company. "The local peasants do not seem to mind."

"The island's peasants your brother would bar from the citadel?"

"He does not mean to be cruel," the girl replies. "He simply thinks it best to conserve our store of supplies. What if we are besieged by the Ottoman Turks?"

"We might only be able to hold the castle for a month or two," Mush tells her. "The walls are weakened, and I do not have enough men to stop a mass attack on several fronts."

"Speak to my brother Gianni… and make him into your friend," Isabella advises. "He commands the Venetian soldiers, but for now, the City Council commands him."

"City Council?" Mush knows nothing of any council, and wonders why they do not speak to him directly. "Who are they?"

"Two old men, appointed by the Doge. They are elected senators back in Venice, and make all the important decisions. One is an admiral, called Bennetti, and the other a rich merchant who is a member of the Spaldini house. They rely on the island to make them a good living, and fear anything that might upset their cosy life styles. My brother Gianni thinks he must obey them."

"Then I must speak with your brother," Mush says, "for this fortress cannot be run by a council of old men."

"As you wish," Isabella says. "When you do speak with my brother, you must also ask his permission to call on me. Otherwise he will have to swear a blood feud against you."

"A blood feud?" Mush shakes his head in disbelief. "What on earth for?"

"Why, for looking at me as you do," the girl explains. "You look at me like you want me, and that is an insult, unless you declare your honourable intentions."

"My honourable intentions?" Mush realises that he is being courted by a very clever young woman, and wonders if it is such a bad thing. "Ah, I begin to see. Very well, I will ask your brother's permission, so that I might lust after you honestly, Mistress Isabella!"

"You would mock me, sir?"

"Of course," Mush says, and she makes as if to slap his face. He catches her hand, pulls her to him, and kisses her. "There, now I really must seek your brother s permission!"

12   A Turn of Fate

It is almost a month now since his sudden marriage, and Gregory Cromwell is still trying to come to terms with his ordered new life. From being a well educated student, adept with both greyhounds and falcons, he has become a member of the landed gentry, an esquire with over twelve hundred acres of lush farm land, six hundred sheep, and two hundred and fifty head of the finest dairy cattle. There are a dozen well kept farms on his estates, and a huge house that once belonged to a local abbot of the old church.

Perhaps the greatest change of all was his sudden move from single man to husband. Gregory was filled with dread when his father wrote, and instructed him to marry, and is even more worried when Ned Seymour collects him, and conveys him to the rural edge of Leicestershire, where he meets his new wife to be for the very first time.

Lady Elizabeth Ughtred is the widow of Sir Anthony Ughtred, and the sister of Jane Seymour. Because of this, Gregory becomes, in the blink of an eye, the brother-in-law of Henry, King of England, and of the Seymour brothers, Ned and Tom. The ceremony takes place in a small village church, where Ned Seymour takes care to see that the big door is left open, as required by canon law. There must be no legal bar to this wedding, and the register is signed by a dozen witnesses.

From the church, they are hurried into a flower bedecked coach and driven, at a furious pace, to their first abode together. The couple are marched into the great hall, and are left alone to occupy their new home, having yet to utter a word to one another, other than 'I do'.

Gregory Cromwell is relieved to see that his wife is of a most comely appearance, and has a fine, shapely, figure. He is even more relieved to find that she is an experienced, and most accomplished lover, once they retire to their bed chamber. After a night spent satisfying his every wish, the young Elizabeth pours out her life story.

She is the young sister, bartered away for a title, to a man who preferred gambling and drinking to tending his estates. Ughtred was fifteen years her senior, and kills himself with drink by the time he is thirty eight. She is left with debts, and two children, who are lodged with relatives.

A politically inspired marriage has been imposed upon her, she concludes, but with the most fortunate of outcomes. She thinks Gregory Cromwell to be very good looking, and thanks her lucky stars that he is not another weak old man.

Gregory sees that his life has been put in order for him by his father, and he will spend his days with an attractive woman who seeks only to please him. He is not yet eighteen, and fancies that this is what his elders know to be love. The love will come over the years, of course, but for now, his lust for his new bride will guide him down the right path.

"Tomorrow, I will write to my father, and sincerely thank him," the youth says to the young woman in his arms. "Then you shall write to your dear relatives, and instruct them to return your two children to you at once."

"You would do that for me?" Elizabeth asks. Second husbands, especially those who take on pretty wives, seldom wish to be reminded of any cuckoos in the nest, and children of first marriages are seldom made welcome in the new order of things.

"It seems that a turn of unavoidable fate dictates what I must do," Gregory tells his new bride.

"Do you rue your fate then?" Elizabeth asks.

"Not one whit, madam, for you are my wife," Gregory replies, and runs an idle finger down the soft nakedness of her white back. "It is my duty to please you, where I may. We shall become a family of four, and with God's good grace, soon swell that number by several more."

"Oh, sir... for that, you must practice far more," Elizabeth tells him, and moves her lips over his. Given time, she will guide her new husband into a place at court, and help him become a wealthy landowner. With the help of her new father-in-law, the king's first minister, they might even be granted a noble title. She runs a hand down his flat stomach, and takes his responsive manhood into her eager charge.

"Have a care, my love, Gregory mutters. I fear your ardour will quite wear me out, and we do not want you to be a widow again so soon!"

"Oh, sir... I'll risk it!"

*

"You wish to pay court on my sister?" Captain Gianni Lucretto, commander of the Venetian force in Corfu is astounded. "I am sure that will be acceptable, my friend... but why?"

"I admire her, and do not wish to cause offence to the family," Mush replies.

"Have you slept with her yet?" Gianni asks.

"No." Mush struggles to like the fellow, and finds his question to be most un-gentlemanly. "We have only spoken together twice."

"Then bed her, my friend, with my entire blessing," Gianni says. He sees that Mush is confused by this and tries to explain. "I know how Venetian girls are, my friend. Refuse them the man they really want, and they take every man who asks. It is best my sister chooses one strong lover, and be damned to it."

"I would not hurt her," Mush says, and Gianni shrugs his shoulders, as if to show he does not understand the English way of things.

"Take her. She wants you, and that is that." Gianni runs a finger over his sparse moustache. "If she gets with child, I expect you to either marry her, or provide for her and the child."

"Of course." Mush Draper sees that some sort of mysterious bargain has been struck, and moves on to more pressing matters. "It is now three weeks since the infidels landed, and we still do not find them at our gates. Why would that be?"

"The council know why," Gianni Lucretto replies. The Englishman has agreed to take on the burden of one of his seven sisters, and their relationship has, quite subtly, changed. Mush is as good as family to the young Venetian now, and he will not lie to him anymore. "Our spies range far and wide, and report that the Ottoman filth have spread over the island, and control everywhere, save Corfu town itself, and the fortress."

"Why have you not tried to oppose them?" Mush is dismayed at this news. "It accounts for why so few have sought shelter in the castle. They are in hiding, enslaved by the enemy, or dead. You could have raided, and caused the enemy much hurt."

"There was no point," Gianni replies. "If we attack them, they will just come against us all the quicker. For the moment, they harvest in the crops, and take what slaves they can find. This activity keeps them from our gate."

"But they have control of the island," Mush insists. "How can that be a good thing? They hold every safe harbour, and every other stronghold on Corfu. How will my sister s ships ever make safe landfall, when they come back for us?"

"There is no safe route between Italy and the Greek mainland anymore," Gianni says. "We must hold this castle, and hope the enemy grow bored with the venture, and leave. The council think…"

"The council think nothing!" Mush cries. "They are two frightened old men, who hope for a miracle. The infidels have the island. They have us cut off. Why not just let us starve, and walk in when we are too weak to fight them? That is what I would do. Why lose one man, when the enemy are willing to starve themselves to death, without putting up a fight?"

"The council think the Sultan will lose interest, and sail off to raid other lands," Gianni says.

"Then the council are pathetic cowards," Mush snaps. "Do you agree with them?"

"I am not a coward." Gianni would draw his sword on any other man, but Mush is now part of his family, and must be given some leeway. "What do you suggest I do?"

"Prick these infidels, until they become enraged, and attack us," Mush replies. "Then defeat them at our very gates."

"They number over twenty thousand," says Gianni. We are no more than five hundred. How do we overcome those odds?"

"We fought the Condottiero Baglione with as few, and he commanded fifteen thousand men. We drove him back from the walls, then destroyed them on the low ground. The Ottoman army must labour uphill to get at us, then cross a moat."

"You think we have a chance?" Gianni Lucretto is not so sure. "The council will withhold permission."

"Then we do not tell them," Mush explains.

"Their spies will inform on us."

"Do you know these agents?" Mush asks. "No? Then we must remove the council from power."

"I cannot be a part of this," the Venetian says. "The Doge ordered me to obey their will."

"What if others imprison them?"

"I have no orders about such a thing," Lucretto admits. "I would have to ask for advice from the other senators in Venice, which might take six months."

"Then I shall have Tom Wyatt escort your two old senators to a place of confinement, and bar you from speaking with them."

"Without instructions, I fear I must throw in my lot with you and your men then."

"Excellent."

"What do you wish?"

"We slip out at dawn, and strike at the Ottoman Turks unexpectedly. The enemy will not be able to resist the challenge."

"Their commander is no fool," the young Venetian tells Mush. "Barbarossa Pasha will sense a trap. He is a seaman, and will stand off our seaward walls, and bombard us. His army are well versed in siege warfare, and will know how to overcome our resistance. They use devices to storm city walls. They have towers, like the old Romans, and long ladders to scale with. They know how to get close to fortifications without suffering harm."

"You make them sound invincible," Mush scoffs. "I will show you how to beat these Turks at their own game. Then we shall drive them into the sea, and return Corfu to Venetian ownership."

*

"My ships are back in Lisbon harbour," Miriam Draper tells Thomas Cromwell. "They have delivered my brother, victuals, and two hundred men into Corfu Castle."

"Excellent news, my dear." Thomas Cromwell knows that Mush and Tom Wyatt will seal the castle up, and withstand the Ottoman attack. If they hold out through August, and up to Christmas, the infidels will withdraw. The Sultan Suleiman is impatient, and seldom lays siege for more than a month or two.

"Captain Fescue informs me that both ships were lucky to escape the Turcoman invasion force. He writes that the sea was thick with enemy vessels, and that the Turks took every harbour, save that at Corfu Town. He requests that I advise him as to how to proceed. Corfu is taken."

"The rest of the island might very well be in infidel hands, but Mush is safe locked away inside the fortress. You must trust me, dear girl. The walls are over thirty feet tall, and ten or twelve feet thick. There is a broad, fast flowing canal, which cuts the fortress off from the land, and Tom Wyatt has twenty new cannon at his disposal. The enemy will batter away from both land and sea, and all to no avail."

"Then I am only to have my ships return in October, as planned?" Miriam asks. She fears for her brother, but some inner sense tells her he is still alive. "How will they run the gauntlet of the Turcoman fleet?"

"I have sent orders to the English southern fleet," Tom Cromwell tells her. "With the Spanish treasure ships now so easy to find, we can spare enough men o' war to force a passage. The Turks have many galleys, but they cannot stand up to our great sixty gunners. If need be, we will force our way into Corfu Town's harbour, and extract your brother, and any other Christian souls who wish it."

"Then I shall write accordingly to my captains, Master Tom, and have them run some local cargoes, until the time is right."

"An excellent idea, my girl."

"And I need not worry?"

"Fear not, Miriam," Tom Cromwell tells her with a belief backed by wisdom in such matters. "Mush is not a fool. He and Tom Wyatt will do nothing to provoke the infidels."

*

"Master Charnley, how goes it?" The Duke of Norfolk asks of the sly looking fellow who is holding the king's favourite brace of falcons for him.

"Well, Your Lordship," Charnley replies. "The kindness you have shown me brings me into constant favour with His Majesty."

"Favours done… and favours received, eh?" Norfolk mutters. "Does your freedom about the court suit our mutual needs?"

"I find I have access to much private information, my dear sir," Charnley replies. "I can ascertain his movements as I wish."

"Discreetly, I hope?"

"Of course." Charnley returns a wave from the king.

"See that? Even you are in greater favour than I," Norfolk sneers. He finds himself pushed to one side at court, and blames Thomas Cromwell, quite rightly, for his current predicament. It is time to take measures, he decides, and resolves to make a better job of it than his late nephew, George Boleyn. "Are you then ready to strike?"

"All is in order, My Lord," Charnley reports. "I have a dozen men waiting to act. They do not know who pays them, and are all the most murderous rascals you might ever wish to meet. They are in Lincoln, ready to strike without mercy."

"And what of their prey?" Norfolk asks. He knows that he is set on a dangerous course, and speaks in veiled ways of that which he wishes to come about.

"Travelling to the city, as we speak, sir," Charnley says. "I have informed our men, by swift rider, and they will be waiting on the high road. With so many bands of malcontents roaming the northern counties, it will seem to be an attempted robbery gone wrong."

"Will twelve men be enough?" Norfolk asks.

"Twelve against three? I should think so, sir," the fellow tells his master. "They will know how to handle the situation."

"Very well. The moment news comes, I will grant you a hundred acres, and a fine pension, Master Charnley. Fail, and I will rip out your guts with my own hands. Is that acceptable to you, fellow?"

"I shall not fail," the man replies, but his face is drained of colour. The Duke of Norfolk seldom makes idle threats, and he is quite able to kill in cold blood. The prey is as good as dead.

*

Kel Kelton rides as if born to it, and wears the black livery of Austin Friars with growing pride. Since being taken on by Thomas Cromwell, as a reward for forewarning him of a murder plot, the youngster has become a most valued member of the big house's staff. Beside him is Richard Cromwell, who has become almost like a father to him during these last few months.

The great bear of a man, can be casually violent when needed, but has a soft heart where Cromwell's young men are concerned. He is teaching young Kel how to read and write, and promises to instruct him in the law, as soon as he is old enough. The lad is a quick learner, and as loyal as can be wished. He takes instructions well, and has become proficient with sword, dagger, and pistol. His one wish is to marry Maisie, the daughter of Cromwell's most senior cook, and start his own small dynasty.

The girl is a year older, and often gives him the sharp edge of her tongue, but she likes him for his rascally ways, and his utter devotion to her.

"I asked Maisie to marry me yesterday," Kel says, with a casual air.

"Really?" Richard suppresses a grin. "Have you asked permission of Master Tom yet? It is for him to dispose, and he will want to ensure you marry well."

"Master Richard, I was a thief on London Bridge four or five months ago," the youth complains. "My one aim was to avoid being hanged for my sins. Now I must marry well?"

"Maisie is a good girl." This comment comes from the rider ahead, and makes both of his companions smile at one another. "She can make a tart almost as well as Mistress Miriam!"

"Well said, sir." Richard looks at the solid, square set of the man ahead, and admires how well he rides, considering his advanced years. "Would you have her marry this scoundrel?"

"We are all scoundrels," comes the quick reply. I ride on a hundred pound horse, and wear the finest seal skin, and furs. The chain about my neck is worth a fortune, and men hurry to bow down to me... Yet I am a scoundrel. It is a secret known to but a few. Put on a good show, and the world adores you for it."

"They bow out of fear," Kel Kelton calls. "For the very name 'Cromwell' strikes fear into their hearts. Let the good folk of Lincoln know that Master Thomas Cromwell has come to call!"

The first shot sends a lead ball rushing past Kel's ear, and he is leaping from the saddle by the time more muskets fire. Richard Cromwell drives his heels into his mount, and gallops forward at the knot of men who have suddenly barred their way.

"Ride!" he shouts, and draws his sword. Behind him, Kel cocks the first of his two pistols, and takes careful aim. The weapon kicks in his hand, and a running figure twists and falls to the ground. Richard Cromwell rides into the four men blocking the road, and sends them scattering. One fails to duck in time, and Cromwell's sword bites into his neck.

Others are coming at them from both sides, and the crack of guns, and the smell of gunpowder, fills the air. Kel cocks his second pistol, strides right up to a man who is trying to reload his musket, and fires straight into his face. He goes down with blood spraying from his shattered eye, and Kel drops the discharged gun. He draws his sword, and rushes at the next nearest attacker. The man sees him coming and raises his musket to his shoulder.

Kel half turns, to make himself a smaller target, and the man fires. The badly primed musket misfires, and Kel is on him in an instant. Though a foot shorter than his foe, he charges in, and thrusts his sword into the man s chest. The blade hits a rib, and rips up into the fellow's heart.

Richard Cromwell wheels around on his mount, and looks to where Thomas Cromwell is curled up on the ground. He gallops back to him, and slashes at anyone who stands in his way. All of a sudden, the attackers melt away, leaving five of their number dead, or dying on the bloodstained ground. They have achieved their goal, and the greatest minister in the land lies, choking in his own blood.

Kel runs over, and stands guard over the fallen man, whilst Richard leaps from his horse, and takes their stricken charge in his arms. This is not what is meant to happen, he thinks. These men are not robbers, but assassins, paid to murder Thomas Cromwell.

"Dear Christ," the younger Cromwell groans. "Do not let him die." There is a deep furrow across the fallen man s cheek, where a lead ball has scored him, and carried off the lower part of his right ear, but far worse is the shot which has lodged itself in the chest. Blood is welling up out of the grave wound, and Richard is at a loss as to what can be done.

Kel Kelton has no such confusion. He moves from body to body, and takes anything of value. The final villain is still alive, having received nothing more than a torn scalp from Cromwell s slashing blade. Kel grabs the fellow's long, lank hair, and pulls his head back. The thin blade comes out of his doublet, and is pressed against the man s throat.

"Who sent you?"

"Go bugger yourself!" The man snarls, and the youth flicks the blade up, and removes the man's left ear. He screams, and begins to sob. "Mercy, sir, for we did not seek to kill you."

"You go about it in an odd way, you dog," Kel says. "Who set you on us?"

"We were paid to kill only the old man," the frightened villain replies. "We were told to put an end to Tom Cromwell, and did not expect so ferocious a defence. Mercy, sir...agh!" The point rips down, and opens the cheek from the severed earlobe, to the corner of the mouth.

"A name, now!" Kel is shaking with rage, and Richard leaves him to it. He has managed to pull off his blue sash, and is using it to bind the ragged chest wound.

"Lie still, sir ... and we will get you some help. There are tears in young Cromwell's eyes, and he wonders if the dying man can still hear him. "See, some riders approach. Hang on, for God's sake. Do not die on me, old man."

"A name, Kel says, again. or I will take off your nose next."

"Courtney… Master Edward Courtney," the man grunts. "Spare me, for I meant no harm to you."

"Spare you?" Kel Kelton's rage is causing him to shake, and his mind is a whirl of conflicting thoughts. "Be damned to that, you filthy murderer!" The blade bites into the neck, and opens the throat from one side to the other. The man gurgles, and his eyes turn up to the sky. Kel lets the body fall, and turns to face the troop of horsemen bearing down on them.

They are gentlemen of the loyal local militia, out looking for the rag tag remnants of the army of rebels who so nearly brought down a king. They have run into the remains of the men who ambushed them, and taken them all prisoner. One of the militia, an ageing surgeon from Lincoln, jumps from his horse, and runs over to tend to the wounded man. He pushes Richard Cromwell's hand aside, and presses two fingers into the bloody wound, in the hope of staunching the flow.

"Dear Christ, the man says, as he sees the crumpled form in Richard's arms. "They have tried to murder Thomas Cromwell!"

"Will he die?" Richard asks, with tears in his eyes.

"Be damned if I'll let him!" the man curses. Start a fire, and heat a knife blade in it. You, man, fetch me my bag from my horse, and be damned quick about it."

The surgeon, who has much experience of wounds, knows enough to realise that the lead ball must be removed. He also knows that the shot will have carried some rag of clothing into the wound, and that must come out too, to avoid infection.

"Will he live then?" Kel asks, as he drops the surgeon's bag down beside the fellow.

"That is for God to decide," the surgeon says. "All I can do is clean the wound, and cauterise it."

"Oh." Kel does not know what 'cauterise' means. Two men have started a small fire, and are heaping dry tinder on to it. Another draws his knife, and pushes into the glowing embers.

"Find a stout stick, for putting in his mouth, the surgeon commands. Lest the poor wretch bites off his own tongue!

13   Coursing the Hare

"Master Edward Courtney? Pray, might I beg a moment of your time, sir?" Richard Cromwell is at his most affable, and taps the heavy leather purse which hangs from his belt. "I am told you are the cleverest lawyer in all of Lincolnshire. Is that true?"

"I know my business well enough, sir, Edward Courtney replies, eying up this prospective new client. Do you wish to consult with me?"

"No, sir." Richard opens his purse, and counts out five shillings. "I would have you witness my dear uncle's will. The old fellow is failing fast, and has much property, and wealth, to dispose of."

"Is your ailing uncle amenable to making a new will and testament then?" the lawyer asks, shrewdly. Many nephews, and younger sons try to force dying relatives into changing their wills to favour them.

"He is confused, sir." Richard counts out another five shillings, and puts the coins in front of the lawyer. "If you would come along with me to his house, I am sure we can come to some mutually beneficial accommodation."

"I charge one tenth part of the estate, Edward Courtney explains. "It might sound a steep price, but the will shall be so well worded as to secure all the deceased fellow's worldly goods, and property. The fee will also ensure my lips remain tightly sealed."

"Excellent," Richard says. "Take these ten shillings as a sign of my good faith, sir. There is a large estate, and a great deal of ready money to be had. I will be amazed if you do not clear two hundred pounds for this days work."

*

"Will he live?" Kel Kelton asks. The surgeon washes blood from his hands and nods his head.

"The face will not be quite so pretty, once the stitches are out," he says. "The catgut must stay in for ten days, then it must be cut away, before any infection sets in. As for the ball I plucked from his chest, Master Cromwell is lucky. It broke a rib, and punctured a lung.

"That does not sound too good."

"He is strong. The lung will heal, but he will be an invalid from this day forth. His breathing will be laboured, and he will tire very easily. I fear the king's minister must retire from public office, and live out what little time is left to him."

"You pronounce a sentence of death, sir." Kel Kelton is still very angry, and curses how little he was able to do to save his charge. "How long do we talk of?"

"Master Cromwell will be prone to colds. A dose of fever could finish him in a moment. He must reconcile himself to his poor condition, and hope for a few more years."

"It is a cruel world that condemns a man so, Master Yale," Kel says. "Here is your fee."

Joss Yale estimates the purse to be at least ten pounds, and feels uncomfortable at accepting so large a reward.

"This is too much, sir," he says, honestly. "My usual charge would be no more than ten or fifteen shillings."

"The fee reflects the greatness of the service, Master Yale," Kel Kelton replies. "Will you need to return?"

"Only if he takes a turn for the worst."

"And the stitches?"

"You are returning to London, are you not?"

"We are."

"Well, if he survives the journey, a competent doctor, or a trained surgeon can take them out." The surgeon pockets his overly generous fee, and makes to leave. Kel lays a heavy hand on his arm, and causes him to pause.

"This must not be talked about," he says. "Not one word, Master Yale. Can we trust you?"

"Of course," the man replies, rather testily. "You have the word of a gentleman. I trust you know what that is worth?"

Oh, yes… I do that," Kel says, and lets the surgeon go about his business.

*

"Here we are," Richard Cromwell says. "My uncle is lodged within. After you, sir. The lawyer enters the house, and finds himself confronted by a hard looking young thug with a dagger in his fist. He turns, but Richard Cromwell is blocking his only avenue of retreat.

"What is this?" Edward Courtney demands, but his voice shakes with apprehension. "I am an important man in Lincoln, and you would do well to treat me with greater respect."

"I want a name," the younger man says. "Your man was kind enough to give me yours, but only after I took off his ear."

"Christ above!" Courtney sees that his life is at risk, and tries to think of a way out of his dilemma. "I am nothing but a lawyer. I arrange things for people. You want a fresh will for a deranged old relative … and I arrange it. Or someone does you a grave disservice, and I find someone to put the matter right for you. I have never done anyone violent harm."

"No, your hands are clean, just like Pontius Pilate," Richard says, softly. "My young friend has a very short fuse to his powder keg, Master Courtney, and he is without scruples. Refuse him his answer, and he is likely to take out an eye with the point of his dagger. Refuse him a second time, and he will have your stinking pintle off, and nailed to the front door."

"You are trying to frighten me," the lawyer stutters.

"No, sir, I am trying to save you from the most devilish sort of pain," the younger Cromwell says. "Your thugs have wounded a friend of ours, in the belief that he is Thomas Cromwell, and we would have the name of your master. Tell us everything, and you will not be mutilated. Lie, and Master Kelton will do things to you that no man should ever have to suffer."

"A name… now." Kel steps forward, and raises the tip of his dagger to the lawyer's eye level.

"Charnley," Courtney stammers. "Though I must warn you that he is a dangerous man, and not one to cross, sir. I had no choice in the matter. He wanted Thomas Cromwell dead, and paid well for the deed."

"You sent a dozen men against us," Kel says. "Six are dead, and the rest are taken by the Lincolnshire militia. They will hang at the next assizes. We are dangerous men, sir. How much did he pay you?"

"Three hundred pounds."

"Good God above," Richard mutters. "Who can spend such a vast amount, so readily? Why does this Charnley fellow want Thomas Cromwell dead?"

"I know not," Edward Courtney replies. Now he is telling the truth, he cannot stop, such is his relief at not forfeiting an eye, or an ear. "I know only that he is from London, and he has the most powerful friends. He knew things about me, and my business that I thought safely hidden from sight. I was forced into the deed, against my better judgement, sir… I swear."

"You have knowledge of where he lives?" Kel asks, and the lawyer shakes his head.

"No, I do not know where he calls home, Courtney says, truthfully. "I received an unsigned letter, informing me that I was to receive a visit, then another letter naming a place, and a time. We met in a low drinking house in the old wall, and he kept his face covered from me. He hid himself, and kept his name a close secret."

"Yet you know it?" Richard asks.

"He had two big thugs with him. They lounged at another table, and watched us. Whilst we discussed his needs, we drank, and I was forced to go outside to piss. It was then I heard one of the men tell the other to hurry me back inside, as Master Charnley wanted them close."

"So, you marked the name," Kel says. "What then?"

"I wrote to a lawyer friend of mine in Greys Inn, and asked him to find out about the fellow for me."

"And did he?"

"He wrote, saying he would make enquiries, but a few days later he was waylaid in the street, and stabbed to death," Courtney explains. "I understood that this was a message, and made no further attempt to uncover Master Charnley's secrets."

"Is there anything else you can tell us?"

"No, I swear to God above."

"Then do it in person." Richard Cromwell grips Courtney's head in his two hands, and gives it a sharp twist. There is a muted crack, and the lawyer falls to the floor, flopping about like a freshly landed fish. After a moment, the body convulses, and lies still.

"You must teach me that one day, Master Richard," young Kel says. "It could come in mighty useful!"

*

"Damn this bright moon," Tom Wyatt grumbles. 'Its very fullness will hamper our stealthy approach. Can we not wait until it wanes?"

"What, and miss so pretty a prize?" Mush replies. They are lying on the crest of a low sand dune, and looking down at a wide, sandy bay. It would be idyllic, were there not a dozen Turkish galleys floating in the calm waters. "See how each boat is tethered to the next, and see how poorly they are watched?"

"True enough," Tom Wyatt concedes. "We have stumbled on a rare chance to hurt these infidel dogs."

"How shall we proceed?" Gianni Lucretto asks.

"Leave two reliable men with the horses, ready for our swift retreat," Mush advises. "I shall make my way down to the galleys, and set them on fire."

"I shall come with you, Gianni whispers. The night air is still, and all that can be heard is the clicking of *Cicadas*, and the gentle lapping of water onto land. "You do not know how to handle our Greek Fire. Let one drop touch you, and you are as good as dead."

"Very well," Mush wants to act, and does not care to argue the finer points. "I will guard you, whilst you work your mysterious magic. Once the fire starts, we must run for the horses."

"That is when you will be most at risk," Tom Wyatt says. "I will have the men fan out along this ridge, and give musket fire to any who give chase."

"One volley only," Mush insists. "Then you must take horse. I do not want to lose any men because their blood is up."

"God's speed," Wyatt says, and the two young men slip down the sandy dune. He signals to the remainder of the raiding party, and they take up position along the sandy crest.

The galleys, each a fast single mast vessel, designed for the chase, are lined up in a neat row, and there is only one guard standing at the nearest galley's prow. The sails are furled tightly, and lashed to the tall, slender masts.

Mush and Gianni have bright Ottoman robes on, and will pass for Turks, even in the moonlight. They stand, and stroll towards the lone guard, who raises a hand in salute. The fellow is armed with a great curved scimitar, which hangs at his belt, and a short spear, with a barbed steel tip. He asks them something, and Mush laughs, and continues to walk towards him. The guard speaks again, but the tone is harsher.

"*Insh allah.*" Gianni says one of the few phrases he knows, and the man agrees. Mush is close enough now to risk a throw. The beautifully balanced Spanish throwing knife comes out of his robe, and whistles through the air. For a moment, the guard seems transfixed, but his knees suddenly give way. He falls onto the sand, and gives a soft moan.

Mush retrieves the knife from the dead man's chest, and peers down the length of the sandy bay. There are a few camp fires glowing, and he can hear the chatter of Turks, mixed with the usual ribald laughter of soldiers. He beckons Gianni forward, and the young Venetian approaches the nearest galley. He throws back the restricting robe, and displays the small cask he has slung around his neck.

"We must be quick," Mush whispers. "How can I help?"

"Stay back, and let me lay a trail," Gianni says. "You must not let the Greek Fire splash onto you. Keep an eye on those infidels camped up the beach, and I will see to the rest."

Mush nods, and takes up a position behind a small tussock of sand, covered with sea grasses. It is not the best of cover, but need only suffice for a few minutes. Gianni crouches, and runs to the further most galley from him. He slips aboard, and the young Jew is left alone in the moonlight. After a moment he sees Gianni hop from one low deck to the next. As he moves down the line, the Venetian pours out a thin trail of syrup-like Greek Fire, connecting each galley to the next.

He is on the deck of the penultimate craft, when Mush sees a blaze of light approaching. A huge Arab, easily as big as Richard Cromwell, is coming towards the galleys, with a burning torch held up high. He pauses, and stares down the long, even, line of sleek warships. "Ameed?" He takes another few steps, and drops a hand to the sword at his belt. "*Ahlan sadiqi*?" Mush knows that the man is calling for his friend, and that they will be discovered in moments if he does not act. He grunts, and raises a hand from behind the low hump of sand. The huge Arab warrior laughs, and makes a coarse sounding noise with his thick lips. He thinks he has caught his comrade out in an undignified squat, and advances on Mush, chattering away.

The young Jew has no other option, he draws his knife, and throws. The Arab staggers back, and curses loudly. The point has taken him in the shoulder, and he is stung into rage. The curved sword comes out of his belt, and he charges at the small figure who is plainly not Ameed. Mush rolls to one side, and the great sword cuts through empty air. He comes up, with his own sword in hand, and thrusts at the giant's chest. The man chops his blade down, and Mush's blade is snapped off at the hilt. The Arab delivers a back handed blow, which Mush catches on the broken hilt. The power is such that the young man is sent staggering sideways. He tries to twist away, but the sand slides under his feet, and he goes down in a heap.

The big Arab drops the blazing torch, grips his sword with two hands, and raises it. Deliver the blow well, and he knows his opponent will be split from head to waist. It is only then that he thinks to call a warning to his own comrades. He opens his mouth, but no sound comes forth. His eyes roll up into his head, and he falls to his knees. Gianni is behind him, holding the now empty cask in both hands. The blow, delivered with all his might, has cracked one of the staves, and the Turk s thick cranium.

"Are you hurt?" the Venetian asks, and Mush shakes his head. Their big adversary is stunned, and crawling away across the beach, towards his friends. The young Jew picks up the burning torch and runs towards the first galley. He halts a dozen paces away, and throws the torch like a spear. It arcs through the air, and lands on the deck. He would stand, and watch, but Gianni grabs his arm, and pulls him away.

"Wait. We must…"

"Run!" Gianni screams, and they both sprint away, just as the torch ignites the trickle of Greek Fire the Venetian has poured across the timbers. There is a sudden, white flash of light, and the magical mixture of oil, sulphur, and other secret ingredients, ignites with all the raging fury of Hell. A sheet of flame sweeps across the first deck, and leaps to the second galley. By the time they are struggling up the nearby hill, half of the ships are engulfed in fire.

"Down!" Tom Wyatt's shouted warning sends them diving to the sand, and a dozen muskets fire over their heads. Three of the nearest pursuers scream and fall, but another twenty come on without hesitation, roaring their blind hatred of these Christian intruders. Mush is up, and dragging Gianni Lucretto after him. They crest the low hill, and leap onto the waiting horses.

"Ride, men!" Tom Wyatt cries, and the small band needs no second telling.

The raiding party dig heels into horses flanks, and they gallop off into the darkness. Behind them they hear a spattering of muskets being fired, and they can hear the roar of a dozen enemy galleys going up in flames. The Greek Fire burns intensely, even when on water, and the timbers of the once sleek enemy ships are soon nothing but charred embers in the glorious moonlight.

*

"It is like coursing a hare, Richard Cromwell explains. "We close off every escape route, and let the greyhounds loose. We follow the twisting path of our prey, picking them off, one by one. In the end, we will have our buck hare in a corner, and he will have nowhere to turn."

"Yet we have only a name," Kel Kelton says, as they drop Edward Courtney's weighted body into the river. "Charnley. How many men of that name are there living in, or about, London do you think?"

"Will Draper will know where to look," the younger Cromwell says. "He is an investigator. Besides, once Uncle Thomas knows how poor Edmund Ambrose has been treated, he will leave no stone unturned."

"If you say so," the youth mutters. Over the weeks, he has grown very fond of Cromwell's double, and sometimes forgets he is not with the real man. "Master Ambrose must be avenged. No matter what the cost, we must find this man, or else they will think Austin Friars is growing soft."

"Let us not lose our heads," Richard replies. "It might take a while, but there is nowhere to hide once we Cromwell lads are on the trail. Damn!"

Master Courtney, despite the stones in his doublet, refuses to sink. Instead, he floats away, down the wide Humber, and will end up floating out to sea. That will frighten a few fishermen, no doubt. "Did you take everything from the body?"

"Everything," Kel answers. "Give him a day in the water, and his own mother would not recognise him."

"Good lad... you learn well."

"Do you think Master Ambrose will live, Master Richard?"

"He will be cared for," Richard replies. "My uncle will cover every expense, and pay for the best doctors. Edmund Ambrose may be an old rogue... but he is an Austin Friars rogue!"

14   The Hornets Nest

Isabella Lucretto has not left the watch tower of the fortress since her brother, and his war party, left that morning. Now it is almost midnight, and she still stands and waits. It is only a couple of days since Mush spoke to her brother about her, and she has yet to give herself to the handsome Englishman. She wonders what she will do if he does not return from this mad raid.

A half hour later, and she spies a group of horsemen, riding hard for the main gate. Men begin to cry out orders, and the drawbridge is lowered. On the other side of the *Contrafossa*, bands of Ottoman Turks have been arriving since noon. They are busy pitching tents, out of cannon fire range, and preparing for the rest of their army to arrive.

Mush Draper sees that the Turkish force, no more than four or five hundred strong, are busy digging narrow latrine ditches, and are not expecting anyone to come charging from their unguarded rear. He shouts out a command, and the small war party, a mixture of English mercenaries, and un-blooded Venetian gentlemen, draw their swords, and spur their mounts into a mad charge for the main gate. The Ottoman soldiers are startled to see the drawbridge begin to come down, and run for their weapons which are stacked in neat piles. The mixed English and Venetian force ride into their rear at full tilt, and gallop through them. One or two of the braver Turks try to snatch at horses bridles, or draw their swords, and are cut down for their trouble.

The entire party are safe inside the fortress, and the heavy drawbridge is being wound back up, before the disarrayed besiegers can organise a serious counterattack. They run back and forth outside the walls, scream threats, and discharge a few muskets into the night air. This only stops when a young Venetian merchant on the platform above the main gate loses his short Italian temper, and fires off his ornate fowling piece at them. There is a great cheer from the garrison s defenders when the poorly aimed shot hits an enemy officer on his heavy breastplate, and knocks the fellow from his horse.

The small advance army withdraws to a safer distance, and will resume digging latrines, and building firing platforms for the expected Ottoman cannon, once dawn breaks over the island. For now, there is an uneasy stalemate, and each side's sentinels watch their enemies from a safe distance. It is first blood to the Christian garrison, but dawn will bring ever more men to swell the ranks of the Ottoman Turks.

*

"How many are there?" Mush asks of Tom Wyatt. The poet consults the parchment upon which he has been counting each new arrival to the enemy camp.

"About three thousand foot, and a thousand horse, so far," he reports. "We seem to have kicked open a hornet's nest last night."

"I doubt it," Mush replies. "A dozen galleys might carry five hundred men, at most. These fellows are coming in from every direction. I think they have just decided that it is time to settle matters, once and for all time."

"A comforting thought," Gianni says. "The last of our spies returned last night, before our own escapade. He reports at least thirty large cannon being dragged here by teams of oxen. They will be here by noon."

"They must finish digging gun pits first," Tom Wyatt tells them. Each cannon must be firmly bedded in, and have a protective wall built before it."

"Why?"

"Because, if they can reach our walls with their guns, we can reach their guns with our own ordinance." The poet is something of an expert when it comes to cannon, and he is happy to share his knowledge with his younger friends. "Their gunners must fire up, against our fortifications, whilst we are raised above them, and can reach further. With luck, we might be able to keep their cannon quiet for a while."

"These infidels do not know the meaning of fear," Gianni says. "They are driven on by a blind faith in their god, whom they call 'Allah'. It is said that a prophet, named Muhammad, brought them God's word… long after Christ, and that they do not fear death. If the cannon are stilled, they will simply charge our walls with swords and ladders, until they get in."

"Every army has its great warriors, and its fanatics," says Mush, "but most ordinary soldiers want to live through a battle so as to be able to fight another day. If we make it too difficult for them to break in, they will lose heart. It is one thing to charge against a host similar to your own, but these men must climb a slope, ford a canal, and scale a thirty foot wall, before they even get to us. They will waver, and they may even run away."

"Let us hope so," Tom Wyatt says, "for here are their cannon." The poet lets out a small groan. "Twenty pounders. God is not on our side today, my friends!"

*

Mush has prepared their defences well. He has massed his best men above the main gate, and set the rest to guard the outer wall at ten pace intervals. The stretch of repaired wall will not withstand a prolonged bombardment, so he elects not to man it. Instead, he has steel helmets placed at each embrasure, and orders pikes and spears to be leant against the inner parapet. From the other side, it seems as though he has two hundred men holding the weakened part of the wall.

"They know about the damage to our wall," Tom Wyatt tells Mush as he watches the enemy preparations. "See how they drag their two biggest guns to face the weak part? Their spies must have warned them. Once those two twenty pounders open up, your shored up fortification will collapse like a tower of playing cards."

"Good of you to let me know, old friend," Mush mutters. "I have warned our men to plug the gap, if that happens. If we can bring enough musketry to bear, we might break their first charge."

"I fear we must come up with a better scheme than that," the poet replies. We must force their great ordinance further back, and confound their purpose. Perhaps you should grab some sleep, and let your mind rest. Lady Isabella did not let you slumber last night, I warrant."

"It seems we are pledged to one another." Mush yawns. The young woman, though completely inexperienced, gave herself with a willingness that left no time for sleep. "Have you an idea, Master Poet? Shall we rhyme these unbelievers to death instead?"

"*Let me loose an arrow into the air, may it land where best it dare.*" Tom Wyatt extemporises, and smiles. "Let me have six strong men, with picks and shovels, and I might save your flimsy wall for another day or two."

"Choose whoever you would have," Mush replies. "I trust your judgement. What part am I to play in your little ruse?"

"Man the stronger part of our walls, and prepare yourself for the unexpected," Wyatt says. "If I am successful, it might provoke a sudden riposte. Warn Gianni to be ready, and put your best men on the firing platform over the gate. These fellows are not great strategists, and will come head on, rather than employ any clever ruses."

"Very well. Then let us get to it," Mush replies. "We will do our part, Tom, so pray do yours, whatever it may be!

*

"I have been a damned fool!" Thomas Cromwell pounds a fist down onto the breakfast table in Austin Friars' crowded kitchen, and seems about to burst into tears. "I should have given my poor look alike a larger bodyguard."

"You were not to blame, sir," Richard says. "Who would suspect such an attack, in broad daylight? Kel and I should have kept closer to Master Ambrose."

"And the miscreants?"

"Dead, to a man," Richard replies. "Young Kel killed three of them himself. He is a fine lad, uncle."

"He shall be raised in our service," Thomas Cromwell agrees. "Do we know who ordered the foul deed?"

"We found an unscrupulous lawyer in Lincoln, who gave us a name. It seems that this Charnley is our man, but that is all we know of him." Richard tells the truth, but does not mention Courtney's fate. In hindsight, the young Cromwell thinks he should have brought the man back to Austin Friars for further questioning.

"I will find the fellow. Colonel Will Draper is the head of the King's Examiners, and has access to all walks of life, be it at court, or beyond. Is there no given name?"

"None."

"How did this lawyer know Charnley is a Londoner?"

"He asked help from a friend who worked in Greys Inn, as a lawyer."

"Worked you say?"

"He is dead. Slain in the street, because of his probing ways, I think." Richard does not see how valuable this information is, and Will Draper nods his head in satisfaction.

"Then we have only to ask the lawyers at Greys Inn, and we shall have the dead man's name. With that knowledge, I can start to search out what he was up to when he died. He found something, and it got him killed."

"Then get to it, Will," Thomas Cromwell says. "For they will not settle at one failed attempt. Until this Charnley is run to ground, I cannot sleep safely in my bed."

"You should use your chambers at court," Will says. "You are easier to keep an eye on in Whitehall Palace, or even in the confines of Greenwich. Men have found their way into Austin Friars before now. Remember how close that swine Sir Francis Weston came to murdering you?"

"Yes, it was Kel who saved me then too," Thomas Cromwell says. "Have the lad come to me, Richard. I will reward him at once."

"He is quite content with his current position," Richard tells his uncle. "The lad fears being sent too far a field, lest he loses sight of the precious jewel he cherishes."

"I shall give him money."

"Then let it be as a dowry, Uncle Thomas, says Richard.

"Ah, I begin to see. I wondered why he was always to be found in the kitchen, yet never seemed to put on weight. Does our dear Maisie feel the same way?"

"She will say not, out of sheer contrariness."

"And if I compel her into this marriage?" Thomas Cromwell asks, even though he would never do such a thing to one of his own people.

"She will complain that you are an ogre, but that she must obey her beloved master," Richard says. "It will be a splendid match. Kel loves her, and she needs that sort of devotion. He is a lucky lad. I wish…"

"As do I, nephew," Thomas Cromwell tells him. "Lady Jane Rochford would make you a fine wife. Perhaps, now Gregory is related to the Seymours, Henry might relent. It would be an easy matter to get you a knighthood, and she would not be able to refuse you for being a lowly commoner."

"I cannot force her, Richard Cromwell says. These things must run their course. I must roll the dice, and let them fall where they will."

"Yes, love is a game of chance," Thomas Cromwell muses. "I am constantly surprised at why we fall in love, and how we cannot stop loving, even in the face of some terrible danger."

"You think that Lady Rochford is in some sort of danger, uncle?" Richard asks. He misunderstands, because, like the rest of the world, he is not privy to his uncle's profound love for Jane Seymour."

"Oh, no. I was simply musing… over hypothetical lovers and their ways." Thomas Cromwell thinks how it is but a few short weeks to the queen's final confinement, and how the world is about to change, whether they like it, or not. It is as if love is a fuse. Light it, and you must take the consequences.

"Then must I tell Kel to press home his suit?" Richard Cromwell asks. "Do we offer him any help?"

"No, let him face up to it like a man," Cromwell says. If he can take on assassins, he can convince Maisie to marry him!"

*

"Is it safe?" Gianni Lucretto eyes the strange configuration dubiously. "I mean to say, my friend… it looks like a thing of great folly. Are there enough ropes?

Who knows? Tom Wyatt says. I have never tried this before. Though I have seen a similar device in Rome. They call it a mortar, and its job is to throw cannon balls over, rather than through a wall. The poet's invention consists of a four foot deep hole, into which one of his precious twelve pound cannon has been tipped, with its twelve foot long muzzle pointing skywards. The huge metal beast has been lashed into place with strong ropes, and heavy timbers. Besides the large hole is a narrow trench, some two feet deep.

"You mean to fire a cannon into the sky?" Gianni asks. "You are mad. Why shoot at the moon?"

"What goes up, invariably comes down, the poet mutters. "I must double charge her, and hope she stands the strain.

"May God be with you… but not I," the young Venetian says with a smirk. "I shall be hiding somewhere safe, like the powder room." He picks up his musket, and trots off towards the weaker stretch of the wall.

"Mush, how are they getting on?" Tom Wyatt calls up to his comrade.

"They are almost in place, Mush replies. "Soon they will start to bombard the walls. I fear they know we cannot reach them with our smaller twelve pound ordinance."

"Stand clear!" The six men under Wyatt's command drop their shovels and run for cover, as the poet touches a lit wick to the short fuse at the cannon's priming hole. He has only enough time to throw himself into the narrow trench, before the fuse ignites the double charge of black powder, which blasts the wadding, and a twelve pound shot up into the air. The poet has spent some time calculating the height, and trajectory of his improvised mortar, and fears only that the barrel will fall over and crush him.

Mush, and the men on the fighting platform above the gate, gasp in amazement as the ball arcs up and up, over their heads, and then falls. It hits the hard ground twenty feet short of the enemy cannon positions, and bounces over the Turks heads. The shot bounces twice more before ploughing into a company of foot soldiers, where it kills one man, and maims a half dozen more.

The defenders leap up and down, crying out insults, and one man even turns, and shows his bare backside to the infidels. For their part the

Turkish gunners examine the crater made by the shot landing, and return to preparing their own gun. Tom Wyatt can hear bells ringing in his ears, and he staggers to his feet and examines his precious cannon. It appears to be unharmed.

"A fine try, my friend," Gianni says. "You landed but a dozen paces short, and the bounce shattered one of their formations."

"Close enough, the poet replies. Get to it lads. I want that shot in place at once! His six men re-appear, and carry a wooden stretcher between them. On it is what looks like another twelve pound lead ball, but with a length of fuse tied around it.

You are going to try again?" Gianni asks, and the poet shakes his head.

"This one is hollow, and packed with black powder and clout nails," he explains. "Stand well clear, my friend. "The barrel might not stand another double charge. He supervises the primer cone being reset, and sees the wadding is rammed home tightly onto the double charge of powder. Then they heave the hollowed out shot up, and balance it on the lip of the big gun. "Count of three lads," the poet mutters. "One… two…" He touches his lit wick to the fuse wrapped around the shot. "Three!" They release the shot, and leap for whatever cover they can find. Tom Wyatt puts the wick to the primer, and falls into his trench.

The primer powder ignites, and the double charge explodes in the cannon, sending wadding, and ball, high into the air again. The twelve pound shot arcs high, watched by both sides. The Turkish gunners gesticulate, and speculate how close the ball will land. Behind them a column of foot soldiers throw themselves to the ground in terror.

The ball's fuse is too short, and instead of bouncing first, it explodes ten feet from the ground. The blast rips the cannon ball apart, and sends the pieces tearing into the unprepared Turkish gunners. The twisted pieces of lead, and handful of clout nails wreak havoc amongst the enemy. A dozen men are cut to pieces, and as many more receive horrific wounds to their heads and upper bodies. On the fortress walls, Venetian and English defenders cheer for dear life.

An Ottoman officer sees how his artillery must be forced further back, and rages at his surviving gunners. They are the sons of whores, and stupid dogs, he tells them, who must skulk away and drag their massive guns out of range. His rage grows, and he demands an immediate attack on the walls. His men have long ladders, and grapples, he sees, and coupled with their bravery, he thinks that should suffice.

"*Allah Akbar*!" The blood curdling yell sends a thousand men rushing at the Venetian fortress. The wide moat will not stop them, for they are soldiers of Allah, and He will give them a certain victory.

"Christ save us," Gianni says.

"Hold your fire," Mush commands. "Let no man loose his weapon until I will it. Let them run to us, my friends. They will come to the moat, and have to think again. If they get their grapples onto our walls, wait until they are on the ropes before you cut through them. If they get their ladders across and up to us, let them climb, before hacking them down. Let them do all the work, lads, and victory shall be ours."

The wave of screaming men cover the half mile from their own line to the offending moat, and slow down. Others run through them, in pairs, and each pair carries a roughly lashed together raft. They throw them into the water, and jump in afterwards. In moments a hundred crude rafts are crossing the fifteen feet of sea water, and men with ladders are wading up to their necks.

Some Turks reach the fortress side, and start to hoist up ladders. The top of one ladder lands against the gate wall, a foot away from Mush. He draws his pistol, leans over, and fires down at the first man to start the climb. He falls back, and three more men take his place.

"Fire!" Mush shouts, and muskets begin to crack. Some of the enemy fall back dead, and Venetians with long spears uses them to push away the ladders. Men are screaming, either in fear, or the throws of death, and the one sided carnage goes on. There are piles of fist sized rocks piled on the parapets, and after letting off their muskets, the defenders start dropping them down on unguarded heads. "Lower the drawbridge!" Mush's command is obeyed at once.

In the inner courtyard, sixty of the best marksmen Mush has at his command are lined up in three rows. A sergeant at arms waits until the bridge is down, and Turks are swarming across it, before he gives the command.

"Front rank, fire! Kneel. Second rank, fire. Kneel. Third rank, fire!" A cloud of smoke wafts across the drawbridge, and as it clears at scene of carnage presents itself. The lowered wooden bridge is piled high with a mass of dead and wounded, and the sergeant gives another order.

The men lay down their muskets, and draw their knives. They advance, and collect the Ottoman arms, rob their purses, and slice gold earrings free. Any who are found to be alive have their throats cut, and the bodies are rolled into the fast flowing moat, where they will swirl down to join the sea.

"Drawbridge up!" Mush commands, and the firing party retreat back inside the fortress. The gate is closed once more, and the ill judged attack peters out. The Ottoman charge has cost them over three hundred dead, and many more wounded, and all to no avail. "Gianni… how have we fared?"

"No casualties," Gianni shouts back. He turns then, as one of his men shouts out. The huge cannon, having been fired for a second time, has broken loose from its moorings, and toppled over.

"Capitano…the Englishman!" Men are running from all directions, and Mush throws himself down a ladder to the ground. He sees now how dangerous the task was, and that Tom Wyatt has risked his life to give them a small respite.

"You mad fool," he shouts. "Dear Christ!" Men with shovels are digging around the cannon, which has toppled across the shallow trench. Sand flies in all directions and the Englishmen dig with fervour. After a moment, one of them throws aside his shovel, and starts to scrabble with his hands. More join in, and a cheer goes up, as the poet is dragged from his shallow bolt hole.

"God's bollocks," the poet cries, and spits sand from his mouth. "Wine, before I choke to death. Get her back up, lads. I think she will serve us again.

"But with a longer fuse," Mush says.

"Another six inches… I promise," the poet replies, and they embrace. "I do not recommend being buried alive, my friend. How went the battle?"

"Done. They have lost many hundreds."

"Yes," Gianni Lucretto says, "but there are thousands more gathering, and they will come with more than ladders and a death wish next time."

"Then we must prepare more traps for them," Mush Draper decides. "They think we have a mortar, so will keep their cannon at a safer distance. That means their bombardment will be less accurate. Tom can mount his cannon to cover any mass break through with chain shot. I doubt these infidels have tasted so modern a weapon."

"Even so, they will swarm over us, like ants," Gianni replies. "The best we can do is make it a hollow victory for them. One way or another, the Ottoman Turks will take Corfu Castle and we will all die."

"What about the women?" Tom Wyatt asks. "Can we not parlay with these fellows, and get them safe conduct back to Venice?"

"Perhaps," the Venetian tells him, "but they would demand something in return. They have no honour."

"We might be able to slip a small boat past the blockade," Mush says. The women, and four good seamen to guide them."

"Isabella will not go," Gianni says. "God knows why, but she loves you, my friend."

"Then, if the time comes, I must tie her up, and throw her into the boat," Mush decides. "Come the final battle, I do not need her death on my conscience."

15   Death's Sting

"Thomas, a word if you please? The king is grinning like a schoolboy, and holding out a document. "Can you explain this strange communication to me? Thomas Cromwell, who has been about to join in conversation with Rafe Sadler, breaks off, and crosses the throne room to stand by Henry and Queen Jane. Jane is large with child, and must soon disappear into confinement, he thinks.

"Sire?" He takes the paper, and reads. It is a letter written by the mayor of Lincoln, and sent by the weekly courier. After the usual preamble, the mayor reports the sad death of Lord Cromwell on the high road out of Lincoln, and offers His Majesty his sincerest condolences. "Ah, yes. I must inform Your Majesty that reports of my demise are somewhat exaggerated. At this moment, I feel particularly alive, and I am glad to have avoided death's sharp sting. The mayor of Lincoln has been too swift in offering his honest regrets at my passing."

"How could such a thing come about?" Henry asks. He smells a juicy tale, and wonders if Cromwell will relate it to him.

"I sent a delegation to Lincoln… regarding the local unrest over the church, and they were attacked by a large gang of unruly malcontents."

"The Devil you say!" Henry loves a spicy story. "Are there still those who defy my new Church of England then?"

"My nephew and two others fought them off & killing a dozen of the rogues, but one of my fellows was sorely wounded. He lives, I am pleased to say, and will make a full recovery."

"They thought you were with them?"

"It seems so, sire," Thomas Cromwell says. "First reports indicate that I was the intended victim. I have taken the liberty of asking Colonel Draper to investigate, as he is your own Royal Examiner, sire."

"Of course," Henry says. Use the man as you will. He is a most capital fellow. Do you recall how we once fought… toe to toe… and he almost overcame me? A hundred such men, and I would invade France with impunity."

"Then François is indeed a lucky man, sire." Thomas Cromwell bows, and withdraws. He finds it physically painful to be in Jane's presence, without being able to exchange a pleasant word, or throw her a tender look. He returns to Rafe Sadler, who is deep in conversation with Sir John Russell, and Sir Richard Page.

"Sir John," Cromwell offers him a quick bow. Should you not be on your way to Hampton Court? The king will be setting off later today, and you must announce his coming."

"It seems that I am excused," Russell replies, with a thin lipped smile. "I was hoping Master Sadler could explain why."

"And I have been stood down from my duties too," Sir Richard Page says. "We have had our differences in the past, Master Cromwell, but I really do think…"

"It is none of my doing," Thomas Cromwell says. "What do you know about the matter, Master Sadler?"

"Orders directly from the king," Rafe replies with a shrug that shows how much he is also in the dark. "His Majesty has a list of positions he wishes to re-appoint, ranging from Master of the King's Horse, and Wardrobe Master, to Head Cook, Master of the Clocks, Gentleman of the Privy, and even the boy who lights the fires, and cleans the boots. He gave it to me this morning."

"May I see it?" Cromwell asks. Rafe Sadler glances about, and sees that no one is paying much attention to them. He rummages in his folio, and brings out a paper, written out in Henry's own hand. The king s minister takes it, and peruses the new appointments. The names are, for the most part, unfamiliar, and he does not see why Henry has taken the trouble to involve himself. "The king seeks to remove his cook, the finest in England…a man he stole from me in the first place… and as for the lads who do these menial tasks about the palaces… I am at a complete loss. Let me look further into it, gentlemen. I assure you both that you will not suffer by this."

Thomas Cromwell takes his leave, and is crossing the outer court area when Charles Brandon, the Duke of Suffolk, comes hurrying after him. The duke is flushed, and looks ready to do murder. Cromwell sighs, and waits for him to catch up.

"Is this your doing, Cromwell?" the duke demands to know, and waves a document in his face. "This… *preposterous* imposition on my friendship… is the last straw."

"Oh, do shut up your blustering, Charles," Thomas Cromwell snaps. "Though I confess to liking you, I do not consider you to be a real friend. Nor have I made any imposition on you. He reads the document, and shakes his head in disbelief. "Ireland?"

"Ireland." TheDuke of Suffolk is almost shaking with disgust.

"You are to be the new Governor General of Ireland?" Cromwell begins to see it all now. The serpent is showing its fangs. "Why then, the country is lost. When do you sail?"

"I went to Henry."

"And?"

"He says I must agree to it… and it is my duty." Suffolk is distraught, and rings his hat in his hands. "He says that great changes must be made, for England's good."

"He sends his best friend to Ireland, and dismisses half of his staff… for England's sake?" Cromwell thinks hard. Most of the changes are positions filled by his own agents, or men of good office, who can be counted on to support him with the king. "This is not for England s sake, but for the sake of some other."

"Then it isn't your doing?" Suffolk feels a pang of fear run down his spine. If someone thinks to attack Cromwell, then the old minister must be in trouble. "My first inclination is to step back from you, Master Cromwell, but I find I cannot. If you are in trouble, I feel compelled to help you."

"You show surprising loyalty, My Lord," Cromwell says. "If you would, please glance at these new names, and see if anything suggests itself to you."

"Of course." Suffolk takes the paper, and reads. After a few moments he points to the third name. "The new Master of the Robes is to be Sir Martin Keogh, who is married to a cousin of the Duchess of Norfolk. I see also that James Fyfe is to become a Royal Equerry."

"Do I know him?" Cromwell asks.

"He is new to court," Suffolk replies. "I believe he was, until recently, a secretary to our present ambassador in Scotland. He is related to the Seymour family through a distant cousin."

"Who?"

"Some bastard son of the late Lord Willoughby's brother."

"Lady Maria de Salinas' late husband?" Cromwell is even more confused. "How would Henry even know the fellow?"

"I do not know. This young man here is, or was, a squire to the Earl of Surrey. Here is a distant cousin of Isabel Neville."

"Enough!" Cromwell draws himself up, and juts out his jaw line. "We are under attack, Charles. The recent attempt on my life has set things into motion before their time. We must plan out our response, and see what we can do to keep your feet firmly on English soil."

"Amen to that," Suffolk says. "For if I must go to Dublin, I would want a thousand Austin Friars men about me. It is a hard country to rule over, I fear."

"Calm yourself, sir. We will win out, and I will not forget whose side you have chosen to support. Might I offer you my hand, Charles?"

The duke finds a tear coming to his eye, and takes the proffered hand. He is touched to have a real friend, rather than the shallowness of his relationship with the king.

"I seek only to be on the winning side, Master Thomas, he says, affecting a brusque manner. He has played the part of friend to Henry for so long that he struggles with sincerity. "To date, that has been your domain, sir… pray, do not let me down now!"

*

Rafe Sadler moves through the inner and outer courts with practiced ease. He stops, here and there, to reassure a bemused courtier who thinks his livelihood is to be taken from him, or ask a pertinent question or two. It seems that the proposed new appointments have a common theme.

"Well, my dear friend, was I right?" Thomas Cromwell asks, over dinner that evening. It is a select gathering at Draper House, and those present all have a way of life to protect. Suffolk sits at the minister's right, and Miriam, her husband, Will, Richard Cromwell, John Beckshaw and his wife, Pru, and Eustace Chapuys, make up the small compliment.

"It appears so, sir," Rafe says. "Sir Martin Keogh is the Duchess of Norfolk's cousin, and related to the husband of Lady Salisbury. James Fyfe is a bastard nephew of the late Lord Willoughby, and his father was a close friend of George Plantagenet, the late Duke of Gloucester. Others are either related to Isabel Neville, or allied to the Pole family. Some … like the new squires, and masters of horse and hounds are young men who once were in the Earl of Surrey's service. One was a steward of Harry Percy's, who later worked for Lady Salisbury."

"Then they are all, in some way, allied to Lady Margaret Pole, the Duchess of Salisbury?"

"The new kitchen staff used to be in the household of Reginald Pole," Rafe tells the gathering. "I cannot understand why the king would wish to surround himself with relatives and servants of the old Plantagenet regime."

"I doubt he knows," Miriam says. "When did the king last choose a servant? Why, even Rafe here was foisted on him. I wager that Henry has no real idea who these people are."

"Then he must be told," Will Draper says.

"Better to ask, my friend," Eustace Chapuys says. "Kings do not like to be instructed. I suggest Thomas speaks with him."

"I shall see him on the morrow," Thomas Cromwell assures them. "Now, Ambassador Chapuys… might we turn to other business? Is the emperor satisfied with our arrangement?"

"He is, my friend, though I fear it will not last into another season," Chapuys replies. "The sudden rush of wealth has gone to his head. He is using some of the gold to put more cannon onto his treasure ships. Next year, he will instruct our naval forces to resist you, despite our current alliance."

"It will cost him money," Richard says.

"He is under pressure from Anton Fugger," Chapuys explains. "The banker twists the knife, and demands protection for his gold ships… or else. The fellow has seen his income drop by two thirds these last few months. He will raise the interest rates on our loans if we demur."

"Refuse to pay any more," Miriam says.

"He dare not," the little Savoyard explains to her. "The Fuggers have the mining rights for the next seven years, and New World gold production accounts for three quarters of the emperor's current income. His lands are not as fertile in tax revenue as is England, Mistress Miriam. Anton Fugger can foreclose, and bring down the empire. It is only held together by good will these days."

"Never mind, it was profitable whilst it lasted, Cromwell says. How goes the war against the Sultan Suleiman?"

"The emperor's army makes good progress in the Provençal district, because the French army are in northern Italy," Chapuys says with an ironic smile. "As one army moves, another replaces it on the board. Some cities are bewildered with how many lords they have had this last year."

"You soundly defeated the Ottoman Turks at Genoa." Cromwell is pleased to a see the small look of surprise on his friend s face.

"I have only just heard," the ambassador says. "Your spies do you proud, Thomas. Admiral Doria broke their navy, and drove them away, but they will be back, once they finish with Corfu."

"Then they have landed there?" Cromwell asks. "I confess to not having any knowledge of the island this two weeks past."

"Nor I," Chapuys says. He does not know about the secret expeditionary force, and speaks without thinking. "My guess is that the island is fallen, and every Christian soul is either dead, or enslaved by now."

Miriam catches her breath, and looks across the table to where Pru Beckshaw is seated next to her husband. The girl gives a small shake of her head, and a smile, to signify that the ambassador is wrong.

"You doubt Eustace's word, Mistress Pru?" Richard Cromwell asks, and the girl blushes at being singled out.

"I know Master Mush is well."

"How so? Suffolk demands."

"I just know," she replies.

"Ah, women s intuition is it?" Suffolk scoffs, and is surprised when no one else laughs at his remark.

"Brother of a king … not brother… I see a cowherd in your lineage," Pru mutters, and flutters her eye lids.

"How dare you!" Suffolk is on his feet, his face suffused with rage. "You mean to insult me, madam!"

"Would you call my wife out, sir?" John Beckshaw growls at the duke. "For if so, I must champion her."

"I meant no offence," Charles Brandon says, hurriedly. "Will Draper's men have acquired a reputation for settling things violently, which he has no wish to test. "Mistress Pru merely took me by surprise. I understand what she says about my kinship to Henry… but the rest is … confusing."

"Is it, Charles?" Thomas Cromwell asks. His agents keep him abreast of things, and of late they have mentioned how Suffolk dallies with a milkmaid on his estates. "I hope you have made provision, as is fit for a gentleman to do."

Brandon has the good grace to blush. The girl is with child, and he has settled her and her family on a farm close by. It is quite likely that the child, if a male, *will* spend his days herding cattle.

"Mush is alive," Miriam pronounces, "and Corfu must still be in good hands."

"Amen," Tom Cromwell says, though Pru's vision might also mean he lives, but in a state of captivity. "Now, who is for some of this splendid apple pudding?"

*

"Your Majesty, might I speak with you?" Henry, who has been flirting with two of the ladies of the court, turns away from them to greet his minister. He is shocked to find Cromwell is down on one knee. Though it is the usual way to present yourself to the king, Henry prefers a less formal approach from his senior advisors.

"God's Grace, Thomas," he says, and takes Cromwell by the elbow. "Get up. What possesses you to grovel at my feet? Are we no longer friends?"

"I was not sure, sire," Cromwell replies, as he lurches upright. "Such things have come to my ears that I feared your beloved friendship was lost for all time."

"What is it?" Henry demands. "What makes you speak to me thus? Have I ever been anything other than a loving lord to you, sir?"

"Forgive me, sire … but Master Sadler gave me your list of new appointments, thinking me already ware of them. I was shocked to see how you dispose of some loyal fellows."

"Time for a change," Henry says, softly. "Let those I release be given a small pension. I suppose I should have let you know the way of my thoughts."

"*Your* thoughts, sire? Thomas Cromwell sighs theatrically. Then you truly do intend casting off My Lord Suffolk?"

"Ireland is a prime post," Henry replies.

"Usually, but the current state of the country demands the presence of a strong general. Charles will be gone for at least two years, My Lord."

"Oh, I did not know." Henry frowns. "I shall rescind that one then. He shall remain in England."

"Then poor Sir John... replaced by the bastard son of a Plantagenet, and Sir Richard Page by a cousin of Margaret Pole's husband."

"Are you sure?" Henry is beginning to see that he has been duped in some way. "I was told that these men are all honest, and fiercely loyal to the crown."

"Yes, but which one?" Tom Cromwell asks. "Every one of your new appointments are either allied to the old Plantagenets, or affiliated with the Pole family. Some used to work for Reginald Pole, and his mother, Lady Salisbury."

"Dear God, I wonder how such a thing has come about," the king asks. It seemed to me that the names did come to me from many sources."

"Suggested by whom, sire?"

"To be honest, they were suggestions made by some of the stout fellows I hunt with. Not gentlemen, you understand, but the commoners who work about us. Why, one is almost a friend, despite his low birth."

"Might you name him, sire?"

"Why, Charnley, of course. You must know the fellow, Cromwell. He speaks well of you, as do his men... though he says how the commoners would prefer to see more of their own class close to me, and tending to my everyday needs. We have spoken often over the last months, and I became convinced that the voice of the people should be listened to. What harm if an honest fellow is promoted to serve me?"

"No harm at all, sire, unless these 'honest fellows' all love the Pole family, and would therefore see a Plantagenet back on the throne of England." Tom Cromwell sees it all now, and realises how clever the plot is. Replace all the men around Henry with their own, then cut down Cromwell. The king would be surrounded by enemies. "This Charnley is now known to my agents, and they would speak with him, most urgently. What do you know of him, sire, and who is his lord?"

"To be truthful, I do not know," Henry admits. "The fellow is always at hunts, or out at falconry with us. He has a merry, jesting way about him, and is never short of a skin of wine tied to his saddle. I simply assumed he was one of the usual stewards and lackeys that attend such functions. He might be anyone s man."

"No matter, we will find out who he serves once he is found," Cromwell says. "In the meantime, in light of this news, might I suggest we hold off on these promotions?"

"Of course." Henry sees he has been played for a complete fool, and his unbridled evil temper comes to the fore. "In fact, arrest every name on the list… for they are all traitors. Have them taken up, and put to the question."

"Your Majesty, there are over fifty names on this list." Thomas Cromwell has never been in the business of murder for murder's sake, and the thought of this wholesale, and unwarranted, slaughter makes him uneasy.

"Break them, sir!" Henry will not retreat from his decision, once it has been made. "Find out what you can, then have them all hanged. No, they shall have a traitors death. Let them be drawn and quartered also. Let it be through the streets, so that all know how I will not suffer traitors."

"What of those I find to be innocent, sire? It is a lawyers trick, which gives him the ability to spare all, save the obviously guilty men, but Henry is not to be duped so readily.

"How innocent can they be?" he asks. "After all, they are on the list!

Thomas Cromwell feels the cold horror of what must happen creep into his bones. He will spare the women on the list, and save others where he may, but he must still countenance the horrible torture and death of a score or more.

"As you command, sire." He turns to leave, then turns back to confirm something with his king. "What if we take this Charnley rogue, and he gives up his master to spare his life?"

"Then that is all to the good. Find this man, make him tell his secrets, and his lord shall die a traitor's death along with all of the rest," Henry says. "Whomsoever it be, he has planned to give me over to the enemy camp. Had they succeeded in killing you, my throne would have been taken from me. Am I so hated, Thomas?"

"I do not hate you, sire," Cromwell says, though, he adds silently, *I do not love or respect you either.* "Now, with your permission, I have much to do."

"Thomas, do it quietly. The queen is due in a few weeks, and I would not have her upset."

"Not for all the world, sire," Cromwell says. "All shall be done with the greatest discretion."

*

Charnley is not an easy man to find. In fact, the man does not exist, for he has been made up by Roger Blount, a scoundrel of the first order, who has allied himself to the Duke of Norfolk. He has ingratiated himself with the duke, as Charnley, and made himself a useful member of his entourage.

It is Blount who suggested the murder of Cromwell, and it is Blount who suggested surrounding the king with new faces. It has taken months, but the plot is still on course. Cromwell, it transpires, is still alive, but his position will be weakened once the new appointments are made. His will become but one voice amongst many, and his power will diminish.

Norfolk is pleased with the scheme. He dislikes Thomas Cromwell's power, and fears for his own position at court. With the power of Austin Friars broken, the duke believes he would return to favour, and be in a position to dictate who ruled, and how.

He could wait for Henry to die, and put a Roman Catholic Mary on the throne, or select his own grand niece, the infant Elizabeth for the position. Either way, he would be the natural choice to be regent, and the position would allow him to wield great power once more.

Of course, Blount thinks, if Henry were to have an accident, whilst hunting, the duke would have to take control, and might turn to the Plantagenet Pole family for an heir. With Mary married to Reginald Pole, the two dynasties are united, and the royal blood line would last for ever. As an aside, Blount thinks, he will become very rich, and might even receive an earldom for his efforts.

Such ideas go through the minds of unscrupulous men, and Blount is more lacking in morals than most men. He cares not for the fact that such an alliance would result in civil war, nor does he give a fig for Henry, or his family. It irks him that Cromwell still lives, but thinks he will triumph, once his new appointments are made.

It seldom crosses the rogues mind that he might have been out thought by a cleverer fellow, and he thinks his plan is still running along as he wishes. He finishes his wine, and slips out of the small tavern set by the river s edge. He uses a different name on each side of the river, and seldom sleeps in the same house two nights running. This makes him almost invisible to the casual eye, and difficult to trace, even for trained agents.

Blount is a fraudster, a thief, and a killer, and his career has seen him commit the most evil deeds across England, Wales, and Ireland. His only vice is wine, and he prefers to drink in those few inns and taverns which stock the rarer foreign vintages. To this end, he rotates his carousing through a shortlist of four establishments, and is known by a different name in each. In short, he does everything he can to protect his own life, whilst scheming the deaths of others.

A broad beamed boat is bobbing up and down at the wooden jetty, manned by one of the many licensed ferrymen. Such men find an acceptable mooring, and wait for enough passengers to turn up to warrant a trip across the Thames. One such customer is wrapped up in a heavy cloak on the rear cross plank, and already snoring and in a drunken stupor.

Cross the river for a penny, sir? the boatman asks, as soon as he sees the newcomer. It'll be my last trip tonight, for the tide is strong, and the water will be too choppy later."

"Are you leaving now, or must we tarry?" Blount knows these scoundrels like to fill their boats, to make more money, and they seldom leave either bank unless they have at least six pennies worth of fares.

"No need, sir," the man says. "See, here are another two gentlemen now. I will make the run for four pence if they are willing. Are you for the other bank, good sirs?"

"We are, master boatman," the bigger of the two says. Are you ready to push off?"

"A penny a piece, and I am all yours, gentlemen," the ferry man says. "Pray be seated, unless you require a cold bath too."

"Get on with it, you rogue," Blount says, as he hands over a copper penny. We would all like to be safely in Southwark, well before the moon comes up!"

The broad beamed boat eases from the shore, and is taken by the current almost at once. The boatman knows his business, and waits until they are a dozen feet from the bank before he sends his oars biting into the choppy water. He feathers one, and heaves on the other, until the prow of the craft turns, gradually, away from the Chelsea bank. Both oars bite into the river now, and the ferryman pushes his craft towards the far shore.

Once in Southwark, Blount has a dozen bolt holes to choose from, and wonders which one to favour. He has a wife waiting in one, who thinks herself to be married lawfully to Oliver Cox, a leatherworker from Putney, but she is with child again, and likely to be in a temper. Then there is the room he keeps at the *Lamb o' God*, and the comfort of one of their regular jades for a shilling. Yes, he thinks, that will do nicely, and he settles down at his ease. Even with the tide in his favour, few rowers can do the crossing in under fifteen minutes.

A chilly evening, is it not... Master Charnley? the larger of the two men observes.

"Cold enough," he replies, then slips a hand into his cloak, where he finds the handle of his knife waiting."Though you mistake me for another, sir."

"Do I?" The man frowns and scratches at his beard. "You are not Master Charnley?"

"My name is Alexander Bunter, my friend," Blount replies with an easy smile. "I fear I must look like a lot of people."

"I think not, sir," the big man replies. "My friend here knows you for who you are. He tells me you run with the Duke of Norfolk's hounds."

"I hunt with many different people," Blount says, as he eases the knife clear of his belt. He can kill one with ease, and decides to take the bigger one first. Once he is done, the second will soon follow. "What business is it of you two?"

"We four," the big man says. "You are our guest, sir, and we would know something from you."

"You have the wrong man." Blount grips the knife, as he realises that the 'drunkard' behind him has stirred, and is pressing the point of a sword into his spine. "What is this damned wickedness… I am an honest man!"

"You work for Norfolk," the big man says. "Now others begin to uncover your secret, sir. Let me make it plain to you. If your position with the duke becomes difficult, would you consider changing sides?"

"How do you mean?" Blount asks. "He is relieved at the turn of events, and realises that he might yet survive the crossing. These men are here to buy his loyalty, rather than to kill him.

"Say you are for Norfolk, and another offers you more," the big man says. "Perhaps a large estate, and couple of hundred a year as a pension. Would you join them?"

"You sorely test me, sir," Blount says, "even though I do not know what you mean. Would you offer me so much, simply because I look like someone else?"

"Or more," the fellow replies. "Will you betray Norfolk, or not, Master Charnley?"

"My name is not Charnley."

"No, I presume not. I think you might have a dozen names sir, but let me ask you again… no matter what you wish to call yourself… will you turn on the Duke of Norfolk?" The choice is clear enough to Blount, and he has no wish to be done to death because of a childish sense of loyalty to his current master.

"For so much land, my life spared, and *three* hundred a year… yes," he bargains.

"Just as I thought." The apparent drunkard throws back his concealing hood, and Tom Howard, Duke of Norfolk scowls at his untrustworthy servant. "You would sell me out to

Thomas Cromwell, the moment he finds you, sir. The race is run, Master Charnley, and it seems that Thomas Cromwell has won again."

"My Lord, I only thought to …" Norfolk thrusts, and the clever rogue stares at the cold steel where it protrudes from his chest. He feels no pain, but a deadening numbness spreading over his mind. The big man leans over, and grabs at his hand. Blount cannot keep a grip on his knife, and the fellow pulls it from his grasp. "Oh, damn it sir, you seem to have killed me."

"Why, so I have," Norfolk replies. "Sorry, old fellow, but the trail must end with you. Over he goes, lads!"

The body hits the cold water with a resounding slap, and sinks down into the murky depths. It will resurface, and bob about in the currents, and in another a week it might come up on the far Chelsea bank, or find itself caught on the great stone arches of London Bridge. The head will be unrecognisable, its features eaten away by the slick river eels, and the body will go into an unmarked grave.

16   Jihad

"You have news, Colonel Draper?" Henry is poring over charts of the Atlantic with Thomas Cromwell, who is trying to explain why the capture of treasure ships is now so unlikely.

"Of a sort, Your Majesty," the King's Examiner tells them both. "My men found where our quarry was living in Southwark, under the name of Cox, but they missed him. Then the trail led to him living in Chelsea, under the name of Blount. They made another thorough search, but he was gone. A gossiping neighbour spoke of Blount drinking down by the river, and even named a drinking place. So, we set out to corner him."

"Most exciting," Henry says. "He enjoys a little adventure, even if it is not at first hand. "Hide and Go Seek with treacherous secret dogs. Was the filthy traitor taken, Colonel Will?"

"Yes, sire, but not by my men," Will Draper confesses. "It seems that he took a boat for the south bank, with some others, just before our arrival. We commandeered one of the river barges, and gave chase. We did not catch up with them, but we did find a body floating down river.

"Charnley?" Thomas Cromwell asks. "Or Blount, or Cox?

"Yes, sir." Will stands to attention, and waits for Henry to explode in rage. So much effort, and nothing to show for it. Instead, the king just smiles, and nods his understanding.

"No matter," the king says. "The traitor is dead, and that is enough. Thank you, Colonel Draper. As always, your actions save the day, and I am pleased to have you as a friend. Here, let me reward you. Henry pulls a ring from his smallest finger, and holds it out for Will to take. "This garnet will look well on Mistress Miriam's pretty little hand. Give it to her, I pray, with my sincerest affection."

"You honour me, sire." Will drops to one knee, bobs his head and jumps back onto his toes in one fluid motion.

"Would that I were still as nimble," Henry says.

"You are neat enough of foot, sire," Will replies. "I still wonder how you managed to avoid my blow, and best me at that tournament." It is a clever little lie, that Henry has come to believe, and he recalls his fight with Draper as being one of the best moments of his martial career.

"Ah, but you almost had me, Colonel Will!"

"Almost is never quite good enough, sire," Will Draper says, and begins to make his retreat. Henry smiles again at the false memory of how well he fought, and wonders how much pleasure he would get if it was he who could slip that ring on that pretty little finger. Mistress Miriam is, he fears, out of even his purview. He turns back to his charts, just a little frustrated.

"Tell me once again. Why will we catch no more treasure ships, Thomas?" he asks.

"My source of information has dried up, sire," Cromwell tells the king, for the third time. "Without prior knowledge, our chances of running into one of the emperor's ships are now quite negligible. He has also started arming them with many more deck cannon. Twenty pound guns that could blow even the Great Harry out of the water. It is no longer worth the risk."

"Then what do we do now?"

"I suggest we urgently send a fleet to Corfu, sire," Tom Cromwell says. "The island is under siege by the infidel Turks. As we are in an alliance with Venice and Spain, against France and the Ottoman Empire, it would make good political sense."

"Then we stop irritating Charles, and turn our attention to King François?" Henry asks.

"It is only fair, sire," Cromwell says. "We deal with each of our enemies with equal scorn."

"Then they are our enemies?" Henry often loses track of just whom hates whom these days.

"Sire, they are all our enemies." Cromwell points to an ill defined stretch of coast, north of the Spanish New World. "To the north are vast lands, unclaimed by anyone. With the gold we have taken from the emperor, and the riches we will receive from saving Corfu for the Venetians, we should explore the northern New World, if only to see if we can sail around it to Cathay. Such a new trade route would make you the wealthiest king in Christendom."

"Exciting times," Henry says.

"Just so," Cromwell replies. The king will never speak of the events surrounding Charnley again. It is clear that he has guessed who is behind this latest plot, but does not wish to break with Norfolk openly, for fear of triggering a civil war. "Perhaps we should put My Lord Norfolk in charge of the expedition, sire?"

Henry narrows his eyes, and gives Cromwell a quizzical look, before he begins to laugh. They both know who the enemy is, he thinks, and they both know why His Lordship is to be spared, yet again.

"They say that far off land is full of great bears, wolves and all manner of strange beasts," Henry says. "Might not Uncle Norfolk scare them all away, Thomas?"

"You make a most valid point, sire," Tom Cromwell replies, forcing a smile at the king's heavy handed attempt at a clever jest. "Perhaps we should keep him close to home instead … the better to keep at least one eye on him. Shall I give the job to Sir Hilary Foxton, Your Majesty?"

"What?" Henry is surprised by mention of this poor excuse of a man by Cromwell. "Is Sir Hilary one of your best agents then?"

"No, sire," Thomas Cromwell says, with an unsmiling countenance, "but the fellow does only have the one eye!"

"God strike me down … but he does too, you rogue!" Henry finds this sort of cruel jest to be most amusing, and will repeat it to anyone who comes into earshot until the entire court are sick of laughing.

Cromwell makes a mental note to warn Sir Hilary that the king will almost certainly repeat the jest to him, and advise him to find it most mirthful. By thus laughing at himself, Sir Hilary will become a member of Henry s inner circle, privy to his inner most thoughts. This suits Cromwell, as the visually challenged, weak looking fellow is, in fact, one of his better agents.

*

Miriam Draper has made provision for her two ships to be fitted out with six eight pounder deck guns each, and manned with crews who are ready for a fight. They are all promised a rich bounty, and told they will be supported by three of King Henry's best warships. Her merchant captains know the waters between Italy and Greece well, and think they have a good chance of avoiding the main Ottoman fleet.

Tom Cromwell's agents report that Barbarossa Pasha, and most of his fleet are off raiding soft targets, and will be absent for the best part of September. It is thought that he has left a token force behind to secure Corfu for Suleiman the Great, and that he will not return to the island until the start of October.

"Your ships, along with the king's men o' war will be able to run any blockade the Turks set up, and so relieve the island from its siege," Thomas Cromwell says with misplaced confidence. "Once the Ottomans see five great many decked ships, pouring hundreds of men ashore, they will take to their galleys and flee."

"You make it sound so easy, Master Tom," Miriam says. "I oft times think of how happy dear Mush will be to see us. All these months of boredom he has had to put up with."

"Your brother will be fat and lazy with inactivity," Cromwell says. "I dare say his only exercise will have been in chasing after the pretty local girls."

"Then we shall become richer, without much effort," Miriam replies. "A third of the island's income is a goodly amount, Master Tom. The Doge will keep his word?"

"I have it in writing… and he is a very old friend, Cromwell explains. Our revenue will be paid into a discreet Lombard bank, and discharged to us, as and when we see fit. If Henry gets to hear of it, he will expect more than half the booty for his own very small contribution."

"The king has quite enough already," Miriam replies. "Besides, he has done none of the planning, and avoided fighting. Let him have his legal tithe, and no more. My share will see that my family are comfortable, for the rest of our days. My children will grow up to be fine lords and ladies, and never have to worry about being spat at, or called '*Jew*' to their faces."

"Amen to that," Thomas Cromwell says. "All we need is for Mush to hold the city against what few men the infidels have left behind.

*

Mush Draper stands on the fighting platform above the great gate of the fortress, and looks down on the peculiar scene below. To his right and left, a half dozen of his best musketeers have their weapons trained on the group beneath.

Just before dawn, a lone rider came galloping from the enemy camp, and delivered a request for a parley between the two sides. Gianni Lucretto, who has now taken control from the ageing city councillors, sends back the reply. They will meet outside the castle gate, on the far side of the fast flowing *Contrafossa.*

Gianni rides out, flanked by four Venetian gentlemen in burnished steel breastplates, and long pennant bearing spears, whilst the Turks arrive on horseback, bedecked with magnificent silks, and adorned in fabulous armour made of silver and ivory.

"They look like vain peacocks," Tom Wyatt murmurs, as he admires the vividly dyed fabrics, and intricate gold and silver chasing on their breastplates and cuirasses. "That armour would be completely useless in battle. It might deflect a sword s edge, but a well placed pistol shot would punch right through it."

"They dress in their best finery to show their utter contempt of us," Mush replies. "It is to demonstrate to us that they have no fear of death."

"With eyes that blaze wi the fires of hell,

He stands thus, our un-fearing infidel…" the poet declares, and he receives a ripple of cheering from the men on the nearer battlements. "Not too martial sounding?"

"Not at all," Mush says. "Though I prefer it when you do rhyme love with dove, and speak of pretty maids all a dancing. It is the most awful nonsense, but it soothes the weary heart."

"Sir, you are an utter Philistine!" Thomas Wyatt jibes.

"Not I," Mush returns. "For I am prepared to meet my own mighty Goliath."

"A witty rejoinder, my friend. Let us hope our sling shots are up to these Philistines." Wyatt hoods his eyes with a hand, and stares into the hot sun. "See… the Ottoman gives Gianni something for him to… oh!" The Venetian rips the parchment he is handed in two, and half draws his sword. The Turks make as if to reach for their own weapons, and Mush's men cock their muskets.

"Parley, good sirs," Mush calls down. "Gianni, return to us, and bid your new friends good day." The Venetian and his small party gallop back across the drawbridge, and it is winched back up behind them. The Turks trot up and down for a few moments, to show their contempt, then wheel about, and gallop off, back to their vast tented encampment.

Thomas Cromwell is right in most things, but in regards to the number of well armed Turks left to hold the island, he is sadly misinformed. Since the first skirmish, the Ottoman army has swelled by a couple of thousand men each day. Now, there are over twenty five thousand of them facing the fortress of Corfu, and its five hundred and odd defenders.

"What was it?" Tom Wyatt asks, as soon as Gianni is back inside the walls. "What was on that scroll?"

"A declaration," the young Venetian soldier replies. "Their leader requested that we surrender at once... and without conditions, and when I refused, he gave me the scroll. On it were some Arabic words... speaking of how they must strive in the way of Allah. They call it *Jihad* ... or we would say 'Holy War'."

"Then they mean to attack?" Mush asks.

"Oh, far more than that," Gianni Lucretto replies. "They have declared *Jihad* against us... a Holy War ... unto the death. Their preachers will whip them up into a frenzy, and they will be told that if they die in combat, their souls shall go straight to their heaven."

"Ah yes... where they have seventy two virgins waiting for them?" Tom Wyatt asks."He finds this aspect of an otherwise incomprehensible religion to be quite fascinating, and would be tempted to convert, if not for all the time spent in praying."

"Do not Christian priests promise a place in heaven for all who fight God?" Mush says.

"They do," the poet replies, "but they are never quite so specific. They talk of choirs of angels singing, and a life of eternal bliss. Not of nubile young women."

"And what of their women?" Isabella Lucretto has joined them, and is smiling at their ribald talk. If one of them dies for Allah, does she get seventy two handsome young men to fulfil her desires?"

"Trust you," Gianni says. He knows his sister well, and doubts she would have any problem keeping so many eager young men happy. "I hope you do not intend becoming a follower of Islam, sister."

"Not I," the girl says. "I am going to stand beside my betrothed, and fight."

"You will stay in the tower," her brother tells her.

"Where you have laid a fuse, so that we ladies might be blown up, and spared the wicked attentions of the infidels?"

"Isabella!" Gianni has done just such a thing, and does not want it bandied about, for fear of upsetting the dozen women left in the citadel. "This is no place for you. Tell her, Mush. It is your duty now… not mine."

"She must do as she wishes," Mush Draper replies. "Can you load a musket, my love?"

"And fire one too," she replies. "Let us stand, and fall, together, my dear one." Mush nods. It is unlikely that anyone will survive the first mad charge, let alone the crush of another twenty thousand trying to destroy the fortress, stone by stone.

"How long before they come?" Tom Wyatt asks.

"Soon," Gianni explains. "They will kneel for prayer during this next hour, then their Imams will goad them to fever pitch. I think they will come at us just before sundown."

"Then let us prepare as best we can," Mush tells his friends.

"God help us all," the poet mutters. He has positioned his cannon to face the length of weakened wall, and the main gate. At the last, he will be able to rake the Turks as they break through. His chain shot will cut them down by the hundred, but he doubts it will be enough. As a final defiance, he has planted kegs of black powder all around the two towers, and has fuses at the ready. The final act will be a glorious sacrifice, with not one Christian left alive to bear witness to the bitter end.

*

"They are bringing their cannon right up," Mush shouts down to Tom Wyatt. They know the English gunners are good, but the Turks do not care now how many casualties they will suffer. A half mad Imam has cried out for *Jihad*, and the end is upon them. To die now means instant transportation to heaven, where they can indulge their most carnal desires with the promised number of nubile young virgins.

Tom Wyatt calls for the muzzles of his own cannon to be elevated by knocking wooden blocks under them. Each blow of the hammer forces home the hardwood wedges, and raises the elevation by a fraction of a degree. It is a mad race to be ready, and the two closely matched sides begin to fire at the same time.

Mush ducks down, as a great twenty pound ball smashes into the gatehouse, and falls into the moat. More shots follow, and crash against the huge outer walls. The main towers and the gate are solid, and can withstand the prolonged pounding, but the weakened length of repaired wall is already beginning to crumble, and debris tumbles out into the fast moving *Contrafossa*.

Tom Wyatt's cannon, each manned by a master gunner trained either at sea, or in the Tower of London, reply to the Turkish gunners with devastating accuracy. At such close range he is able to use fused shot, and each round explodes in the air above the enemy cannonades, cutting down the Turkish gunners, and loaders, by the dozen. Round shot smashes into the big Ottoman guns, and damages wheels and limbers. One shot hits a stack of dangerously positioned gunpowder barrels, and the resultant explosion scythes through those Turks foolish enough to advance close behind their big guns.

The exchange of fire continues for another half hour, by which time half of the damaged fortress wall has collapsed in smouldering ruins. Most of the bigger Turkish cannon have been silenced by the English gunners, or have been pulled back out of range.

An eerie silence descends over the battlefield, and Tom Wyatt assesses his casualties. He has enough crews unharmed to man the remaining eight guns, and draws them up across the gap left by the wall s semi-collapse. His other two guns are positioned on the castle's high towers, and have been trained on the open ground before the main gate. The poet knows that round shot is no use at close quarters, and gauges the distance from his guns to the edge of the *Contrafossa*.

"Chain shot," he commands, and his gunners begin to load the deadly things into the maws of the eight remaining cannon. The poet knows the enemy will go for the weakest point, and calculates that his gunners can load and fire three times before the Turks reach the moat. They will bring rafts, and ladders. The moat will hold them for a few minutes, and Wyatt thinks he can put two more lots of chain into them as they ford the swift flowing *Contrafossa*.

"After the last round is done, we fall back to the towers, lads," he says. "If any Turks survive, we will fight them there. They will not give any quarter… so do not think of surrender."

"We are Englishmen, sir," one of the young loaders calls, and the remaining forty men send up a ragged cheer. And 'tis them bastards as will be askin' us for quarter!"

"Well said, lad," Tom Wyatt replies. There is a tear in his eye, but he puts it down to the smoke that drifts across the arena. It seems strange to him that, after surviving all the intrigues of the Tudor court, he must die fighting in a foreign land. His one regret, apart from all the women he has yet to sleep with, is that he has never published a single poem. Survive this, he promises himself, and he will put aright both faults.

Mush Draper watches as troop after troop of foot soldiers form great lines, from side to side of the battlefield. Each line is of five hundred men, and there are already a dozen lines. The front rank of men each carry a crude wooden raft, which they hold before them like huge shields.

"They will advance on us, under fire, until they come to the far *Contrafossa* bank," Gianni explains. "Then, those who still live will stake a rope to the far bank, and tie it fast to the raft. They will launch themselves across. Once the raft has completed its trip, the next man will come across, and lash his raft to the first. They will repeat the process, until they have enough narrow bridges lashed in place, and then they will surge across at us."

"Then we must fire at the raft men," Mush says. "It is madness. They will lose hundreds."

"Perhaps, but as one man is felled, the next will pick up his raft, and continue." Gianni is the pessimist, whilst Mush looks for the best in everything.

"At such close quarters, our muskets cannot miss their mark," he insists.

"How many muskets do we have?"

"Four hundred, and a dozen pistols," Mush says. "With three reloads we can kill a thousand before they even reach the moat."

"We have enough powder and lead ball for fifteen thousand charges," Gianni concludes. "If we fire off every round, and each ball finds a mark…they will still have ten thousand men left."

"Then pray to your God, Gianni," Mush says, "and stick to the plan. Win or lose… we are in for a very bloody time of it."

"Do not let my sister fall into their hands," the young Venetian replies. "Promise me?"

"My word on it," Mush says, "as an Englishman."

The Venetian captain goes off to make the final arrangements. The women, wives and mistresses of the garrison, are in the arsenal, stoically awaiting their fate, along with the two old Venetian senators who have had to be tethered to a post, for fear they would surrender the city to the enemy, and so seek to save their own skins.

"My brother worries like an old woman," Isabella says, when Mush returns to her side. "Has he asked you to save me from dishonour?"

"Of course."

"Ignore him," she says, with a steel-like glint in her eye. "At the end, I will retreat into the arsenal with a firebrand, and thrust it into the remaining gunpowder. It will be a final surprise for the enemy." Mush stares at her in open admiration, and perceives that she is speaking the truth.

"You would truly do that?" he asks.

"A man would hesitate, and think too long about it," the girl replies. "I have no desire to fall into the hands of the Turks."

"Very well." Mush kisses her, and pulls her to him. She sighs, and he whispers into her ear. "We will not die today, my sweet girl. It has been foretold."

"Foretold?" Isabella sees that Mush is quite serious, and feels a coldness clutch at her heart. "How so, my love?"

"There is this girl…and she sees things. What she says comes to pass. She spoke of a chosen one walking out of the furnace."

"And you are he?" The girl does not know of Mush's heritage, and does not understand that he is one of God's chosen people. "Is not Our Lord Jesus Christ God's chosen one? You do not make sense, my love."

"Never mind," Mush replies, and kisses her again. "We shall emerge from the furnace together, and I shall take you back to England with me."

"As you say, my dearest one." Isabella turns her head, and gives a small gasp. The serried ranks of Turkish soldiers, which now fill the horizon, begin to move. Great drums begin to beat time, whilst cymbals and horns sound from all quarters.

"Stand fast, lads," Mush shouts over the din. "They seek only to make us fear them. Their noise will be nothing to the roar of our guns. Let no man flinch, and this day will be ours."

"Rich pickings, lord?" Abel Welch, a young rigger from one of Miriam Draper's merchant ships asks, and the men, crowded along the battlements send up an ironic cheer. He is just fourteen years old, and seeks a life of adventure, and plunder.

"Enough to pay for your first girl, Abel Welch," Mush calls back.

"Fair shares then, Captain Draper?" one of the older, wiser, men shouts.

"Equal shares for us all, after Dear King Hal's lawful cut is taken into account," Mush agrees. "So, strip them bare lads, but make sure they are all dead first, for I want no naked Turks running about our island!"

They cheer again, but this time at the prospect of some very rich pickings indeed. The infidels wear their wealth, and any one of them might be worth ten or even twenty shillings, dead.

"Brave words, my darling," Isabella says. "I wonder how many, like you, will come out of the furnace this day?"

"I do not seek a heroes death for these brave men," Mush tells her, earnestly. "Life … any life, is precious, and not to be thrown away for a hopeless cause."

"You really think we can win?" Isabella smiles, and is proud that this strange man is hers, no matter how short their time together might turn out to be. "You think we can turn so many infidels back?"

"If not, I would have loaded my men onto the nearest ships, and sailed for home," the young

Jew tells her. I do not look for death, like my poet friend."

"Tom Wyatt s soul seems troubled." The girl is young, and wishes everyone to be as happy as she now is. "Is it a broken heart he suffers from?"

"Broken beyond mending," Mush Draper explains. "He was besotted with Queen Anne Boleyn, and he simply cannot push her from his mind. He courts danger at every turn. It is as if my friend welcomes the spectre of death at his side, and cares little for his own self."

"Then you must bid him farewell, before the battle starts," the girl replies. "Lest it be too late afterwards, my love."

"No doubt he will pour scorn on me with his sharp edged poetic verses," Mush grumbles. "But let my tongue be still… for I will only scorn myself if I miss saying my goodbyes."

"Well said," Isabella Lucretto replies. She is only sixteen years old, but has the benefit of a fine Venetian education, and a keen understanding of how a man s mind works. "Go, and bid him good luck in this trying hour."

"This terrible furnace you speak of, my friend," Tom Wyatt says. "Is it not some biblical thing?" He is standing by his eight twelve pounder cannon, and watches the lines of far off infantry creep towards him. Mush, who is busy showing his face at every point, has paused to ensure the poet understands his part in the coming battle, and to say a soldier's farewell.

"You doubt what Mistress Pru sees?" Mush replies, with a broad smile. "I am a Jew, one of the chosen people. That is clear enough, is it not? As for the furnace … she speaks of the great prophet, Isaiah… to whom my God said 'Behold, I have refined you, but not as silver; I have tested you in the furnace of affliction'. I am to be tested, and will be found most worthy in the sight of God. You do see, do you not, my friend?"

"Plain as day," Tom Wyatt says with a distinct sniff. "You are being tested, by a god, whose name you cannot even utter."

"It is too holy a name to be spoken out loud," Mush explains. We use paraphrases, such as adonai , which is Hebrew for My Lord. And it is He who decrees my fate this day."

"Good for Him. My English gunners and I know our duty, Mush. Gianni will keep his Venetians at the broken walls too, for as long as he must. Back to your hearty Englishmen at the gate, and tell them all about this holy prophet, Isaiah. Who knows, but that he might turn up;

> *Come, Isaiah and lend a hand,*
> *to save this poor, beleaguered land,*
> *from the Sultan s mighty wrath,*

and put us on the righteous path.

"Your rhymes grow worse with every passing hour," the young Jew says, with a broad smile.

"Then let some zealous Turk be my final critic," the poet replies, and turns back to his men.

"Good luck, Tom," Mush tells his friend. "May you shoot straight and fast. He turns and runs back to the ladder which leads up to the rampart above the main gate. As he reaches his allotted place, the leading ranks of the enemy come within musket range.

"Best men only!" Mush cries, and a dozen of his finest marksmen raise muskets to their shoulders. Even a well aimed musket ball will go astray at a hundred paces, and these men can find their mark at ninety, providing there is no cross wind. "Mark out the men in the finest robes. See how they have splendid swords, and glittering golden breastplates, lads. Those fellows are their sworn lords … their best officers, and they shout for our deaths, and would have our heads on their lance tips. Let loose, and aim well!"

"A musket cracks, and one of the distant figures falls to his knees. The men on the high rampart cheer, and more shots ring out as they identify the leaders of the Turks. Four or five find their mark, and then they all begin the laborious task of reloading.

The enemy ranks have not wavered, and others quickly take the place of the fallen men. Those of the enemy who are before the gates come on at a slow march, but their right flank sees that the weakened section of wall is in a state of complete collapse.

Many of the huge, two foot cubed granite slabs have fallen into the moat, and provide irregular stepping stones for any Ottoman Turk brave enough to chance a sudden rush. An Imam cries out to Allah, and urges those about him to take advantage of their apparent good fortune.

The line breaks, and Turks, whipped up into a mad frenzy, charge at the yawning gap. The hardiest amongst them leap from stone to stone, whilst others throw wooden rafts into the water, and try to form them into an impromptu causeway for those pressing them from behind.

Gianni Lucretto watches as more and more of the enemy are funnelled into the thirty foot wide gap, and force their way across the rushing *Contrafossa*. A dozen of the bravest men bound from stone to stone, and throw themselves into the inviting breach, followed closely by a hundred more. The Venetian licks his lips, and draws the heavy pistol from his belt. Here it is, he thinks, that chance of glory that all young men dream of. May God help me!

"Fire!" Gianni gives the command, and shoots the nearest Turk down whilst he is in mid leap from one stone to the next. Two hundred muskets, pistols and fowling pieces bark out, almost in unison, and the charging hoard of infidels disintegrate into a rabble of wounded, screaming men. Bodies fall into the swollen moat, and are washed away, and others lose their footing and are plunged into the fast running current, where they fight, vainly, to stay afloat.

The following ranks surge up to the lip of the *Contrafossa*, pause, then raise their muskets. Gianni sees their intent, shouts out an order, and his men fall to their faces, as five hundred rounds of lead tear into their weak position. Despite this evasive action, some of his Venetians are killed, and others wounded. The young captain shouts for his men to return fire, and they manage a ragged volley into the packed ranks of Turks.

So close together are the enemy, that a hundred or more are brought down, many shot through and through. Then the Turks fire again, and again. As each rank discharges their muskets, they step back, and allow those following to form up and send a volley into the unfortunate Venetians. Musket balls sweep over the defenders in rapid waves, and forces them to hug the bare earth in fear of their lives. Gianni signals to those nearest him to fall back, and then crawls back to the battery of waiting cannon.

He reaches the relative safety of Tom Wyatt's position, and waits, impatiently, for those of his men who have survived the onslaught to form up around him. He counts quickly, with fear in his heart, and is astounded to discover that he has lost only fifteen men killed, and another twelve badly wounded. He thanks God, hastily, and raises a hand to draw them to attention.

"Form a double line behind the cannon, gentlemen," he commands, and the Venetians do as they are told. They quickly reload their muskets, fowling pieces, and pistols, and loosen swords in scabbards. Despite all the modern advantages of warfare, the final reckoning is usually left to cold, unforgiving steel. Axes, swords, daggers, and even a half dozen hunting bows are at the ready for the final struggle.

"God is with us!" Gianni Lucretto shouts, and his men cross themselves. Tom Wyatt sees that the enemy s courage has not waned, and they are pouring across the half blocked moat, intent on savouring the final victory. A great, magnificently garbed Arab reaches the fallen wall, and waves a gaudy war banner above his head. He is screaming exhortations at his men, and hundreds rush to join him in a solid phalanx. In moments, a thousand men form into a great arrow shaped wedge, and prepare to bludgeon their way into the very heart of the great citadel.

"Allah Akbar!" the huge Arab cries, and a thousand voices answer him, fervently. Spears bristle from the solid formation, and great scimitars gleam in the last of the evening light. Even the most hardened English gunners take a moment to cross themselves, or shake hands with their comrades. The moment is here when each man must face his own demons, and decide how he will act.

"Fire!" The poet gives the order, and closes his eyes. He has witnessed the effects of chain shot on tightly packed men before, and it is a sight that is hard to expunge from his mind. The eight cannon belch out long tongues of flame, and the huge lead balls hurtle forth.

Each cannon ball splits into two half hemispheres, with a taut length of chain between them, and scythes through the air at chest height. Tom Wyatt hears the familiar whistling noise that is peculiar to this mode of warfare, and opens his eyes.

The magnificently brave Arab is cut in half, and all about him, the deadly chain shot reaps its devastating harvest of death, and destruction. Mens heads are sliced from their shoulders, and those piling in behind the front ranks are cut down in twitching, bloodied, heaps.

After the cannon roar, there is a great, unified scream from all the Turks unlucky enough to have reached the breach, then comes an eerie silence. The bodies are heaped up in huge cones of dismembered heads, arms and legs, and the wounded are stunned into mute horror. A man wanders around with the stump of his right arm spewing out blood, and another stands stock still, but headless.

The English gunners are already ramming home more black powder, and heaving the heavy twelve pound chain shot up, and into the guns great maws. The loader steps aside, and the ramrod pushes his padded pole down the barrel.

"Clear?" Tom Wyatt shouts, and eight gunners reply.

"Ready, sir!"

"Fire!" This time the murderous chains fly over the heaped dead, across the *Contrafossa*, and whip into the massed ranks of Turks, eagerly awaiting their turn to advance. Those in the first three or four ranks are, literally, torn into pieces. Even after the initial force of the shot is spent, the two chained balls still bounce and swirl onwards, breaking limbs, and maiming anyone who cannot get out of the way. One chain decapitates a horse, and cuts in half the high ranking officer on its back, then whirls on until it hits a Turkish cannon and rips off its wheel.

Under such a deadly bombardment, any European army would have wavered, or even broke, but the hate crazed Imams, and a handful of highly respected mullahs exhort their men to one last, unstoppable charge. They will surge forward, through the scything chain shot, as if it were no more than blossoms blowing in the breeze, gain the fortress walls, and overwhelm the defenders.

For Allah has decreed it, and Allah is great.

Mush sees the threat to Tom Wyatt's position, and admires how the Venetians continue to load and fire from between the gaps in the English guns. They need to hold on, and slow down the thousands who are moving against them. For his part, he is running up and down the rampart, sword in hand, trying to encourage his own men.

"Reload, lads," he cries. "See, they are across the moat, and coming to climb our walls. Are we going to let them?"

"Kill the buggers!" young Abel shouts, and drops a lump of stone down onto two Turks who are raising a ladder to the wall. One of the men catches the falling missile full on the top of his head, and falls down dead, only for another to take his place. The top of a ladder appears almost in front of Mush, and he steps across, and waits for a head to appear. The moment it does, the young Jew drives the point of his sword into the Turk's face. He cries out, and falls away. More ladders fall into place, and the English defenders have no time to recharge their muskets.

They turn them about, and use them as clubs, pull axes from their belts, or draw the fearsome short swords that navel men call 'hangers'. As each attacker gains the top of his ladder, he is met by a stab, or a savage blow, and sent crashing down. Mush sweeps his sword down, and it bites into a Turk's shoulder. The man grunts, and falls, knocking three more off the ladder as he goes.

"Here, my love." Isabella, true to her word has stayed by his side, loading musket or pistol, as required. He turns from the wall, to find her holding out two freshly charged pistols. Behind him, a Turk slithers over the wall, and drags a comrade up after him.

They charge at the first enemy they see, intent on doing bloody murder. The young Venetian girl cries a warning, and Mush swings around. The leading Turk charges and Mush parries, and thrusts. The sword goes right through the man, and he twists away, and falls. The hilt is ripped from the young Jew's grasp, and he grabs for the knife at his waist. The second Turk sees his chance and raises a huge, curved scimitar above his head. It is as he starts the downward sweep that Isabella squeezes both triggers of the pistols at once. There is a double flash, and both balls hit the Turk in the chest. He tumbles backwards, and the girl is sent staggering back with the force of the recoil.

Mush smiles his thanks to her, retrieves his sword, and runs back to the wall. All along the length of it, ladders are being fixed, and each fills with fighting men, eager to get over the compromised ramparts. Victory will bring them gold, and death will assure them a place in heaven. Below, hundreds of Turks press to find a place on any one of a dozen ladders, and the fast flowing *Contrafossa* behind them is criss-crossed with makeshift wooden crossing points. Each bridge is heaving with the enemy, and thousands more line the far bank, screaming their war cries, and imploring Almighty Allah to help them to their reward."To his left there is the sudden roar of English cannon, and a third lot of chain shot smashes into the thousands of infidels who are now pouring across the hundred makeshift bridges that span the defensive Contrafossa. The chain shot's butchery is terrible to witness, and the enemy troops are cut down in their hundreds. The water is filled with arms and legs, mutilated bodies, and severed heads. The place of slaughter is almost obscured by vast hanging clouds of gun smoke, immoveable in the still air, but the great tide of screaming Musslemen can still be heard, and the Sultan Suleiman's vast military array comes on at the hard pressed defenders, unabated.

Mush Draper senses that the enemy, endowed with almost magical energy by their strange faith, are on the edge of overwhelming his small force. The thin line of English gunners and brave Venetian gentlemen, and his own rag tag band of soldiers and sailors of fortune, are at breaking point. He grips his retrieved sword, steps back a few feet from the wall, and waves it above his head. On the far off rampart of the Castel Vecchio … the old tower… Gianni Lucretto, who seems to have deserted his men, holds up a spear, with a red pennant at its tip, and signals back.

Mush waves again, then brings the blade down in a sharp, slashing motion. The young Venetian sees, and shouts to two of his men, who are standing ready, with blazing torches in their hands.

"Now, my friends… and God be with us!" The torches arc out from the old tower, and land in the *Contrafossa*. Barrels of the infamous Greek Fire have been breached, and poured onto the running salt water. The thick liquid floats on the surface, from one side of the moat to the other.

The moment the blazing torches hit the water, the dreadful mixture ignites.

Mush watches in horror, as the moat catches fire from bank to bank, and then spreads steadily towards the main gate. The Greek Fire burns like the pits of Hell, and sticks to everything it touches on its terrible progress. Those nearest the point of combustion are incinerated in moments, and the wall of fire steadily engulfs all of those hundreds of Turks packed onto the flimsy bridges. Men turn, and plunge into the water to escape the oncoming flames, but the water is already seething and boiling.

Others run back as specks of the Greek Fire touch their exposed skin, and begin to burn away their flesh. They scream and run about like madmen, and those they crash into receive the deadly potion's relentless touch. Those who are thus afflicted become human torches, and create chaos in all directions.

The troops towards the rear begin to realise that the tide of battle has swung around, and a wild, animal panic sets in. Allah has deserted them, and death now will not send them to paradise. They turn away from the fortress, and its curtain of Greek Fire, and run for their lives. Ottoman officers raise their swords, and order their men back to the attack, but they are pulled from their horses, and murdered by their own side. Under any other circumstances, the defenders would surge out, and rout the enemy sending them scattering to the four winds. It is, however, impossible to give chase, for fear of the blazing water, and the defenders can only stand and watch as the vast army of Sultan Suleiman the Great burns to death before their very eyes.

*

"Eighty-three dead, and a handful of seriously injured," Tom Wyatt reports to his comrades. "I fear that most of those killed were Venetian, although two dozen were from amongst my gun crews."

"And what of the Ottoman Turks?" Gianni Lucretto asks the poet. "How can we ever count their dead? Greek Fire leaves little once it has passed."

"True enough," Mush says, "but my lads were not easily put off from their plundering. The hardiest of them have been busy stripping the dead, and they think almost three thousand perished in the last attack. That means they have lost close to a quarter of their army."

"They are running for those ports still in their hands," the poet continues. "It seems they intend not only abandoning the siege of our castle, but the entire island of Corfu."

"Good riddance." Isabella Lucretto spits on the ground, and puts her hands on her hips. "We must stop them, or else they will be at the gates of Venice, Paris, and even London."

"Captain Mush!" Young Abel, who has become a man during the last terrible hours, is waving for all he is worth, and pointing out to sea. "English sails, sir. Five… no, six ships, cracking on under full canvas."

"Men o' war?" Mush shouts back.

"Four are, I think," the lad confirms, "and one of them is the Great Harry. By God, but that will put the wind up that King Sultan fellow, and no mistake!"

"We must get word to the admiral, and have him sail around the island. I dare say he will be able to pick off a few of the Ottoman stragglers," Tom Wyatt says. "They come, but only when we have done all the hard work. I hope they have a few barrels of decent wine with them."

"Two of them will be my sister's merchantmen," Mush guesses, and full of the best victuals she can find. We shall all have full bellies tonight, my friends."

"Then it is truly done," Tom Wyatt mutters. "Thank God, for I could not stand another such victory as this one. It is one thing to face a man, and kill him before he kills you, but this…this hellish ox roast…" He gestures across the terrible aftermath. "This is a slaughterhouse, and my temperament is not suited to working at the butcher's block."

"Your share of the prize money will keep you safe at home from this day forth," Mush says.

"God and Tom Cromwell willing," the poet replies.

"I have a mind to stay in Venice for the nonce," Mush Draper announces. "It is a fine city, and Isabella might not wish to go to England."

"As you wish," the poet replies. "After all, has not the chosen one faced the fiery furnace, and come out alive?" Pru Beckshaw's odd pronouncement has come to pass, and he wonders at her inexplicable second sight , and hopes she is clever enough to keep her special power a close secret from those who might misuse the knowledge.

"I want to go to the English court," Isabella says with firm intent. "I want to see the rest of the world, and stay by your side, my love."

"As you wish, Isabella," Mush Draper tells her. "I dare say my dear sister will take a liking to you, and find you lots of things to do. I shall be forced to sit in taverns all day, waiting for you to finish your day s work. Why, Tom and I might become a pair of raddled old topers… ruined by gout, and with our purses emptied at the card tables of London.

"Then I shall lock you away in the bedroom," Isabella says. "You must remain the man I fell in love with. As for Master Wyatt, he must return home to his unhappy wife, and child, and try to make his life into a better thing."

"It is all so easy for you young things," the poet says with a smile. "Wait until Mush starts to snore, and chase after other girls when he is let out."

"Chase other women…how, without his *cazzo*?" Isabella says, softly, and touches the thin dagger tucked into the sash at her waist. Mush does not doubt the casual threat, and wonders just what he has let himself in for.

"What a girl," Tom Wyatt whispers to his friend. "I cannot help but look forward to you introducing her to court life. Why, she and Lady Mary Boleyn will be able to share such wonderful stories."

"*Cazzo*," Mush whispers back, and they both begin to laugh aloud. Isabella and Lady Mary together will make the Venetian's Greek Fire seem tame!

"Twenty one days, you say?" The king shakes his head in something close to awe. "There is not a ship in my fleet that can do that, even with the most favourable winds."

"Your Majesty is quite correct, of course," Thomas Cromwell concedes. "The Great Harry is still on her return voyage, and is only now reported to be off the coast of Lisbon. Master Wyatt and Captain Mush Draper used other means to bring us news of our great victory over the infidels."

"Pray explain," Henry asks. "Has our poetic young friend grown angels wings?" Henry admires the poet for his skill with the quill, and the ladies, and resents him for the very same reasons. It is not long since he suspected Tom Wyatt of swiving his wife, Anne Boleyn, and only Cromwell telling him otherwise kept the poet's head on his shoulders.

"Close enough, Your Highness," Thomas Cromwell says, and explains. "They chartered a Venetian trireme and raced from Corfu to the southern French coast in just five days and nights. Tom Wyatt hired another thirty oarsmen, and had them spell their tiring comrades every few hours. In this way they covered the entire distance; some nine hundred and odd miles, in record time.

"A Venetian war galley, by God," the king mutters. "And what then?"

"Horseback, sire," Cromwell tells the king. "Thirty odd miles a day in the saddle."

"Yes, it is do-able," Henry decides. "In past times, I myself have ridden just as hard."

"In full armour, and against an entire French army," Tom Cromwell says, quickly, in the hope of cutting short the false reminiscence. "Those were the days, sire."

"Yes, you fought them in Italy, did you not?" the king recalls. "How did you fare, Thomas?"

"I regret to say, I was on the losing side," Tom Cromwell admits, to the delight of the king. "Whereas you swept the field clear of the perfidious dogs. Might I present the gentlemen to you, sire, so that they can recount the details of their great victory?"

"Was it that meritorious then?" Henry asks. He likes a good, bloody battle tale, but thinks that chasing after a few infidels is poor stuff for heroes.

"Six thousand enemy dead, and a score or more of their war galleys burnt to ashes. The flotilla we despatched took another six enemy war ships as prizes, and the Sultan Suleiman… who styles himself as 'the great' is sent back to Constantinople with his infidel tail between his legs."

"And the cost?" The king is careful with crown funds, and never likes to make a loss.

"The expedition was privately funded, sire," Cromwell tells him. "The Draper Company supplied the merchant ships, and the fighting men. After reimbursing them for this, you come out of the affair some thirty thousand pounds to the good."

"Thirty-thousand pounds profit?" Henry tries not to show his pleasure at the news, lest he is expected to show too much favour in return. "A reasonable profit then. What will Wyatt, and young Draper, expect from us?"

"Your favour, sire, and nothing more," Thomas Cromwell replies. "The venture is, as I say, a privately funded one. If it succeeds, they are paid by the company, and if they fail … it has nothing to do with us. It is the way forward, My Lord."

"Really?" Henry does not quite follow Cromwell s thinking, but wishes to avoid looking stupid. "I tend to agree, but wonder if we are in full accord. What is your thinking on the matter, Thomas?"

"The same as yours, I suspect, sire," Tom Cromwell says, blithely. "Instead of sending expensive fleets off to the New World, hoping to find a North West Passage…or some vague treasure…we let private companies have Royal Charters. They shoulder the entire cost, and the crown takes a cut of the profits. If they fail, it is their loss alone to bear."

"Yes, just as I thought," Henry says, and nods his fleshy head. "It pleases me to have a minister whose thoughts so closely match my own, Thomas. That your intellect is as fine as mine does you great credit."

"Thank you, sire."

"Henry." The king is happy, and wishes to show his love for those who serve him well. "In private, we are always to be Thomas, and Henry."

"You honour me … Henry," Tom Cromwell says. Soon, the king s mood will swing about, and it will be back to 'sire', and 'Majesty' once again. "Ah, here are the gentlemen now. Might I call them over to speak with us, Henry?"

"Why not, Thomas," the king replies. "I am thinking of a knighthood for Tom Wyatt." Cromwell smiles and nods his agreement. It does not do to correct the king, but Wyatt has already been elevated to the rank of knight, some two years before. Before the usual investiture, the poet had written some offending ditty about Anne Boleyn, and aroused Henry's jealousy. The knighthood, though enacted in law, was swiftly covered up, and Tom Wyatt packed off to help the English ambassador in Rome.

"I shall make all the arrangements, Henry," Cromwell says.

"Excellent. Now… who shall tell me of this famous victory?" the king asks. "Shall we hear the professional soldier's tale. Or the clever words of a master poet?"

Mush Draper and Tom Wyatt approach at Cromwell's beckoning, and bow to the king. Wyatt spends his time admiring the king's new boots, and Mush feels his throat dry up at the prospect of describing the horror of battle.

"Come now, Sir Thomas," Henry says, sharply. "Have you nothing to say?"

"Nice boots, sire," the poet exclaims. "I might well write an ode to the calf who provided such exquisite hide for so noble a calf."

"What? Ho… you rascal!" Henry guffaws and slaps Wyatt on the back. "I hope you do not wish to fill them."

"Not I, sire," Tom Wyatt responds, pertly. "Methinks your beautiful lady is attending to that, about now. May God grant Your Majesty a fine son, and he will, one day, fill such large boots, I warrant."

"By God, but you are right." Henry throws his arm about the poet, and hugs him. "I have missed you, fellow. Why did you keep yourself away from me for so long?"

"I went where I was sent, sire, Wyatt replies, truthfully. "It was never my intention to abandon you to lesser poets."

"Dear boy… was it because of her?"

"Sire?"

"La Putain… Boleyn," Henry whines. "Did you love her?"

"Did you, sire?" Tom Wyatt is in no mood to pander to so self indulgent a fellow, even if he is a king.

"Ah, you send an arrow deep into my wounded heart," Henry says to him. "The woman cast a spell on me, or so they do say."

"Then how could you expect a lesser man, such as I, not to fall under her bewitching thrall, Your Majesty?" Wyatt is on dangerous ground, but Cromwell cannot interfere. "I loved her… as did you… but, to my eternal shame, it was a poet's love I had, not a man's."

"Well said, sir." Henry nods sagely, and turns his attention to Mush. "Come now, Captain Draper and stir my old heart with your heroic tales. How came you to turn back the Mussulmen hoards?"

"With fire and sword, sire," Mush says. "Though mostly with the former element. The Venetians call it Greek Fire, and it is a most terrible thing to behold."

"We have read of such a thing, once used to save Byzantium from capture. Have you managed to bring the secret back with you, young man?" the king asks.

"We were not allowed to see its preparation, sire," Tom Wyatt explains. "I am told that only a half dozen of the most ancient, and venerable Venetian senators know the full secret recipe."

"We might bribe one of them," Mush offers, but Thomas Cromwell is already shaking his head at the idea.

"The Doge of Venice would see such an act as a breach of good faith, Your Highness, and he is a valued ally. Besides, Venetian senators are also merchants, and so rich that any bribe we might offer to them would seem pitiable. Dante Umberto is said to be worth five million Ducati."

"Then Venice is really so wealthy a city? Henry is envious, and wonders if he might be better allied to the French. In such a case, he would be justified in capturing the place, and all of its secrets. Cromwell sees the thought pass over the king's face, and explains why the idea will not work.

"It has a navy that almost matches our own, and they can hire mercenary armies from all over Europe," he tells Henry. "If the French get too close to his walls, the Doge simply orders the unbreakable Swiss pike men to guard his city, or pays some Lombard Condottiero to strike at them from the rear. He also has an unbreakable bond of friendship with the new Bishop of Rome.

"That pious old bastard," Henry mutters. The new Pope is a decent sort, as heads of state go, and he makes the English king uneasy with his philanthropic ways. "What kind of a man is it who would give away all he has to the poor, and spend his days in prayer?"

"Attack Venice, and you are Rome's enemy too. If Rome is against you, then so is the Holy

Roman Empire, Tom Cromwell continues. "To sack Venice would then require the help of the Ottoman Empire, and we have just given them a bloody nose."

"Sack Venice?" Henry affects a look of surprise. "The Doge is our most loyal ally, Thomas. I am surprised that you should even suggest such a thing."

Thomas Cromwell has strong shoulders, and takes the unkind words with stoicism. He resolves to slip away at the first opportunity, and pay a visit to the queen's private chambers. Apart from Henry, and the court doctors, he is the only man allowed to visit her in her confinement. Henry thinks of him as a doting old fellow, with an avuncular love of his young Jane.

Mush Draper crosses to the chart table, and unfurls a rough map of Corfu Castle, and the surrounding land. He and Tom Wyatt will each describe the campaign from their own perspectives, and keep the king entertained until dinner is served. Thomas Cromwell makes some small excuse, and manages to slip away.

*

At the insistence of Queen Jane, quarters have been provided for Cromwell at Whitehall, Westminster, and Hampton Court. In this way, she explains, the minister can be kept close to his king at all times. His private chambers at Hampton Court Palace are right next to the kings, and it is an easy matter for him to slip into the queen's outer receiving room.

The usual ladies-in-waiting are clustered about, at their sewing or embroidery, and Cromwell acknowledges each one with a bow, and a few words. The sisters, Mary and Jane

Arundell are flirty things, and as alike as twins, whilst Jane Ashley is straight backed and rather quiet. Cromwell has a smile for each one, and makes a mental note to have them all sent a small gift of gloves.

No, perhaps not gloves, he thinks. It is kid gloves that first brought him to Jane's attention, and started her loving him. He will have Rafe Sadler find something else to give them. Something far less suggestive.

"A delightful piece of work," he mutters to Anne Bassett, as he offers a polite nod to Margery Horsman. "Ah, Lady Norris, are you quite recovered now … excellent, and Mistress Parr… how is that brother of yours… still in France?"

"He is, Master Cromwell," Anne Parr replies, with a knowing smile. "His appointment was most welcome…especially to my father." Cromwell waves away the implied thanks, and thinks how useful the young man will be in Paris. News of the French court is always useful.

"Not sewing, Mistress? he says to the pale young girl in the corner. Mary Zouch shakes her head, and worries at a string of beads with her fingers. The old Catholic traditions are hard to suppress, and many protestants, who readily denounce the papist way of worship, still cling to their prayer beads for comfort in times of great need.

"I am too busy praying for My Lady, the girl says. She has a pleasant west country accent, and it makes Cromwell think of happy days spent at Wulfhall. "We do not want God to be looking elsewhere, do we, sir?" Thomas Cromwell smiles at her simple faith, and wonders where he left his own. Lost behind my account ledgers, perhaps, he muses.

Sir John Russell is standing guard at the closed bedroom door, armed with a sword. Weapons are forbidden to all in the confines of the royal quarters, save for Russell. His normal duties are to gallop ahead of the king s progress, and ensure that everyone knows of his coming. He is the king's man, and today, it is his duty to guard the queen's door against any who might cause her distress.

Cromwell likes the man, and has used him for tasks which might not find favour in Will Draper s eyes. He is not the cleverest of fellows, but he is a staunch sort, and will throw himself into any danger if there is a full purse in the offing.

"Sir John," he says, "guard our lady well. I see the blue calico I sent you has made up well."

"It is ideal for doublets, Master Thomas," Sir John replies. "My tailor says it should last me to my grave."

"Hush, man… no talk of death here," Cromwell warns. "It might prove unlucky."

"Your pardon, sir, I meant nothing by it." Cromwell sees that he has spoken too sharply, and wonders if their audience has noticed his concern for the queen, and noted its intensity.

"Good day to you, sir." Thomas Cromwell turns at the sound of a familiar voice, and is taken aback to find Lady Rochford sitting in a corner, with a book of verse on her lap. As the sister-in-law of the previous queen, her presence might be misconstrued by those of evil mind. "Do you come seeking news?"

"I feel like a doting father," Tom Cromwell tells her, somewhat ambiguously. "Is the queen well?"

"Jane is tired," Lady Rochford replies. "Her labour has commenced, but it is a slow business, Master Thomas. You must content yourself with knowing that she is in capable hands. Your Jewish doctor is with her."

"Adolphus Theophrasus is a Cornishman," Cromwell tells her, for the benefit of all those listening in to their conversation. "It seems that his mother was from those parts, though her husband had Greek blood in his veins. The olive skin is down to his many years of travel in the far away lands of Egypt, and India."

"Of course it is." Lady Jane Rochford smiles sweetly up at him. "Then, your Cornish doctor, who claims to be from *Exeter*, is with dear Jane, and he reports that she is bearing up well, and the child is not distressed."

How long has she … ? Cromwell has great difficulty in speaking of a woman's matters, and hopes George Boleyn's shrewd widow can read his mind.

"Been in labour?" she says, helpfully. "Six or seven hours, I think. I came as soon as I heard. Queen Jane and I have become quite close, since I was so abruptly widowed."

"You mourn oddly, madam," Cromwell replies. Lady Rochford has, until recently, been living at Austin Friars, and conducting a very intense love affair with his own nephew.

"Mourning White is so ageing," she says, with a pert little smile. "Besides, your nephew likes me in red, or yellow."

"Ah, your sister-in-laws favourite colour," Cromwell says to her. "Though yellow never did her any good."

"I am of a different cut than that lady," the duchess replies. "I believe you know that, sir."

"I respect you, madam," says Cromwell. "My nephew has stronger feelings. Pray, do not hurt him too much."

"He will survive," Lady Rochford says. "As must we all."

"Then there is nothing for me to do here?"

"This is women's work, Master Thomas," Lady Rochford tells him. "Jane must do her royal duty, without benefit of any advisor. I suggest you either return to the king's side, at once, or take up sewing. I fear it is going to be a rather long night."

Cromwell wants to go in, and sit with Jane. He wants to hold her hand in his, and tell her that everything will be alright, but instead, he bows to the ladies, nods at Sir John, and retreats from the chamber.

"When he returns to the inner court, he finds that Henry has ordered up his chests of hand painted soldiers. He, Mush and Tom Wyatt are busy arranging them in ranks. The poet places a wine bottle to show where the strategically important Castel Vecchio stands, and the buckler from his belt to signify the position of the Castel Nuevo. A silk neckerchief, provided by the Duke of Suffolk is draped between towers and Turks, to show how the *Contrafossa* bisects the two ill matched armies.

"This is so like the time I was faced with a French army of thirty thousand," Henry pronounces. "I wager it is a tale you lads are too young to have heard?"

"On the contrary, sire," Tom Wyatt replies with expert diplomacy. "Though we would like to hear it from the lips of one who was there."

"Then you shall... by God... you shall, sir!" Henry is in full flow now, and Thomas Cromwell doubts if they will ever manage to get their dinner. "It was back in the year of Our Lord... hmm..."

"The summer of 1513," Tom Cromwell whispers into his ear.

"Yes, that was it. My advisors wanted to go carefully, but I took to my horse... a huge white beast it was ... and told them to be damned. I charged, with a few loyal men straggling behind, and the bloody French turned around, and galloped away. All we could see were their spurs glistening in the sun."

"They still call it the 'Battle of the Spurs' , sire," Cromwell says. Though the thirty thousand were nearer fifteen or twenty thousand, he thinks, and the king was hemmed in on all sides, with over six thousand of his finest cavalry. "A famous victory."

"We should have one last go at the French," Henry complains. "Why, with these fellows, and the likes of Will Draper, we could ride to Paris, and kick François off his throne. What say you to that, Thomas?"

It is one of those moments that can define the future history of Europe, and Henry makes the proposal with the most casual ease, as if he is not putting forward a plan to devastate half of the continent. Cromwell, quite suddenly finds himself in the most appalling situation. To agree would cause chaos, war and famine for years to come, and gain very little, but to disagree would put him out of favour. Henry is excited about the victory over the Turks, and wants one last fling. To deny him, will bring ruin on anyone foolish enough to demur. The wily minister decides to appear enthusiastic, and he slams the flat of his hand down on the table.

"By the Blood of Christ, yes!" he snaps, and even Henry is taken aback by the action. "We should brave the wildness of the Channel in this season, and hurl our fleet against their ports. We can storm them, and start to land our own troops. Yes... but we must be quick about it. Suffolk, how soon can you raise your yeomen?"

"Er...within a month, Master Thomas." Charles Brandon, Duke of Suffolk is appalled at the notion of an unthinkable war, and wonders what Cromwell is doing. "Eight thousand foot, and two thousand horse, to start with. Then another couple of weeks to knock the rabble into shape."

"Excellent. They shall be the spearhead," Thomas Cromwell enthuses. "By the time the French king raises his army, we will already hold Normandy. Norfolk can land in Brittany with his ten thousand. Between the two, we should be able to keep François' sixty thousand in play until Cumberland, My Lords Warwick, and Northumberland, can raise their levies. That is another forty five thousand... but we must leave ten thousand behind to deal with the Scottish invasion."

"What...that rascal James means to invade?" Henry is confused by this sudden military fervour from his most reliable minister.

"He will wait until we are engaged with the French, then march into England," Thomas Cromwell advises. "What say you to that, Charles?" Suffolk takes his cue and nods his agreement.

"The clans will rise, of course, and James shall have thirty thousand men at his back," Suffolk says. "Our token force should slow him down enough. He might reach Nottingham before we can spare troops from Ireland, or the Welsh territories."

"Then what of London?" Henry is alarmed at the prospect of an enemy at his back.

"God will be with us," Tom Wyatt says. "By the time he is at the city gates, we will have taken Paris. The Scots, hopefully, will see the futility of their attack, and fall back to the borders."

"Leaving half of my poor England burned to the ground," Henry says. "No, that will not do. We must consider any war with the French most carefully."

"As you wish, sire," Thomas Cromwell says, and sighs, as if his own desires have been thwarted. "Perhaps we might just send a few thousand men to Calais, and throw a scare into François?"

"That sounds like a most sensible move," the king says. "Are we agreed, gentlemen?" They all are, of course, and a servant arrives with a fresh round of wine to further quench their martial ardour. "Ah, this is the Flemish vintage brought over by the Draper Company. Your sister, Miriam, assures me that I have the entire crop."

Miriam Draper is truthful on this point, mainly because she has no other market for the heady wine. The grapes are bought from both

French and Spanish growers, by an importer in Antwerp. He has them crushed and blended, before allowing a level of fermentation which produces a powerful concoction. The strong wine is too much for the delicate French and Italian palate, and too foreign for the Spanish vintners to accept.

"A hundred firkins, I believe," Tom Cromwell says, as he sips the rich red fluid. "Enough to fill seven thousand flagons. If kept as a special reserve for Your Majesty, and a few close friends, it will last until the next harvest is ready to pick."

"Then our Flemish vintner must make his wine for me alone," Henry says. "For truly, I will drink him dry!" It is a very weak jest, but protocol demands that every one in earshot laughs aloud, and those out of range, but aware of the existence of a jest made by the king, must applaud him with polite clapping, and the odd 'bravo, sire' thrown in. Henry's face turns to stone when not one person laughs. Even Suffolk is silent. He takes offence at this disgraceful affront to his royal dignity, and turns to snap at Cromwell.

Thomas Cromwell is not listening either. Instead he, like the rest of the silent court, have their eyes fastened on the great oak entrance, where a lone figure stands. Henry realises that something unusual is occurring, and curbs his childish bout of temper. He watches as the man walks towards him, and the crowd of courtiers parts like the Red Sea for a Tudor Moses.

Adolphus Theophrasus, scion of the renowned Athenian School of Medicine, doctor to King Henry, and consultant physician to Jane Seymour, Queen of England, advances with controlled gait, and a mournful look on his aged face. He pauses, exactly four steps from the king, and offers him a stiff bow.

"Your Majesty… I come to your presence from the queen's bed chamber."

"Yes?" Henry can feel tears welling up and forces himself to remain as aloof as he can. He has spent the last twenty odd years having to listen to apologetic doctors and midwives prattling on about dead children. His dead children haunt his sleep, and seem to dominate his waking hours, until he does not know why God chooses to punish him, rather than some other deserving fellow.

"Queen Jane is delivered, sire." Doctor Theophrasus glances at Thomas Cromwell, who seems to be even more anxious than the king. "The child, may God be praised, is fit and well." Not a soul in the room is breathing, and the tension is palpable. "Congratulations, sire, you have a fine son!"

"He lives?" Henry is crying with delight, and starts slapping everyone on the back. "Then God does not look upon me with disfavour, Thomas. The new church, my defiance of Rome, and my decision to put English bibles into the hands of free Englishmen, has proven to be the righteous path."

"God be praised," Tom Cromwell says. "You have assured the future of your bloodline, sire. The Tudor dynasty will last for a thousand years." In the distance there is the sound of jubilant cannon fire, and the cries of common men in the streets about the palace. It seems that the whole of England is celebrating an end to years of uncertainty, and the promise of a much better future for every Englishman.

"I must see the child," Henry decides. "After dinner perhaps? See to it, Thomas."

"As you wish, sire." Thomas Cromwell has two questions; one for the king, and one for someone else. "How will your son be known?"

"Edward…Prince of Wales," Henry says. Cromwell bows, and takes the doctor by the elbow. He leads him to a quiet alcove, and leans close, so that none might overhear.

"Adolphus, pray tell me that which the king has forgotten to ask. How fares the queen?" The physician nods his understanding at the remark, for Henry has what he wants, and seems to have quite forgotten about his young wife.

"It was not a difficult birth," he tells his friend, "but it was a protracted one. The boy is large, and strong, because he has been well nourished at Queen Jane's expense."

"Then she is unwell?" Cromwell wants to run to her side, and beg his answers from her own lips, but he knows that can never be. "What ails her?"

"Nothing that bed rest will not cure."

"You promise me this?"Tom Cromwell asks.

"She is weakened by the birth, and is such a slight girl," the doctor replies. "I have told her to stay abed for at least two weeks, until she can stand unaided."

"The queen will be expected to appear at court, with the child," Tom Cromwell says.

"Refuse them, Thomas." The doctor shakes his head. "No traipsing around after Henry, no running when he calls, and no breast feeding. I have a good woman who can nourish the child, and act as his wet nurse. The boy is strong, and can fend for himself, but our girl must have her rest."

I shall do all I can to see that she rests herself, Thomas Cromwell agrees. "Will you support me against the king in this matter?"

"Of course."

"Then all will be well, old friend," Thomas Cromwell concludes. "Henry will listen to our reasonable advice."

"Just so." Adolphus Theophrasus drops his voice to a murmur. I am going to call in on the queen before dinner. If you were to be walking with me … ?

"It is not proper." Thomas Cromwell is, quite possibly, the father of this new prince, yet he must observe the rules, as if he were no more than a common court lackey.

"Is it not?" The doctor winks at his friend. I doubt the king will begrudge two old men a few minutes with a girl who is so precious to them. The boy is in a cradle by her bed. Do not forget to steal a glance at our new prince."

"Yes, I shall, with pleasure, old friend," Thomas Cromwell says, with his heart racing in his chest. "Edward, born a prince, and set to become our future king!"

~end~

Afterword…

A reader s view on Tudor Crimes

'I am now addicted. The characterisation is fantastic and the plots so fabulously convoluted that I sit with my eyes hanging out in exhaustion, unable to switch the bedtime lights off till I know what has happened.'

'Throughout the series the characters have morphed and grown. The danger rises, and life is breathed into the history we know so well. These books are VERY good indeed and I literally can't wait for the next one, though my heart trembles for the future of the denizens of Austin Friars.'

'Knowing the reality of history adds an almost unbearable tension as the plots unfold, and I find myself hoping against all hope that Anne Stevens chucks history to the four winds and from someone like me, who is particular about the facts, that should give you some insight into just how good these books are.'

The best reviews are often those penned by ordinary members of the reading public. I cherish every comment made by every one of you, and take on board both the praise, and the constructive criticism.

After the success of "Winter King" I felt obliged to return to the world of Cromwell and Henry, and explore how far the characters could be developed. It soon became apparent to me that the era had taken control of the story, and that this Tudor saga must be played out to the very end.

The histories of Henry VIII and Thomas Cromwell are entwined, and to tell one s story is to tell the other s. There is a wealth of historical fact available, and enough scholarly conjecture, to fill many volumes. It would be remiss of me not to follow the path to its inevitable end.

A book is nothing without a reader, and I send my heartfelt thanks to you all.

Anne Stevens.

Further suggested reading:

And Angels May Fall by **Steven Teasdale**

Hospital smell. It was the same all over and defied even the best descriptive powers. Donna couldn't place the aroma and decided it was most likely a mixture of disinfectant, decaying flowers and gangrene spores. It stopped short of pleasant but didn't quite make it to cloying and, with a deep breath, she was able to cope with the odd visit.

'Fancy some nice juicy grapes?'

'Are you winding me up, Inspector Proud? ' Finlay growled. 'I fell through a pub window, so why would you think a paper bag full of unfermented fruit would do it for me?' He poked at the brown paper bag and noticed the neck of a half pint bottle of Scotch hidden away. The sight of the single malt contraband raised his spirits.

***

Donna Proud is a complete mess of a person… but she is very good at her job. People are disappearing, and turning up in pieces, and it doesn't take much to realise that the Grist brothers are flexing their muscles.

Kyle Grist is the most perfect example of the literary psychopath I have ever come across. (S.O.Lamb)

Throbbing, violent and realistic... Donna Proud is here to stay.

5 out of 5 stars: Highly recommended! by David Cameron   [Kindle Verified Purchase]
'Brilliant read. The book draws you in straight away. The characters are believable and the story line is fantastic. AAMF would make a great TV drama!'

Soul Eater by Steven Teasdale,

This is the second Donna Proud novel, and is out now, only through Kindle/Amazon.

What use is evidence when it points to your murderer being over a hundred years old? Donna Proud knows that she is going to tested to the limit if she is to track down the Soul Eater. The hard headed DI has seen the devil, and defeated him once already. After taking on a monster like Kyle Grist, how could this mass murderer from the past phase her?
Gruesome deaths from the past are coming back to haunt the present, and Donna has to stop the Soul Eater, before his mad blood lust destroys everything she holds dear.

I love Donna Proud, and Soul Eater is another winner......
[Tessa Dale author of The Black Jigsaw.]

Books by Anne Stevens in the Tudor Crimes series:

Winter King
Midnight Queen
The Stolen Prince
The Condottiero
The King s Angels
The King s Examiner
The Alchemist Royal
A Twilight of Queens
A Falcon Falls
A King s Ransom
Autumn Prince

Also by Anne Stevens:

'King's Quest' is the first novel in her "Georgian" sequence. Out now in e-book and paperback format.

Printed in Poland
by Amazon Fulfillment
Poland Sp. z o.o., Wrocław